STITCHING

A Novel of Love and Immigration

by

Kim Nelson

Book 1 in the Abruzzo Annals Series

Printed in the USA
First Edition
1 2 3 4 5 6 7 8 9 10

ISBN: 978-0-692-52449-7
          (Reprint)

Dedication

This book is lovingly dedicated to my grandparents, Natalena and Giacomo Mazzochetti, who crossed an ocean to live in a foreign land in order to build a new life in America for their family.

Natalena Mazzochetti

CONTENTS

INTRODUCTION

I sat on a picnic bench at the western end of Battery Park in lower Manhattan on a spectacularly beautiful day in late December, 2014. It was the week between Christmas and New Years and it seemed like a million people were visiting lower Manhattan that day. I had gone to see the new Freedom Tower, the building that replaced the World Trade Center Towers which were destroyed in the 9-11 attacks in 2001 and to pay my respects at the Memorial. I think many other people had the same idea as the weather for such an outing was most inviting.

I walked the mile or so from the Memorial to Battery Park in the crisp, chilly outdoors through neighborhoods that a little more than a decade ago had been covered with the grit and debris of skyscrapers that had been assaulted and destroyed in an unexpected act of ferocious terrorism. The sun shone brilliantly, made even stronger by its reflection off the waters of the mighty Hudson River on its relentless trip to the ocean. From my vantage point I could see the Verrazano Bridge, connecting Staten Island to Brooklyn, the outline of New Jersey in the distance, and the main attraction which was the reason I had come in the first place—the Statue of Liberty and Ellis

Island. These sites were among the first things immigrants saw when their ship steamed into the harbor at the end of their journey, the human cargo of one of the world's greatest peacetime—and voluntary-- migrations.

There she was, Lady Liberty, regal and rigid in the sunlight, light green from the patina that colored the copper statue, immune to the heat and cold, the rain and the wind, dressed in her palla, holding her torch high for all to see as a welcome signal to the world. From my seat about a nautical mile due east, she looked rather small and was dressed hopelessly out of date in her ancient Greek gown, but she completely dominated the tiny spit of land that formed the base of the statue, raised high on her granite pedestal. I could see her clearly in half-profile as the wind whipped up the waves of the river. What emotions those immigrants must have felt seeing her: hope, fear, anticipation, joy, dread, promise, trepidation as they faced the entrance exam at Ellis Island after their long journeys. Most of them only came with one satchel containing all of their worldly possessions and the equivalent of $20.00 to their names. Imagine that! Starting a completely new life in a foreign country with one suitcase and $20.00. How many of us could do that today? I thought of how many prayers were invoked as their ships glided by Lady Liberty, blowing their horns in salute.

I flashed back to the 1950s when I was growing up in a nice, middle-class town in New Jersey. We lived in a three-bedroom, two-bathroom house, my brother, sister and I, with my parents who were as firmly entrenched in middle class life as anyone could be. My father commuted by train to Manhattan every day to his job on Lexington Avenue and my stay-at-home mother would often have cocktail parties for his clients. Yet two or three weekends a month, we would pack up the station wagon and enter a whole different world.

We would drive an hour west, cross the Delaware River, and enter my mother's home town of Easton, Pennsylvania, which might as well have been on another planet. We were going to see our Italian grandparents, aunt, uncle and cousins.

Nunu and Chuchu lived in a brick row house on Ferry Street a half block from the waterfront in an industrial neighborhood generously labeled "working class" by my father. We always had a lot of fun with this side of the family—they were loud, boisterous, opinionated, stubborn and theatrical. It was a house of contradictions. The living room was full of aged furniture with tabloid newspapers on the coffee table that broadcast the latest story of a two-headed fetus born to some unfortunate woman. Opera was playing on the radio. Sunday dinners were orgies of homemade Italian food and gossip. Even though we the kids were relegated to the children's table, we could see what was going on and very early on learned every Italian swearword in the dialect of the Bruzzais.

I was a studious and thoughtful child and was the only one really interested in my grandparents' background. I liked to think that made me my grandmother's favorite; she spent many hours telling me about her life in the Old Country. I cut my teeth on these stories and over the years, I learned a great deal about her past. The only thing she didn't talk about was how she got to the United States. That story belonged to my mother.

My grandfather was another story. He hardly spoke any English after many years in the U.S. so he was hard to communicate with. He was also a heavy drinker so the relatives didn't leave the kids with him. We learned later that after thirty years of marriage, much of them fraught with knock-down, dragged out fights and much drama, they divorced. As I grew up in my comfortable, WASP-y world and watched the relationship between these two people, I was mystified at its complexity. It amazed me that I was related to them; they were so literally foreign to what I knew growing up.

In 2005, I made one of many trips to Europe. But this time was different. It was time to find my roots, so I made a pilgrimage to Citta St. Angelo, my grandparents' town in Abruzzo. A relative who knew I was going sent me a family genealogy dating from 1531 that listed 15 generations of ancestors from the same town. A coat of arms of minor nobility accompanied the document! With great anticipation, I entered the town and walked the streets that they had walked growing up, entered the cathedral, ate at a local cantina, and saw my grandmother's ancestral home. I even stayed at a local hotel owned by a distant relative. What amazed me was that in spite of the cars, electricity, computers and other modern amenities, the town seemed to be frozen in time, a hybrid of then and now, this perfectly-preserved stage for the stories my grandmother had told me in my childhood. I was so moved by the experience that as soon as I returned to the U.S., I began writing this novel, the first in a multi-generational series I call The Abruzzo Annals.

My maternal grandparents were a part of that great migration to the promise land of America and what follows is an embellished tale based on their story. Most of it is true. Some of the story has been expanded to satisfy the booksellers and the commercial market. The astute reader will probably be able to tell the facts from the fiction. My research for the book about their Atlantic Passage colors the pages of Josie and Giacomo's experience, but in truth, in 1917 my grandfather came to the States first, as did so many men before and after him, set himself up and sent for my grandmother. This is how it was done; the scout ant would go first, reconnoiter and pave the way for others. The New York Metropolitan area continues to this day to be the great magnet for immigrants who start their lives on American soil in this fashion.

In the early twentieth century, hope and promise for a better life drove these poor but courageous people to leave their families and homelands in a great gamble to improve their and their children's future. My brother and sister and I are the second generation witnesses to my grandparents' sacrifice and hard work. This book is dedicated to them, my Nunu and Chuchu, Giacomo and Natalena Mazzochetti, without whom we would not be living our own version of the "American Dream."

11

Part I: Italia 1923

Chapter 1   The Gift

The shipping crate was due any day now. Josephina Mattola rushed home after school, fully expecting to see a wagon drawn by one, maybe two horses, in front of her house and two men unloading the unwieldy crate. It might take two horses to bring it all the way up the hill and down the cobblestone streets to the other end of the *Via Maggiore* where her house was located at the end of the alley. For a week she had said, "Today's going to be the day," but each day she was disappointed. Her parents had reassured her that it took a long time to travel from Rome on the train to Pescara, the nearest city in the province of Abruzzo on the Adriatic coast, then for the shipping clerk to make the proper arrangements for delivery.

After all, even though one could see Pescara and the coast from the hilltop town that was known as the City of Saint Michel Angelo, they were worlds apart from her little town. *Citta St. Angelo* was one of hundreds of similar towns in Italy at the turn of the twentieth century, towns that had been almost frozen in time since the Middle Ages, when feudal dukes and kings built them on hilltops at the foot of the Appenine Mountains for their homes and fortresses. Enclosed by a sturdy wall, a single road wound up a hill for about a half mile, the only access and egress to the village at the top. This town had one distinction that the others did not: it was the seat of the local Catholic bishop's diocese, and the bell tower of his cathedral dominated the skyline. From the bell tower, a discerning eye could see the naval activity for miles up and down the coast of the Adriatic Sea and much of the traffic coming up the road through the foothills from Pescara. Such a view offered a distinct defensive advantage to the medieval rulers who ran the town in centuries past. But in 1919, the bell tower was no longer used as a lookout and was off limits for 17-year-old Josie, so she had to wait for her gift in the street.

As the sun was setting that day in late November, she heard a commotion in the street outside her house that prompted her to dash down the stairs, taking two steps at a time. There it was! The massive draft horses were sweaty and winded after the climb, stomping and snorting impatiently as the men smoked and cursed under the weight of the shipping crate. Her father chided them, "*Lentamente, prudente!* I'm not paying you if it's damaged!" More grunts and curses streamed from the workers. Finally, the box was deposited in the house, the men were paid, and Josephina stood poised like a bird of prey with hammer in hand, ready to tear it apart. Her father re-entered the house and laughed out loud.

"Josie, wait for your mother and I'll open it."

"No, Papa, I want to have it all set up by the time she gets home!"

By evening, the wooden crate was in pieces on the floor, packing was strewn about, and a brand new treadle sewing machine was ready to go to work. It was painted shiny black with gold letters on the side of the arm. The machine was set snugly in a table with a wrought iron base that was supported by two legs made of iron worked into the shapes of leaves and vines. The foot pedal was decorated with the same leafy vine pattern. When she came home, *Signora* Mattola, amazed at the sight of this new technological wonder, set the thread and bobbins in their places, then turned to Josie and said, "Give it a try, *cara*."

Josie sat down, transfixed by the whirring of the machine and the speed of the needle, felt intuitively that this would change her life, for there would be no more making clothes by hand, no more needle pricks and blood drops on the fabric, no more uneven stitches, only perfectly-made garments that *she* would create and wear.

"Thank you, Papa! Thank you, Mama! I can't believe it's so wonderful!" Her black eyes sparkled with the joy that only an exceptional present can bring to a young person. That look was compensation enough for her doting father. Yet *Signor* Mattola had one more surprise for his only child. He was prone to indulgence of his beautiful daughter, the child that had given his barren wife so much pleasure when they adopted her from the orphanage years ago. Not only had she grown into a talented, well-behaved young lady, but she was maturing into a lovely woman--as some said, a beauty. The kind of child that two homely, stout, and decidedly average-looking parents could never have produced naturally.

"Josie, this is also for you," her papa said softly as he handed her a sizeable parcel wrapped in brown paper, tied with a string. He watched her as she ripped off the paper to discover a large, neatly-folded piece of English wool fabric, heavy with promise, dyed brown with gold flecks woven into the design. Fabric that would make an excellent winter coat. Underneath the fabric was lining material and buttons that coordinated perfectly with the colors of the wool.

Josie almost fainted with delight. She knew all too well that the sewing machine and now, this most excellent fabric, represented probably six month's worth of her father's wages. She flung her arms around his neck, kissed him, then kissed her mother, and went back and kissed him again, muttering "*Grazie*, Papa, *grazie*. Wait 'til you see the coat! It will be beautiful. I can't wait to start!"

Signor Mattola smiled knowingly at his wife and nodded slightly. So far, their lovely daughter hadn't given them a bit of heartache. Yet. . . If it took a sewing machine to keep her out of trouble, it was more than worth it.

Chapter 2 The Coat

     Josie was so wound up that sleep was nowhere in the near future that evening. There was so much to do to prepare for the construction of her new coat. She took her old coat out of the closet on her way up the stairs, tenderly spread the new wool fabric on the floor and measured and marked it against the old garment with some chalk. First the front, then the sleeves, then the back pieces took shape on the wool. "I must leave room for big seams," she reminded herself. Her mother had always taught her to measure twice, cut once so she double-checked the pattern, planning slight modifications in the style as she went along. The collar was the biggest challenge. She had seen a coat with the same collar in a newspaper photo that an opera singer from Milan was wearing. Instead of a tailored, notched collar that was added onto the neckline of the front and back pieces, Josie designed a rolled collar that was one entire piece of fabric cut on the bias. She was so happy that her father had provided extra fabric in the bundle which allowed her to make a collar such as this one. The collar would give the coat a soft, feminine appearance and would be so different that no one in town would have one like it. The flecks of gold in the fabric of the front and back panels danced vertically against the chocolate-brown background, but the flecks in the collar ran at a forty-five degree angle, which would add contrast and a little drama to the coat's overall look. She also decided to make longer sleeves that could be cuffed at the wrists.

Soon the rhythmic sound of the pinking shears could be heard under the closed door as she cut the pattern pieces on the wooden floor. "Click, ah. . . click, ah . . . click, ah." One by one the pieces of wool emerged like a disjointed puzzle waiting to be stitched together. Before she went to bed, Josie used the wool pieces to cut the same shapes out of the lining material. Now everything was ready for tomorrow. As she lay in bed waiting for sleep to come, she visualized the finished garment in her mind, thinking that it might be her best work yet.

A jumble of thoughts about her life streamed through Josie's head as she waited to fall asleep. She knew how lucky she had been to be adopted by the Mattolas. Their childless condition had an unintended effect on her upbringing; most Italian families had many children, but she had no siblings with which to share her parents' affections. Her adoptive family was not rich by any means. Her father worked as a functionary, a sort of clerk, in the local government and her mother, as tradition dictated in those times, stayed at home and raised her child. Having only one child allowed the Mattolas a little more financial freedom than most of their friends and neighbors, who often lived from paycheck to paycheck, only one step away from the economic chaos that had befallen some of the families she knew. Even though her father did not make a lot of money, he had a steady job and a paycheck that could be counted on every week. Her family was frugal and did not spend money foolishly. Josie had already attended school longer than most girls her age because her parents could afford to send her. Custom held that Italian girls didn't need much education since they would be married at the age of 15 or 16 and settle into domestic life. There was no need for "book learning" for marriage.

Italian mothers made sure their daughters were taught the three most essential skills in preparation for marriage: cooking, cleaning and sewing. Her mother had taught her well and she was prepared. Josie knew her mother had a well-stocked hope chest full of linens, towels, curtains and bedspreads just waiting for her nuptials. She reminded herself that she was a simple girl, a very lucky, simple girl, who aspired to no great future other than marriage and raising her own children. Once or twice she had dared to dream of a future where she could share her sewing talents with the world, perhaps as a tailor or even a clothing designer. After all, *someone* had to design the clothes that people wore! Those thoughts of a career in fashion design were just that, thoughts. Josie didn't have the vaguest idea of how to make them a reality. But tonight all thoughts of career, marriage and children were pushed aside. The coat was the only thing on her mind. She would start sewing tomorrow.

Josie could not foresee that the creation of this coat would set into motion circumstances that would alter her life in ways she could never have imagined.

Three days later, Josie Mattola closed the front door behind her and stepped into the narrow alley in the crisp morning. It was 7:30 and children of school age were pouring out of *Citta St. Angelo*'s old row houses carrying their books and supplies on their way to learn about the world. Josie walked easily past the younger children to meet her girlfriends Celia and Gina at the intersection of the alley and the *Via Maggiore*, the long main street that bisected Citta St. Angelo into the eastern and western sections of the town.

As she approached them, Celia's and Gina's eyes flew wide open and they pranced up and down, shrieking excitedly.

"Josie! *Que bello cappotto*! Where did you get this new coat?! Did you make this on your new machine?" They made her turn around to show them the back.

" Of course I made it. Do you like it?!"

"It's the most beautiful coat I've ever seen!" Gina sighed, not a little envious. "And the style—did you design it yourself?"

"*Si*. I saw it in a picture in Papa's newspaper and I copied it. It's not too modern, do you think?

The two girls looked at each other in amazement.

"We knew you could sew, but this is . . . *magnifico!* " Celia exclaimed. "You're *sooo* lucky!" Gina nodded vigorously in agreement. "But we'd better get going or we'll be late! *Andiamo!*"

The three girls moved through the ever-thickening crowd at a brisk walk, chatting as they traveled. The air was very cold for the sun had not crept above the two and three-story brick houses that lined the street, houses that had stood in the same locations for hundreds of years. Each house shared common walls with the next in the Mediterranean fashion and every single one had a red tiled roof. Some had balconies jutting out from the second floor with lines strung across the alleys with clothes drying on them. Some of the houses in the central part of town were larger, more elaborate structures with entrances to loggias, or courtyards opening into the street that had large gates or doors closing them off from the traffic; these were the homes of the wealthy and were known as the *palacios*, or mansions. They passed shopkeepers descending from their residences on the second and third floors who were just opening up the bakery, butcher shop, stationery store, tailor shop and other places of business. There were a few carriages and wagons in the street, but because the entire length of the town was less than a mile, most people traveled on foot. Many residents didn't even own horses or mules since there were few places in the town to stable them. Once in awhile the girls would see one of those new-fangled machines called automobiles parked in a courtyard of one of the *palacios*. No one took them seriously because they were noisy, smelly and broke down a lot.

After awhile, Josie, Celia and Gina were aware of more and more looks cast their way by children and adults alike as the town came to life. In a small town, the minutest details of life do not escape the eyes and lips of its occupants, and today's news was Josie's new coat. By the time they reached the school at the other end of the main street next to the *Catedrale*, the coat was the talk of the town. Sister Angelina was waiting outside to greet them even before they marched up the steps to the school building next door to the massive church.

"*E vero*, I see you have acquired a new coat, *Signorina*."

Josie lowered her eyes in respect. "Yes, Sister, I have. I . . . ah, I made it myself." A fleeting pang of guilt passed over her.

"Mmmmm. *Dica,* you made it yourself, eh? By hand, I assume?"

"No, Sister. My father bought a new sewing machine for—us." It somehow seemed more legitimate to Josie to include her mother as a co-recipient of such a luxurious gift. Had the Sister heard about the sewing machine too?

"Ah, you are a fortunate daughter to have such a generous father."

"Yes, Sister. I know I am."

"It is a lovely coat, *Signorina.* You sew very well." Sister Angelina managed the slightest hint of a smile that broke through the forest of wrinkles that grew in the corners of her mouth. "*Allora,* go quickly now or you'll be late."

"Yes, Sister," the girls chimed in unison and ran up the stairs.

By lunchtime, the entire upper grade levels of the school knew that Josephina Mattola, daughter of the town's civil clerk, owned a brand new treadle sewing machine. And that she had made a fully–lined winter coat of mostly her own design out of English wool that her father had given her. Josie had expected to stir up some excitement, but she was amazed at the buzz that her windfall had generated. Amazed and a little overwhelmed, to tell the truth. She had never been the center of so much attention before, and although it was pleasant at first, she couldn't help but feel the looks of jealousy that were being thrown her way, especially by the girls in her grade. She dismissed them as inconsequential, figuring they would tire of it and life would soon resume its usual steady, dull rhythm.

At the close of the school day when she was preparing to leave, she donned her new coat and gathered up her books. Maybe, she thought, the walk home would be less dramatic. She knew, as most teenage girls instinctively know, the half-life of gossip. She waited until all of the students left the classroom, then turned towards the door to find Gina and Celia. Where were they?

Instead, the imposing figure of none other than the Bishop filled the doorway. The words he intoned were a command, not a question. "A word, *Signorina* Mattola."

Chapter 3   The Gardener

Giacomo Constanza was walking up the steps of the Bishop's residence next to the *Catedrale* on a cold morning in late November carrying his gardening tools when he spotted three teenage girls wrapped arm in arm walking towards the school building. The one in the middle was the tallest and the most attractive, he thought, not sure whether it was her good looks or the new, fashionable coat that she was wearing that lent her an air of confidence beyond her years. She had thick reddish-brown hair that had a hint of curl to it and large, dark eyes that seemed especially alive for that early hour. She threw her head back and casually tossed her hair in the wind while she laughed at something her friends said. He generally paid little or no attention to the town's teenagers because most of them, he thought, were spoiled brats who didn't know what a good day's work was and were, in his humble opinion, overindulged by their parents at every opportunity. This girl caught his eye mostly because of her new coat though, which although probably homemade, looked surprisingly stylish and well crafted. Perhaps her father had bought it from a catalogue, who knew?

He walked into the inner courtyard and began to prune some dead branches off the Bishop's leafless fruit trees. Of all the plants in his garden, the Bishop loved his fruit trees the most. They must remind him of his home in Sicily, he mused. It was important not to cut the viable parts of the tree since at this time of year with no leaves or buds, it was hard to tell the difference. It would be a grave error to trim off the end of a branch that would in a few months flower and then turn into a piece of fruit. But he had been taking care of growing things for many years, and he cut with the confidence of an expert. He was glad he had brought his gloves--it was cold.

Soon he saw his employer approach him across the courtyard. *Il Vescovo,* the Bishop, moved with the aspect of a man in charge of the world, and so he was. One didn't become a Bishop in the Catholic Church without ambition, diligence and good fortune. The Bishop had all of these qualities, and connections, too. Giacomo had heard rumors of a minor misstep earlier in the Bishop's career which prevented him from being appointed to one of the larger Italian dioceses, or even to one of the coveted cathedrals in Rome, closer to the Holy Father. Things could have been worse for the Bishop, he rationalized; *Il Vescovo* could have been sent to Tunisia or some God-forsaken land in the Orient. That was now many years ago, and it seemed as though the Bishop had succeeded quite well in his career. At least he was still in Italy, close to, yet removed from, the center of power and authority in Rome.

Not that that guaranteed a large, willing flock of penitents. Catholicism was the "official" religion of Italy but many people were only nominal believers. Some never saw the inside of a church between the day they were baptized and the day they were buried after the mass their families thought they'd better include in their loved one's final send-off. Most of the town's population paid genial respects to the church, baptized their children, send them to school or catechism classes, participated in First Holy Communion, got married in the Church and then found excuses to stop going. The Cathedral was only one, albeit the most important one, of the six churches in the town and was the church of choice for the wealthier townsfolk of Citta St. Angelo. The farmers and residents of the outskirts of the town attended a country church located on the road to Pescara. Giacomo's family went to the "Peasants' Church," but he himself did not attend. Ever. Giacomo had no use for religion.

His lack of spiritual participation did not deter the Bishop in the least from employing him as a groundskeeper. There was no one more talented with trees and plants than Giacomo Constanza. He had the gift, a natural ability to bring things to life. He was a short, gruff, uneducated man of about thirty who was not afraid of physical labor and had a deep copper tan, even in November. Giacomo spoke little and seemed like he was ready to jump into a fight at the least provocation, most likely as a result of serving in the trenches during the Great War. Like most farmers, he knew how to fix and build almost anything, and could do it with the most basic tools and supplies. The Bishop had heard that he liked his wine, but since the idea of dining with the help was unfathomable to him, he could not confirm that rumor. Thank God, the Bishop thought, that we have such people to grow our food and work our land. And thank God he always shows up for work, no matter what the weather.

The Bishop gestured lightly for him to join him. He greeted him with a genial handshake as Giacomo bowed slightly to him.

"Do you have time for a special project, my son?" he asked.

"*Certamente, Signor.*" Giacomo always smiled deferentially at the Bishop's special projects since they often meant an extra fee. "Follow me, then."

They walked into the Cathedral that was dedicated to the town's patron saint, the Archangel Michael. In Catholic lore, the Archangel Michael was God's favored angel and was given the job of

"Defender of the Faith." Compared to other Catholic cathedrals, this one was relatively simple in its ornamentation, having a large painting of Christ above the altar and a number of lesser sculptures of saints and angels at the base of the painting. The walls were a dingy brown, except for the wall that faced the street which was filled with windows made of plain, clear glass. Rows of moveable chairs were lined neatly in the space before the altar and even these looked beat up and dusty. It looked like everything needed a good cleaning.

In the back of the church's nave on a high pedestal all by itself stood a five-foot tall statue of the town's namesake, the Archangel Michael, made of painted limestone. The Archangel stood with one foot in front of the other, his torso twisted with one arm raised high above his head, brandishing a long, slim sword. Spread elegantly behind him were a pair of open wings with feathers carved in the greatest detail. Shoulder-length hair flowed part of the way down his back and a halo that was painted gold sat atop his head. A scabbard held in his other arm was balanced against his foot. He was tall and determined, ready to do battle against the forces of Satan. Giacomo thought his halo looked a little like a dinner plate screwed into the top of his skull.

The most unusual part of this statue, to those who saw it for the first time, was the fact that the Archangel Michael was dressed in what appeared to be clothes—not sculpted clothes of stone but clothes made of real fabric. He wore a faded green cloth tunic that stretched to his knees with a thick, ornate belt around the waist. Over the tunic was a dark blue, almost black cape gathered fully about his shoulders and attached around the neck by a gold-colored clasp. Trimmed with golden thread at the borders, the cape fell gracefully behind him to his ankles and somehow magically did not interfere in the least with those handsome wings. His legs were covered by medieval-style tights or leggings. The effect would have been quite impressive if it hadn't been for the layers of dust between the fabric's folds and some very obvious frayed seams. No one in the town thought it was unusual for the legendary leader of God's angel minions to be dressed like a doll, as this was a common occurrence in that part of Italy. Figurines of all sizes, ecclesiastic and secular, were often decorated in clothing to make them appear more realistic. It was considered a lesser art in the countryside and it was widely practiced among the faithful.

Giacomo followed the Bishop to the back of the church and waited for his instructions. He thought the statue looked silly and almost sad, even though it was probably the town's most revered artifact. Everyone knows how rich the Catholic Church is, so why didn't they hire a tailor? At least clean his clothes! Giacomo thought it best to keep these thoughts to himself.

The two of them stopped at the base of the pedestal. "Are you able to do a small job for me, Giacomo?" *Il Vescovo* smiled and his eyes lit up. The thought of denying the Bishop's request was not even a consideration.

"Of course, Excellency."

"The Archangel needs some new clothes, do you agree?"

"*Si*, yes, new clothes."

"In order to remove the old clothes and replace them with new ones, we need a ladder, more like a scaffold, so the seamstress can work on the statue. Can you build such a scaffold around Michael Angelo? Within the week, perhaps? The seamstress does not weigh very much ..."

Giacomo could not believe his good fortune. An extra job that he could perform indoors. "It will be done as you request, Signor. *Grazie*."

"By Saturday evening, then? Good. Let me know what materials you'll need." He turned abruptly and was gone, his shoes clicking a rhythm on the stone floor.

31

Giacomo immediately began designing the scaffold in his mind. It must have steps to the level of the statue's head and a platform that allowed the seamstress to walk completely around the statue but not touch it. It must be very sturdy! He didn't want to think of the ramifications of a broken statue or an injured seamstress. I'll put a railing on the platform, too, he planned.

The next morning the sound of hammering and sawing wood reached the Bishop in his chambers at an ungodly early hour. That Giacomo wasted no time.

Now to hire the girl.

Chapter 4   The Archangel

Josie took a nervous step back as she bowed slightly to the Bishop and murmured, "*Buona sera,* Father." She didn't know what else to say.

"It has come to my attention that you have a new winter coat, young lady."

"Yes, Sir. I do."

"May I see this coat, *per favore.*" It was not a question.

"Of course." She picked the coat up off the chair next to her desk and handed it gently to him, spreading it across his arms like a child.

The Bishop held the garment up for inspection and quietly marveled at the design, craftsmanship and execution. He studied the lines of the coat, so unlike any coat he had seen being worn in this town. The lining was integrated almost perfectly into the outer shell of the wool fabric, the buttons were straight and true and the collar—so unusual to see a collar like that. In particular, he made note of the tight, even stitches that could only have been made by a machine.

"Mmm. How did you acquire such a coat?"

Josie took a deep breath. "I—I made it, Father." She was one step away from a panic attack. Her heart was pounding as she tried unsuccessfully to keep from blushing and breaking out into small beads of sweat. She wasn't exactly sure if she had broken any rules, published or unpublished. A visit by the Bishop could only mean that something very important was in the works. He had never even spoken to her before.

"You have done a remarkable job on this, *Signorina*. How did you manage to get the stitches so even?"

"Oh, well, ah, Sir, my father bought a sewing machine for my mother. And for me. She—we—do a lot of sewing at our house." Had she said too much? She couldn't be sure.

"A sewing machine, eh?" The rumor was confirmed. One of his best parishioners had a sewing machine and a daughter that was an accomplished tailor. He would have to pay a visit to *Signor* Mattola very soon.

"Am I in trouble, Sir? Did I do something wrong?" she asked carefully.

"No, my dear, not at all. I had heard a rumor about this very coat and wanted to see it for myself. I can see you're very proud of it. A good job, a good job, yes. By the way, is your father going to be home this evening after supper?"

"Yes, of course." She was dying of curiosity now. "Why do you ask?"

"I would like to visit him and your mother for a chat. I have a proposal to discuss with them. Around six-thirty, then?"

"Six-thirty, yes, *grazie*, *Signor*. I'll tell them to expect you. *Grazie*." She bowed again.

He left her standing there in a panic. What had she done? Would her father take the sewing machine away? How did this all happen so fast? Where were Celia and Gina? They were nowhere to be found. The rumor mill would be in full production by this time.

Before she turned toward home, she decided to walk into the cathedral next door to collect her thoughts. She and her parents were parishioners there, so she was familiar with every nook and cranny of the church. It was true that it was a little run-down these days, but she still enjoyed the sense of history and longevity she felt attending mass there. It was like an old friend, always available for consultation. She stood in the doorway to the nave of the church but for some reason did not approach the altar. It was good that there was no one in the nave; she didn't want to be seen and have to talk to anybody right then. She wandered over to the statue of the Archangel Michael, paused at its base and looked up into his face. The events of the past few days overwhelmed her as she breathed a silent prayer of supplication to the figure looming high above her, spreading his wings as if to engulf her in his mercy and protect her.

"Please intercede for me, Saint Michael. I don't know if I did anything wrong but please protect me from what's to come!" She couldn't be sure, but in that moment, she thought she felt a light stirring of warm air drift past her face and hair.

The walk home was the coldest and longest she could remember.

Chapter 5 A Commission

At precisely six-thirty that evening, one of the very few automobiles in the town pulled up in front of the Mattola home. Without fanfare, the driver opened the door and the Bishop stepped out. Up two steps and he was in the warmth of the Mattola's parlor where the stove was full of coal and there was not a particle of dust to be seen. Even the crucifix with the body of Jesus hanging on the wall had been cleaned and polished in a frenzy of housework. Water for hot tea was boiling on the stove and a small selection of biscotti was waiting on the good china platter in the kitchen. The Mattolas greeted the Bishop politely with the greatest of respect, barely hiding the fact that this was an extraordinary occurrence for them as both parents and parishioners. Josie was banished to her room upstairs, where all thoughts of eavesdropping were dashed by the annoyingly loud creaking of the aging floorboards of the top two stairs. The driver, although invited in, waited outside at the request of the Bishop.

Signor Mattola gestured to the Bishop and he took a seat on the sofa with the skirt of his black cassock spread fastidiously around him.

"May God bless this house and your family, *Signor* Mattola."

"*Grazie*, Father. And you as well. We are honored to have you in our home." He and his wife nodded in deference. *Signora* Mattola served the men some tea, leaving the platter of sweets on the table.

"You no doubt are wondering about the reason for my visit." The Bishop took a sip and a bite and paused. His eyes scanned the small room and fell on the new black sewing machine that seemed oddly out of place next to the well-worn furniture, rugs and curtains. The Mattolas nodded. "*Si*, Excellency."

"I have been told that your daughter, Josephina, is a talented seamstress."

They both brightened. "Yes, Father, she is very accomplished," Mr. Mattola agreed.

"And is that the machine that she sews her garments on?"

"Yes. God has blessed me with a few extra lire which I have saved over the years to buy this machine for my wife and daughter," Mazzola looked at his wife in agreement. She nodded slowly and said, "There is only one other machine like it in *Citta St. Angelo*, Father, and that is at Impresario's Tailor Shop, although it is an older style machine." Her husband shot her a glance that said, "That's enough." He hoped the Bishop didn't chastise him for not giving more to the Church. But that wasn't what was on the Bishop's mind tonight.

"God has indeed been gracious to you two. And to your daughter. A lovely girl, very polite . . . I examined the coat that she has made on this machine of yours and found it to be of excellent workmanship. Did she have any help?"

Just when the Mattolas thought it was safe to relax a little, the suggestion of fraud jarred the parents' mood. "Oh, no, Father; she made it all herself, even the design, I swear," *Signora* Mattola crossed herself.

"If you are certain that she has done all of the work on the coat herself, then I have a proposition for you."

"Certainly, Father, anything you ask."

"I would like to hire your daughter to construct a new set of clothes for the statue of the blessed Saint Michael Angelo in the *Catedrale.* The clothes he wears now are old and frayed and do not represent the Commander of God's Angelic Host and Defender of our Faith in the proper light. I am proposing that she design a new set of clothes similar to the ones he wears now but with a few modifications, for which I will pay her what you consider a fair price. I will provide her with all the material and supplies she needs. And I would like to have this project completed by

Christmas. Will you permit her to undertake such a commission?" The Bishop sipped his tea patiently.

The Mattolas looked at each other again and, almost as one, let out an imperceptible sigh of relief. What an honor to be commissioned by the Bishop to create clothing for the town's patron saint! Even if the compensation was far below market wages, the Mattolas couldn't have been more flattered. Their daughter had brought such honor to the family. Mr. Mattola beamed with pride.

"I am pleased to give my permission, Excellency. Josephina will do an outstanding job for you, I will guarantee it. This is a great honor for our family. She will begin tomorrow after school. Thank you, Sir."

"Well then. We have an agreement. She can come to my office tomorrow after classes. *Molto grazie, Signor e Signora.* I will not keep you up any longer. I'm sure you would like to discuss our conversation with your daughter, eh? Please impress upon her the seriousness of this task in God's eyes. *Buona notte.*"

He shook hands with Mr. Mattola and bowed his head gently to the missus. In a second, he was gone into the night.

As soon as Josie heard the car's wheels on the pavement, she ran down the stairs to face her parents.

She was wound up like a wire stretched to capacity and was expecting the worst, without knowing what that could possibly be. She looked anxiously at her father and bit her lower lip.

"Josie, the Bishop has asked you to design and sew a new set of clothes for the statue of Saint Michael Angelo in the *Catedrale*. The Bishop is actually going to pay you, too! You are to start tomorrow after school. And you must have the job finished by Christmas Eve. He will provide all of the supplies that you'll need but you will have to use the new sewing machine. Congratulations, daughter! You have a commission!"

"Eeeiiii!" Josie almost fainted. She couldn't believe her good fortune. She was sure that she had gotten into some kind of trouble, maybe for acting too proud of her accomplishment or for designing a garment that was too different from the normally drab coats worn by the townspeople. She remembered her prayer to Saint Michael the day before and pondered how quickly he must have interceded on her behalf. She crossed herself and silently thanked the Archangel who from this point on would be her personal favorite saint.

Never before had so much attention been drawn to her or her family than during the past week. Ever since the sewing machine arrived, a whirlwind of

41

excitement had engulfed the Mattola household, far beyond anyone's expectations. Did she deserve all of this? she asked herself. Whatever the answer, she knew she had a job to do and the impact of the commission began to sink into her young mind. She told herself she had to be grown up now, responsible like an adult. No childish games or excuses. She could not mess up this job or her parents would be so shamed that she might as well leave town for good. Could she do a worthy job? Yes, she was sure of it. Could she finish it before Christmas? Yes, she *had* to. A calmness overcame her and she realized that she was ready. She was up for the challenge!

"*Bene*, Papa. I'll start tomorrow." She hugged the only mother and father she had ever known with tears in her eyes. "I won't let you down."

Chapter 6   The Cape

Josie climbed the scaffold yet again to check her measurements. She was spending most of her spare time these days either sewing, measuring or sleeping, it seemed. There was barely time for homework, and no time at all for her friends. Celia and Gina would gossip with her in class but she quickly lost interest in their chatter. She felt like she was on the edge of the adult world now and didn't have time for frivolities. She had to maintain her focus.

This commission posed some interesting challenges; she was finding that making clothes for a winged statue was not exactly like making clothes for a human. It was those darned—rather, *blessed*—wings! As she climbed up and down the new wooden scaffold that the gardener had built, she tossed around the problem of the tunic and the cape: how could she get them to lie correctly over the wings? The original set of clothes had been sewn in pieces around the wings and were stitched by hand onto the statue so that they were permanently attached. That was why they were so dusty—no one could take them off to clean them without tearing them apart. Josie wanted to make the clothes portable so that anyone could remove them and wash and press them. So her design had to allow for the tunic to open in two places in the back and expand enough to clear the wings, yet be fitted enough when in place on St. Michael's body to look like one piece of clothing. Even though the situation was similar, the cape was easier to address since it was draped over the shoulders and didn't have to be removed over the statue's head.

Josie came up with a solution. She designed the back of the tunic so that the wings slid into the gaps between three strips of cloth. The tunic fell just to the statue's knees and would be covered in the back by the cape, so a few simple hook and eye closings on each strip could hold the strips together. But the cape was longer and was lined. Since the cape just had to cover the back of the statue and not fall over the shoulders in the front, Josie thought up a design where the cape would be made entirely of wide strips of lined fabric attached to a semicircular yoke that was held closed at St. Michael's throat by the clasp from the first cape. She was pleased with this idea; it gave the cape a sense of movement and interest while letting the wings poke through naturally at conveniently-placed openings in the design.

She showed her idea to the Bishop in a sketch. At first he hesitated, wondering at this young woman's creativity, but decided the design might be too unconventional. He would think about it, he told her. In his office, he searched the iconography, looking at pictures of the saint in several art history books. Nowhere did the books show the kind of cape Josie had designed, but the books were very old and who would object to a small update? The next day he relented and gave her permission to use the new design, smiling at her eagerness to translate it into fabric. With this hurdle overcome, the Bishop had just one more request of his young seamstress who was creating such a fine, new look for his *catedrale*'s patron saint.

"*Signorina* Mattola, would you add one more item to the cape for me?" he asked her solemnly. "It is an unusual request, and I would like you to keep the knowledge of this item to yourself, do you understand?"

"Yes, Sir, I will not tell a soul." She was not being paid to question such a patron as powerful as the Bishop, but the thought of why he would ask her to keep a secret did cross her mind. "What would you like me to add?"

"I want you to sew a small pocket into the lining of one of the panels that covers St. Michael's right shoulder. A pocket that cannot be seen from the outside, eh? Think of it as a place to put a pocket watch if he were alive in our times. Make sure to put a closing on it so the "pocket watch" won't fall out. Only you and I will know of the existence of this pocket. This must remain our secret design. Do you understand?"

"Yes, Father. Only you and I." Maybe he wants to put a holy relic in the hidden pocket! she speculated. At any rate, the secret would be theirs.

The day that Josie completed the outfit, she asked the Bishop to meet her while she fitted it to the statue. In the dim light of the afternoon, the two of them stood at the base of the pedestal as the Bishop spoke a simple blessing over the red tunic and the black cape.

"Lord God of the Universe, bless these garments which your servant Josephina has created to adorn your holy archangel Michael. In the name of the Father, the Son and the Holy Ghost, Amen." Josie followed with a breathless "Amen" of her own.

She climbed up the scaffold, cradling the garments like a newborn child to her breast. With the greatest care, she slipped the richly-decorated brocade tunic first over the tip of the angel's sword, gathering it as she slid it down his arm to his head, undoing the hooks and eyes to fit it around the other arm and the wings, then reconnecting the tiny clasps. She heard the quiet "tick" of the metal as each hook slid into place, accepting the eye of its mate. Bending down, she pulled the tunic toward the angel's knees all the way around his body, smoothing the fabric as she went.

Next she added his belt and arranged its buckle in the front, pulling the fabric folds of the tunic so that they were even and symmetrical.

But before she added the cape, she asked the Bishop to approach the scaffold. From below, he looked up at her as she silently opened the cape, exposing the lining of the right shoulder section to reveal a pocket measuring about three inches square. A flap of fabric neatly overlaid the opening, a button and buttonhole added for the time when something precious and holy would find its way into the secret space. She put her index finger up to her closed lips, signaling that she was bound by her honor never to speak of this to another soul.

When the cape was lifted onto the statue's shoulders, the clasp was closed, and when Josie was satisfied that the folds of the fabric fell just right, she descended the platform and joined the Bishop in silence at the foot of the pedestal. Together they stepped back to better appreciate the image they saw before them.

In the dying light of the afternoon, the statue seemed to radiate its own internal glow. The red tunic and the black cape with the clasp about his neck made the statue seem to come alive. Maybe it was her imagination, but Josie thought that Michael Angelo stood a little taller in his new outfit. He certainly looked well dressed for spiritual battle.

The Bishop finally spoke. "*Signorina*, your work is magnificent. I am so pleased . . . You are very talented for one so young."

Josie blushed furiously at the compliment. "*Grazie*, Excellency."

Il Vescovo continued. "The Church is most grateful for your work. I will settle up with your father later this week."

He smiled at her and she noticed a distant look in his eyes. "We shall rededicate the statue at Christmas mass but until that time, the statue will remain covered. Thank you again." He extended his hand and as Josie went to shake it, he placed both of his hands around hers and held it for a moment. She looked into his eyes and nodded, understanding the gesture completely. Their pact was sealed.

Standing quietly in the far corner of the church, the gardener Giacomo observed the exchange without a word.

Chapter 7   The Introduction

The next morning, Josie decided to stop at the *catedrale* to made a final
alteration to the back of the tunic on the statue. She knew that the gardener would be coming to take down the scaffold soon so she had to do it quickly. That gardener always responded promptly to the instructions handed down by the Bishop.

She had seen him once or twice during the course of the project, peeking in the nave to see what was going on. He even came and interrupted her once to tighten up the railing on the scaffold steps. He didn't say much to her, he just looked at her in a funny way like he was studying her and didn't approve of what he saw. He was always so *serious,* she thought. She wondered what his life was like since she knew he didn't live in the town. Was he married? Men of his age usually were. Did he have children? Did he live in a big house? Where did he learn to build things so well? She was naturally curious but did not think it was proper for her to initiate conversation with him, so she kept her distance. She was pretty sure, though, that he was watching her work on more than one occasion.

Yesterday he had actually talked to her. She was amazed that he would be the least bit interested in what she was doing, but he was. He came silently to the base of the statue while she was on the scaffold altering the tunic and nearly startled her to death.

"*Signorina* . . . " he mumbled with his hands in his pockets.

"AYYY! Don't sneak up on me like that—you almost made me fall, *Signor*!

"Oh, I—ah—I'm so sorry, very sorry. I didn't mean to scare you, I just, ah—well, I just wanted to ask you how much longer you thought you might be working on the garments. I mean, when do you think you'll be done with the job, not today, but, you know, uh—when will it be done?" His face was rather red.

Josie was shocked that he had spoken so many words to her at one time. Up to that point, he hadn't said more than a single word to her. She put down her sewing kit and climbed down the scaffolding. She noticed that he had turned away from her as she descended as if he was embarrassed. When she reached the stone floor, she moved around to the front of him where she could see his face and smiled gently at him. Awkwardly, he moved back a step.

"My name is Josephina Mazzola. The Bishop told me your name was Giacomo. Giacomo Constanza. So, *Signor* Constanza, what do you think of the new clothes?" Her eyes twinkled as she introduced herself.

Josie couldn't believe she was saying these words to this strange man.

"The clothes? Oh, they're very well made. He—uh— really needed new clothes. They're—the clothes are very nice." Giacomo had relaxed a little but still had trouble looking her in the face. "You are a good seamstress, *Signorina*."

"*Molto grazie, Signor*." There was another pause. Josie summoned up more courage and asked, "Do you live in town, Giacomo?" Josie astounded herself with her new-found boldness. Her mother would be mortified if she knew she was talking to him. But she was curious, even interested in this strong, silent and mysterious person.

"I live four miles outside of Citta St. Angelo, toward the north, on a farm. Why do you ask?" He couldn't imagine why she would be interested in his home's location, unless . . .

"I haven't been to many places outside of the town, is all. I don't get to travel much. I don't know anyone with your last name in Citta St. Angelo and I just wondered where your family was from." She really wanted to know more about *him*, for she was finding him intriguing and the more they spoke, the more interested she became. Although he was not handsome, she liked the way he looked. He had very dark longish hair with a slight wave to it, the broad shoulders and thick arms of a working man, and rough hands. Although she was about an inch taller than he was, he seemed wider in bulk than she. He had the beginnings of a shadow of beard growth that made his teeth seem even whiter than she had first observed. All in all, he was rugged-looking, fit and muscular. It seemed important to her to get him to smile at her for she wanted him to be comfortable around her.

Giacomo was sizing up the conversation as he watched this young woman's attempts to get him to open up. He *had* been watching her work but, truth be told, he was certain that a girl as attractive as she was would not be interested in an older man like him, with few prospects. She was smart and a little outspoken for her age, but the most attractive thing about her was her confidence. He was drawn to her confidence and easy way of being; it made him feel important. She was genuine and unpretentious, not at all spoiled like he thought she was when he first saw her walking down the street in her new coat. That kind of sincerity was infectious. He wanted to be around it, more and more. As her work was coming to an end, he wondered whether he would see her again. He wondered if he dared think of asking her to meet him for a cup of coffee. Or to come to her house and meet her parents. . . but one thing at a time. He was getting way ahead of himself and had to check his thoughts.

He did want to keep talking to her, though. She had such a nice smile . . .

It was safe to talk about his family, he thought. If she was interested in his family, then he would talk about his family. She might as well know right away.

"You're right, Josephina, my family is not from Citta St. Angelo. They owned land to the north of here for many years, but because of some bad investments, we lost some of it. My father and mother are now dead and my three brothers and I live in the house on our farm. We grow wheat and hay and have a few cows. My brothers are married and the house is pretty crowded right now." Giacomo paused to recover from the effort of talking so much.

The question that burned in Josie's mind had to be asked. She was dying to know the answer, but she didn't know why it was so important. "And you are married, Giacomo?"

Giacomo's face seemed to soften and a wistful look settled in his eyes. He sighed slightly and looked directly into her eyes. She's so young, he thought, what does she know of the pain of life? The kind that never leaves your soul, even for a second?

"No, Josephina Mattola, I am not married." He paused briefly, remembering. "My wife died in childbirth six years ago."

Josie's hand flew to her mouth and she gasped. She had overstepped her bounds and had pried into this poor man's personal life without mercy for his feelings. Her attempts at flirtation had backfired and now it was *her* turn to be embarrassed.

"Giacomo, I am so sorry. I didn't mean to be so rude. Please forgive me, I am so sorry. . . " her voice trailed off and she didn't know what to say. Suddenly the tone of the conversation changed dramatically. She felt awful.

He saw the impact that the information had on her. She seemed genuinely moved. He didn't tell many people about that dark chapter of his life but somehow he felt he could tell her. He thought she needed to know. No matter what happened in the future. She needed to know that much about him.

"It's all right. You didn't know. You don't have to be sorry. It was a long time ago. A long time." He moved a little closer to her and lightly took her hand. Then he kissed it softly, closing his eyes, as if to honor the two people he had lost those years ago. When he opened them, Josie saw the trace of a tear.

"I have to go now. It was good talking to you, *Signorina.*" He was gone as quietly as he had come into the sanctuary, leaving her in silence at the base of the statue.

Chapter 8   The Assault

She waited until the mass was over and the
faithful filed out. Most of the daily worshippers were
old, arthritic women dressed in black, some of whom
were the grandmothers, or *nonnis*, of her friends. She
nodded a greeting to the ones she knew, all the while
studying their reaction to the covered statue. A few of
them glanced up and noticed St. Michael Angelo's
covering, but for most of them shuffling by, the only
thing new was the scaffolding as the full impact of the
change was not yet apparent. Josie was counting the
days until the unveiling of the statue at the High Mass
on Christmas Eve.

As quiet descended on the cathedral once
again, she gathered a few sewing tools she had brought
in a carry-all bag. But she stopped what she was doing
when she heard some voices in the courtyard, low
voices of men talking or maybe arguing, she thought.
The voices stopped and started again, and although she
could not make out what was being said, she thought
she recognized the voice of the Bishop. Footsteps on
the stones could be heard, then more voices. Josie
thought she had better go. She packed up her
equipment and moved to a corner of the church, a
shadowy corner near the entrance to the nave where

she could leave unnoticed. Something wasn't right, she thought; maybe she'd stay just a minute more.

Then she saw the Bishop come in through a small door across the length of the center aisle. He looked to the left and right, checking to see if there were any people in the cathedral before slipping in. The basilica seemed empty. As Josie watched from her hideaway, she saw another man, a man she had never seen before, walk in quickly behind the Bishop and take his arm, walking slightly ahead of him and sort of leading him. He mumbled something to the Bishop, who did not look very happy about the situation. This man *was* a stranger; he was tall and powerfully built, with dark hair and eyes and wore brown pants and a dark jacket. He also had a dark cap on his head and a large, bushy mustache sprouted from his upper lip. Why was he holding the Bishop like that?

The two men walked briskly toward the statue. The stranger was now behind the Bishop as he pushed the Bishop up the scaffold stairs. Josie could hear them now as the stranger snarled, "Go get it, be quick and no one will get hurt." At that point Josie suspected that whatever the Bishop was after, it was against his own will and that she was probably witnessing a robbery. What should she do? She couldn't let them know she was there or she would be endangered as well. She couldn't move without drawing attention to herself; even if she could get to the entrance, the large wooden doors would make a lot of noise in the stillness of the church and she would no doubt be discovered. Time seemed to suspend itself as she watched the events in front of her unfold. It took a supreme act of will to keep from crying out or moving her body. She stood transfixed, riveted to the spot, helpless, frustrated and scared.

The Bishop was now at the top of the scaffold around the back of the statue. He was parting the sections of the black cape, turning them inside out, searching for something. He's looking for the watch pocket! Josie figured that he had put something valuable in the watch pocket for safekeeping last night after she had left; he must have forgotten exactly where the watch pocket was located. This WAS a robbery! That's why the strange man had forced him to walk alongside of him.

Josie began to breathe harder and harder and her restraint was crumbling. It was so hard to be still! What could she do? Why didn't someone come into the church? She looked silently to her right and saw nothing but windows—no escape for her there. The strange man raised his voice a little and said, "You better hurry up, Padre, or you're a dead man." "No!"

Josie thought. She was screaming inside and her head was pounding, ready to explode.

Just then she caught a movement outside the window closest to her out of the corner of her eye. Lo and behold, it was the gardener, Giacomo, trimming some hedges. Could she catch his attention? She rotated her body quietly so that she was facing the window and smiled a large, toothy grin. Raising her hand, she waved at him in a minimalist gesture, hoping to be noticed. For what seemed like an interminable amount of time, she stood there grinning and waving until at last he looked towards the window and saw her. She thought, he thinks I'm flirting with him or making a joke! He nodded and looked away again and she moved both hands up quickly, palms facing her chest, and wiggled her fingers as if to say, "Come hither, man!" He definitely took notice of that. A little smile crossed one side of his mouth as Josie saw him think for a second about what he should do. She smiled again and tossed her head. He put down his shears and started to move toward the door. *Finally,* she thought!

Giacomo walked into the church entrance as quietly as the big doors would let him. An odd place for a romantic tryst, he thought, but kind of exciting. At the very same time, he saw a stranger starting to climb up the scaffold and give the Bishop standing at the top an ultimatum: "Time's up, Padre. Say your prayers!"

Giacomo Constanza was not a big man, but he was a quick man and in an instant, he shot over to the scaffold, grabbed the stranger by the jacket and whipped him around, smashing him in the face with his fist. The Bishop shrank back in fear, which gave the two men more room to fight. Using the element of surprise to his advantage, Giacomo smacked the man above him down onto the steps that he himself had made. His cap flew off as his head hit the wood, but this just served to make him madder. As he stood up and tried to get a foothold, Giacomo threw the full force of his body against his knees from below, tackling him and causing him to lose his balance. The stranger cursed and exhaled an "Ooof" as he was hit. He fell over Giacomo, rolled down the steps and landed with a 'crack' head first on the stone floor at the base of the statue. He did not move again. A small amount of blood trickled from the man's nose and ear. It was over in a minute and an eerie silence returned to the cathedral.

The two stood there in utter shock as they looked down at the body of the dead man on the church floor. Neither one thought of Josie Mattola, who was still standing in the shadows with both hands over her mouth, unable to make a sound, hardly breathing and completely unable to comprehend that a man lay dead on the floor of her church.

Chapter 9   The Decision

For a long moment, the Bishop and Giacomo looked at each other, not daring to speak. Finally, Giacomo said, "Excellency, are you all right? Are you hurt?" as he climbed the steps to help the older man down from the scaffold.

"Yes, my son, no, I 'm all right. I . . . can't thank you enough for saving my life, but dear God, a life has been taken and I am responsible and . . . in God's house. . . " his voice broke, trailing off in a cloud of confusion. Giacomo seemed to be suddenly possessed as he left the Bishop and in a matter of seconds, he locked the doors to the sanctuary. He returned to the man on the floor, kicked him to make sure he was dead, and then turned to the Bishop.

"Father, are we alone?"

"I—I think so. Yes, I think so."

"Did you see Josephina Mattola here?"

"Josephina Mattola?"

"Father, I was outside and I saw her through the window. She gestured to me to come into the sanctuary just as all this was going on. Do you know where she is?" The Bishop looked dazed and did not seem to comprehend what Giacomo was saying. He seemed incapable of decision or action.

Josie could not contain herself any longer. She stepped out from her hiding place and walked hesitantly over to the men. As she looked Giacomo in the face, her eyes pleaded with him to be discreet before she spoke.

"Father, I saw everything. I was, uh, about to make one last alteration on the statue's tunic when I heard you two arguing out in the courtyard. I tried to leave but you walked in before I could. I'm so sorry, I didn't mean to eavesdrop, I didn't know what to do and I was so scared . . . I was afraid he was going to kill you! I saw Giacomo outside and I , um, got him to come inside to help you . . ." The impact of what she had just witnessed hit her all at once and she started to sob.

The Bishop looked down at her tear-stained face. "Don't cry, my dear, don't cry! You saved me, Josie Mattola. If you hadn't been here, it might have been very different—for all of us. Thank you, *Signorina*, thank you. You were so brave. And Giacomo, thank you too. But I have to think what to do about this. Would you two be kind enough to stay for a while?" They both shook their heads as they looked questioningly at each other. Each was anxious to see what the Bishop was going to do.

"Giacomo, please keep the doors locked for a little while longer."

The Bishop walked down the center aisle to the altar, fell on his knees and began to pray. Giacomo and Josie stayed in the back of the church; Josie sat in one of the church chairs, while Giacomo dragged the man's body toward the small door that exited into the courtyard. He took the man's jacket off and covered his head and chest so Josie wouldn't have to look at the distorted neck and indented skull. Surprisingly, he thought, there is hardly any blood. The Bishop was still praying so he went over and sat next to Josie.

"How are you holding up, *Signorina*?" he asked tentatively.

She hung her head. "I've never seen a dead body, or a man killed right in front of me. You must be very strong, *Signor* Constanza." she paused. " Are you sorry you killed him?"

He kind of snorted. "No. He was going to hurt the Bishop. And you, if he found you. And he probably would have found you."

She tossed that thought around in her head. Now that her safety was assured, she didn't really feel like she had been in any danger. But earlier . . .

"I'm glad I was able to get your attention at the window," she admitted.

"I have a confession, *Signorina*. I have been watching you for awhile now, long before I saw you today in the window. You—" there was a very long pause before he spoke. "You are a very good seamstress."

Josie blushed. She had never been this close to a man that she was not related to before. She studied his face, his hair and his neck that showed through his open shirt. He was not like the boys in her grade at school, he was a *real* man. He had tiny wrinkles at the edges of his eyes and a tuft of coarse black hair stuck out from his shirt. He smelled like a working man who needed a bath. A real man who had just killed someone, she reminded herself. Not that the dead man didn't deserve it.

"Here comes the Bishop, *Signorina*. I wonder what he's going to do."

Chapter 10   The Arrangement

Il Vescovo was praying only part of the time he was kneeling in front of the altar. The rest of the time he was thinking. A man killed in his church, even in self-defense, presented a real problem. If he called the police, there would be many, many questions, some of which he did not want to address, questions that would involve two other people, to whom he owed his life. What to do? Whatever he did, he had to act quickly. At mid-day the cathedral was usually empty on a weekday but one couldn't count on having no visitors at all. A dead body in the shadows was hardly conducive to spiritual enlightenment.

He turned slightly and sneaked a peek at his two unwitting co-conspirators. They were politely talking to one another in muted voices. All else was quiet in the church, at least for the moment. He crossed himself, asked for forgiveness, rose and walked toward Josie and Giacomo.

"Josie, would you give Giacomo and me a minute alone? Please just wait in the confessional booth." She nodded in agreement and walked into the booth, drawing the curtain after her. The Bishop gestured Giacomo to join him in the pew-chairs. The dead man, now covered by his jacket, lay just a few feet away from them. They moved their chairs in a small semi-circle as if to corral him off.

"I have prayed for the three of us, Giacomo, giving thanks to God for our survival and I asked Him what we should do. I'm sure you understand that it is of utmost importance to avoid a scandal in God's Holy Church." Giacomo looked very solemn as he shook his head in agreement.

"There are several ways we can proceed here," the Bishop continued, "but I need your advice and cooperation. Would you like me to call the police to report the attack, Giacomo? I can tell them that you fought off the man to protect me and that this whole thing was an accident. What do you think?"

Giacomo didn't know what to say, but his gut reaction was not to involve any outside authorities. Nobody trusted the police. It was bad enough that the deed took place in a church. He knew the capacity for gossip in the town and no matter how the story got out, it would not be repeated accurately and he was afraid of the consequences. More important, however, was the impact on the Bishop. If he got into trouble, he might no longer want to employ Giacomo as his workman. Then, what would he do for work? He barely considered the impact such a scandal would have on the young Josie and her family. Without a moment's hesitation, he told the Bishop, "No *policia*, Excellency. I think we should handle this ourselves."

The Bishop nodded in agreement. That was just what he wanted to hear. Now, time was truly of the essence. "Do you think you can help me, ah, remove the body?" the Bishop probed, looking for the slightest hesitation from the younger man.

"Consider it done, *Signor*. I was just digging a large hole in the garden for the root ball of a new fruit tree, but it seems to me that tree could use some— fertilizer. I can do it quickly and no one will know. But, your Excellency, I must ask you one question."

"Yes, of course."

"Did you know that man?"

The Bishop pursed his lips, expecting the question. "That man was an evil, despicable person who has caused trouble for most of his life. He is not from this area; he is from Sicily. I knew him and some friends of his many years ago before I was a priest. You might say he came to settle a score. And now it is settled for good."

Giacomo grunted. He seemed to accept the explanation.

"You should talk to the girl, Excellency."

"*Si, si, e vero*. But before I do, I want to ask your opinion of her."

"My opinion? Why?"

"Because," he paused, looking for just the right words. "I think that it is time for you to consider taking a wife."

"A *wife*?!" Giacomo was astounded at the thought, especially right now.

"Hear me out, now. She is from a decent family but doesn't have many prospects. She was adopted as a child, you see. So no one really knows where she is from or who her real parents are. Her adopted father and mother are good members of the congregation here. I could speak to them on your behalf . . ."

This was the most conversation he and the Bishop had ever had with each other and it was beginning to make Giacomo nervous.

"Excuse me, Excellency, but I have nothing to offer a wife. I have no home of my own other than the house I grew up in. There are seven of us kids and when my parents died, they left the farm to my three older brothers. They have families already living there. My younger sister lives there too. It's quite crowded, in fact. I'm only a poor gardener who—"

The Bishop patted his hand as if to say, I know, I know. "Where there is faith, there is a way, my son."

Giacomo wondered what that meant. He didn't see how any amount of faith was going to help him in this situation. Faith didn't pay the bills, at least not in his world. But the Bishop's next statement was incredulous.

"How would you like to start a new life in America?"

Giacomo raised his eyebrows high on his forehead and let out a restrained laugh in disbelief. "People like me don't go to America, Excellency."

"Oh, but you're wrong, Giacomo. There are many people, even from our own town, who have gone to America and have done well, made better lives than they could have made here in Italy. You have skills and you're a hard worker, my son."

"Excuse me, Excellency, but I can't afford to go to America and I can't afford to get married. " Now Giacomo thought the events of the morning had made the Bishop a little touched in the head. The Bishop, however, was sitting up very tall with his hands folded in his lap.

"You could afford to do both if the Church was to pay your way. Out of gratitude for your service and, shall we say, your continued discretion?"

It took a few seconds for the idea to settle into Giacomo's mind. A bribe. *America.* A wife. She *was* young, nice looking, seemed like a hard worker. The Bishop would know. Arranged marriages were customary throughout Europe and were very common in their town. Would she agree to go with him, practically a stranger, to a foreign land? It seemed unlikely, but so did the idea that he would "accidentally" kill a man earlier today. America. Hmmmmm. America. The idea would not go away.

The Bishop was waiting for an answer. Giacomo needed more time to think about this intriguing, preposterous, absolutely insane idea, but time was a luxury that he did not possess right now.

"Excellency, I need some time to think about this. It's so—sudden—and I, uh, am not sure if Josie Mattola is even interested in me and going to America . . . it's a lot to take in right now, you know?" his eyes were darting nervously from the Bishop to the girl and back to the Bishop again. He ran his hands through his hair.

The Bishop sat very still and waited. Not very patiently.

The silence was deafening. A cloud of expectation hung over the two men.

Giacomo took a deep breath, exhaled slowly and said, "All right."

Chapter 11   The Marriage Proposal

"What is taking them so long?" Josie wondered. The air was getting so close in the confessional booth that she started to sweat. What in the world were they talking about? She thought her teachers were probably wondering why she was so late for school. It would be hard not to tell anyone about the day's events, especially her mother. And Gina and Celia would pressure her to tell them why she was so late. She wished they would hurry up and settle things.

Finally, she heard the Bishop's footsteps as he reached the confessional, parted the curtains and asked Josie to step out. The dead man's body was still on the stone floor although it had been moved again to an even less conspicuous spot and his face and upper body were now covered with construction canvas. Josie glanced uneasily at the body; it struck her as strange that no one had come into the cathedral in all this time.

The Bishop smiled reassuringly. "Josie, please sit down with us." She obeyed and took a seat next to Giacomo in the pew-chairs. She thought the two of them seemed unusually composed. The gardener looked at her sideways and cast a peculiar smile at her, as if he had a secret.

71

"*Signorina* Josie," the Bishop began, "Giacomo and I have worked out a solution to our situation involving this disgusting thief who tried to rob our Lord God's sacred church this morning. You need not know the details, they are not important. But just know that you are safe now and there will be no further discussion of today's events to anyone, not even your parents and especially not with your friends. This is for everyone's safety. Do you understand?"

Josie figured the Bishop would again ask her for her silence. She nodded in assent. She remembered how the town had gossiped about her new coat; she could not even imagine how the townspeople would take the news of a killing in the cathedral. "Yes, Excellency, I understand completely," she said as she put her right hand across her heart and bowed her head gently over it.

"What will happen now?" she asked.

"Now, young lady, I have agreed to intercede in another matter of great importance to your future. This man, Giacomo Constanza, has asked me to help him find a wife. I can attest that this man is a hard worker and that he is strong and loyal. He has just told me that he is planning to emigrate to America, where he has prospects for work and knows some *paisanos* from our town.

He paused for a moment to let the information sink in, gauging Josie's reaction. She sat impassively, waiting for the rest of his speech, wondering what this had to do with her.

"The wife he chooses must agree to leave with him for America within two days. He has asked me to ask you if you would be willing to take his hand in marriage."

Josie covered her mouth with her hand as she gasped, "Marriage! ME?"

Giacomo looked at the Bishop in distress as if to say, "I told you so." The Bishop, still seated, took Josie's hand and soothingly intoned, "Josie, I know all of this is coming as quite a shock to you. It is so sudden, yes? Believe me, I would not make such a bold suggestion without asking your father first, but I want you to know Giacomo's intentions and his interest in you now so you can give his proposal some serious thought. A decision must be made quickly, for the ship that is sailing to America is leaving from just outside of Rome very soon, and you must make travel plans immediately. May I present this idea to your father tonight? Are you willing to marry Giacomo and resettle in America?"

Her head was reeling as the shock of the sudden proposal began to sink in. No one she knew had ever gone to America, the land of unlimited opportunity, the home of movie stars and automobiles, New York City and Hollywood. Everybody knew about *America*. It never occurred to her to want to travel so far away from home, her parents and her life in *Citta St. Angelo*. And this man—what did she *really* know about him? Could she sleep with him? Could she have his children? Would he protect her and their family? Could he provide for them?

The Bishop sighed benignly. "My dear, I don't have to tell you that an opportunity like this is a very rare thing indeed. Not many people like you and Giacomo get the chance to start a new life in the greatest country in the world."

She was getting a little queasy in the stomach. Overwhelmed by indecision, she couldn't think calmly about taking a step of such magnitude. A marriage to a stranger was one thing, but adding to that the immediate departure for a foreign land where she didn't speak the language or know anyone was daunting, to say the least. Josie felt flattered, confused and frightened all at once. She looked first at the bishop, then at Giacomo, then back at the Bishop. THIS IS INSANE!

"I—I think I should ask my father about this, Excellency.. I—it is a wonderful opportunity and . . . but I am not sure . . . it is a huge decision!" She looked earnestly at Giacomo's face for any sign of happiness, joy, relief—any emotion at all that would give her a hint of what he was feeling. He was keeping them closely guarded in front of the Bishop, but he did smile back at her. If ever she needed help from St. Michael Angelo, it was now.

The Bishop looked at Giacomo sitting in the chair with his head down, nervously clutching his hands, and suggested, "*Signor*, perhaps I'll leave you two alone for a bit to discuss the offer." He rose and before they knew it, the two of them were alone.

Josie was speechless. Her heart was pounding so loud she thought it could be heard throughout the whole church. Giacomo now looked stern and worried. Neither moved for what seemed to be an eternity. Then Giacomo said, "*Signorina* Josie, I know I'm just a farmer from the country but I have been interested in you since I first saw you in your new coat. I think I have fallen in love with you since then." He took in a huge breath and let it out slowly, then took her hand in his.

" Would. . . you—ah, I mean—could you possibly consider the thought of marrying me and coming with me to America?" He looked at her sheepishly.

The effort overwhelmed him, and she saw beads of sweat forming on his forehead and face as he continued. "I will work very, very hard to take care of you and any children we may have. The Bishop has offered to sponsor us, and I think you and me, we could be very good together in America . . . "

Josie was so moved by his speech that her heart warmed to him, knowing the supreme effort it must have taken him to make such a proposal. Without debating with herself any further, she acted from her heart, leaned into him and whispered, "If you ask my father for my hand, I will say yes."

Watching them from a distance, the Bishop knew there had been an agreement when the two of them relaxed and started smiling at each other. He slowly made his way back to the couple, and said a silent prayer of thanks as the girl and his gardener rose to meet him. He congratulated both of them.

"Then we shall meet with your father tonight and formally arrange the marriage. I will perform the ceremony in the church tomorrow morning, and we will then go to the town office to make it legal. You can begin packing as soon as possible, but remember to pack lightly. You can't bring any more than one suitcase. And of course, your new coat. You'll have to leave the next day."

Her future was being dispatched so matter-of-factly. Get married, get on a boat and go to America and live there with the gardener. No Christmas with her family, no celebration of the saint's new clothes. It seemed so logical when the Bishop said it. What did all of these men know about her deep inside? She had the feeling that her life was moving too rapidly, spinning out of her control and that she was powerless to bring it back.

"One more thing, Excellency. Where in America will we be going?"

Giacomo and Josie both looked at the Bishop whose future he now held in his hands. Josie was surprised and touched when Giacomo softly took her hand in his and held it as lightly as a piece of fine porcelain. She looked at him again, her eyes large and searching for reaffirmation, but he remained stoically focused on the Bishop's next words.

"You will live in a place called Easton, in Pennsylvania."

Chapter 12   The Wedding

Once again, promptly at 6:30 that evening, the Bishop's car came to a halt at the home of Signor Mattola and his wife and daughter. This time, two men disembarked into the chilly evening air, and as they entered the home's modest living room, there were again pastries and tea for the guests. Giacomo Constanza had obtained a suit to wear and had bathed, shaved and washed his hair. From an old family jewelry box, he had obtained a gold ring with a small sapphire stone set in between a few diamond chips which he had at the ready in his breast pocket. He had even polished his old shoes. All in all, he looked fairly presentable, Josie thought. As introductions were made, Josie watched silently from the sidelines, studying Giacomo's body language. He didn't look very comfortable. Neither was she, under the circumstances.

As they were seated, the Bishop explained to Josie's parents that Giacomo was looking for a wife because he was leaving in two days for America. Josie had of course told her parents what to expect from this conversation and the Mattolas were not completely surprised. Italian tradition dictated that the man of the house give any unwed females permission to marry. A high ecclesiastical figure such as the Bishop rarely if ever entered into marriage negotiations. This was a very rare exception. The Mattolas had pumped Josie earlier with questions: Where did you meet him? How long have you known him? Has he been honorable with you? What does he do for a living? . . . the usual parental scrutiny. True to her word, Josie did not mention anything about the events at the church that morning.

Signor Mattola seemed satisfied with her answers. His only comment was that Giacomo was from a farm family that he knew nothing about. There really wasn't enough time to meet the relatives or even investigate his family's background under the circumstances. If the Bishop vouched for him, that was enough for Signor Mattola. But Josie's mother was crushed. She had envisioned planning a wedding and reception for her only child and now she would be lucky to get a luncheon together under such short notice. And then, she would be gone! Both parents recognized the wonderful opportunity to go to live in America that had inadvertently landed in their daughter's lap. Although the man was quite a bit older than Josie, older men marrying young women was common in those times. They were confident that the Bishop would not put Josie in a bad situation. It was just so . . . sudden! They had both wondered if there was more to this quickie wedding that met the eye. Josie had assured them that there had been no fooling around—how was a parent to know? One had just to go on faith.

The Bishop was winding down his explanation of support for the union, then turned to Giacomo and asked him to get Josie. She had been standing the whole time in the corner of the room next to the new sewing machine, her hand casually stroking the black neck where she had stitched together the garments that had brought her to this point in her life. The Bishop and her parents watched him as Giacomo strode toward her with the ring in his hand.

"Josephina Mattola, will you, ah, will you marry me? I promise to take care of you and if we have some, a few, uh, children," he stammered in a shaky voice. He looked to the Bishop for reassurance. The words were simple and direct, fitting the man that uttered them.

Tears welled up in Josie's eyes and she let go of the sewing machine. She swallowed hard and thought, this is it. There was no turning back after she answered. She glanced at her parents and the Bishop. She looked down at the ring, gave Giacomo her left hand and he slipped the ring onto it. She let out a sigh as she said, "Yes, I will marry you."

"Tomorrow, then, at the *catedrale,* say at ten? " the Bishop was satisfied.

The two looked into each other's eyes for agreement, found it and said, "*Si*, ten." Signora Mattola started to cry softly.

At 9:30 the next morning, the Mattolas left their house followed by a small band of friends and relatives, including Celia and Gina. At the head of the group walked Josie, resplendent in her mother's wedding dress and veil and carrying a bouquet of yellow daisies. Her dark hair was gathered at the top of her head and curls fell softly down the back to her neckline beneath a short white veil. Her mother had given her a pretty gold crucifix to wear around her neck as a wedding gift. She had on her new coat and her only pair of dress-up shoes as she led the procession down the alleyway and over the cobblestones of the main street to the cathedral. The shopkeepers came out to the street to wave to the wedding party as they marched past, shaking their heads at how beautiful the bride looked and wishing her well. By now they all had heard that the girl who made the new clothes for the Archangel was marrying and going to America. As she walked through the town, she felt like a minor celebrity, one who was

81

leaving this provincial outback behind for a big, exciting new world. A *very* lucky girl.

They cheered at her and yelled "*Buona Fortuna!*" at the top of their lungs. Some yelled "America! America!" A few threw flowers at them as they passed and sometimes a coin or two.

They entered the cathedral and met the Bishop at the back of the church. As the party was seated, they acknowledged the few relatives from the Constanza family who had made the trip to the cathedral to witness the marriage. The Constanzas stayed together and didn't mingle much with the rest of the guests. Giacomo stood at the altar with the Bishop in the same suit he had worn the night before when he had proposed. Signor Mattola walked toward the altar with his beautiful daughter on his arm, still a bit perplexed by the whole event. He kissed her with tears in his eyes and whispered something in her ear, then handed her to Giacomo. She heard her mother crying again and caught a glimpse of Celia and Gina sitting together, dabbing at their eyes. The Bishop intoned the Latin liturgy of marriage as he had done so many times before, but now with exceptional interest in the couple who would take the secret of his past with them to America and, he hoped, bury it there.

At the end, he turned to Giacomo and declared, "You may kiss the bride!"

Josie trembled as Giacomo lifted her veil and gave her her very first kiss. He smelled like cigarettes and shampoo as they awkwardly grasped one another in a hug. She thought, "He's so much older than I am, he must know what he's doing," and he did, since he had had relationships with other women before Josie.

They turned and faced the congregation and all began to clap and cheer in celebration as they walked down the aisle as man and wife. They slowly walked past the statue of Archangel Michael and Josie paused for just a second to offer thanks; as she did she noticed Giacomo didn't look at the statue or at her. He kept his eyes forward as he said, "We should go."

The bride and groom walked out of the church and led the group back through the town, arm in arm, to the Mattola's house, where a hastily-prepared lunch buffet had been set for the guests. The whole town seemed to be out in the street cheering them on and vying for a glimpse of the lucky couple. Two boys ran up to Giacomo and tapped him on the back and old and young townsfolk threw rice, pennies or flowers at them, chanting *America, America! Remember us in America!*

Congratulations and wine flowed easily as the bride and groom went from room to room greeting the guests. There was fresh fruit and cheese, sliced ham and olives, meatballs and pasta and lots of wine. The

Bishop had arranged for the party to be catered against the strenuous objections of Mrs. Mattola. His argument had been firm and solid: how was she to get the luncheon together in such a short time? He did have a point. The Mattolas did manage to buy the biggest cake in the town's bakery. It was covered with white icing and the baker agreed to add some embellishments and topped it with a white dove. Each of the guests received a small packet of candied almonds, a token of good luck from the bride and groom. There was no time to hire a band but they danced to the sounds of records played on a victrola borrowed from one of the neighbors.

There was no consoling Gina and Celia for the loss of their friend. They looked Giacomo up and down suspiciously, taking in with disapproval the man responsible for 'kidnapping' their friend. He tried to talk to them but they just stared at him like he was from Mars. Gina did manage to get close enough to say, "You'd better not hurt my friend!"

Josie moved from group to group, smiled and thanked everyone for their well wishes and gifts, promising to write to all about the trip to the United States and their new life there in great detail. Giacomo followed her from room to room, stiffly and solemnly, looking a bit out of place as though he hoped the whole ordeal would be over soon. He was on his fourth glass of wine when people started to leave. His relatives were giving him the eye.

Giacomo pulled Josie to the side and said, "*Cara*, my relatives are leaving in the wagon now— I'm going to go back home with them to pack and get ready for the trip. I'll have to stay there tonight so we'll have to postpone our wedding night for just a little longer. We can wait, no? I'll pick you up in the morning, early so we can get down to Pescara and catch the train to Rome. I have everything we need from the Bishop; you will be ready, eh?" He leaned over her and gave her a kiss like she'd never experienced before, full of wine and desire. She laughed at his seriousness and thought to herself, "He thinks I'm going to back out. But he's mistaken. We're married now and I go where he goes."

"I'll be ready, Giacomo. I'll be waiting for you."

That night, after all the guests were gone and her parents had cleaned up, they sat in the quiet parlor looking exhaustedly at each other. No one said anything—they were too tired. Josie had just counted her wedding money which totaled an impressive $100.00. Most of the guests didn't have time to buy a gift and they wouldn't have had room to take them anyway so they gave money, a small amount here and there but it had added up to a sizeable sum.

"Papa, would you keep some of this money for me, just in case I ever need it? Can it be our secret? Just for an emergency?"

"Of course, *mia filia*. No one needs to know." Josie thought that he was the best father in the world at that moment. She got up and embraced the only parents she had ever known and started to cry. It was all so overwhelming!

Her mother patted her hair and soothed her fears. "It will be fine, *cara*, you'll see. Everything will be fine. Now tell me—are you all packed? Don't forget to sew some of this money into your coat lining tonight. It's time for you to go to bed. Giacomo will be here early and you want to look nice for him, your new husband. Come, I'll help you get undressed." Josie nodded automatically and wearily climbed the stairs for the last night she would spend in her family's home.

Chapter 13   Departure

Saying goodbye was the hardest thing of all. Josie had not expected it to be so difficult; but in fact, she had not had time to think about it at all. There was packing to do, friends and relatives to see, and of course, the wedding. Her new husband was not very much in evidence, which in a way was fortunate in that it gave her more time to prepare for the journey. It was so hard to decide what to bring! All she knew about her destination, Pennsylvania, was that it was in the Northeast part of the United States which meant that it had warm summers and cold winters, Similar to the climate of Abruzzo, except the winters were colder and longer. She could only bring one suitcase but found out later that a shipping trunk was made available, a wedding present from the Bishop, and her mother helped her to fill it with domestic items--several sheets, towels and a few more pieces of clothing—and some nonperishable foodstuffs. She chose the sturdiest pair of shoes she owned, two dresses of a practical fabric, two sweaters, her undergarments and sleepwear, and a few personal items. She left some room in the trunk for Giacomo's cargo too. Giacomo had obtained the necessary papers when he went with the Bishop to the town clerk's office to sign the marriage documents.

The morning after the wedding, Celia and Gina came to her house for a short visit. The three friends had not had any time together since the incredible news of Josie's marriage and trip to America was announced. They sat in her bedroom on the bed, not knowing whether to laugh or cry, so they did both.

"What's he like?" Gina prodded. "Is he a good kisser?"

"Yes, Josie, you must *tell* us *everything*! We didn't know you two liked each other! You kept it hidden very well from your best friends!" She jabbed Josie in the ribs with her elbow.

"It all happened so suddenly—one minute he was just another man, and the next, I guess Fate stepped in and said, 'You two should be together.'" Josie figured that was as true a statement as the circumstances would permit. "The Bishop says he's a good, strong man who will be a decent husband and father, and Mama and Papa approve, so we decided to get married. He's very different from the boys at school, much more mature, serious, hard-working. . . "

". . . and experienced!" Gina's eyes grew wide as she put on a mock-serious look. They all burst into peals of laughter. "I'll bet you aren't his first woman, *e vero*?"

Josie thought about that. "Noooo, I'm sure I'm not. But listen!" Her voice lowered to a whisper. "

Mama took me aside when all the guests left after our wedding dinner and she gave me a talk about the 'facts of life' ."

The girls were all ears now. No one had ever given them the "facts of life" talk. Their voices all dropped to a level of high secrecy, as if national security was at stake. "What did she say?" Celia and Gina both breathed in unison.

"She said that men are a different breed of people than women are. They are the heads of the household and women must obey what they say. When you have children with a man, he is supposed to be the disciplinarian and you are supposed to be the loving, caring one. She said I should take care of his needs all the time, even in the bedroom. If he wants to eat, I should feed him. If he wants to sleep, I should let him sleep. I should do whatever he says or whatever he wants me to do when we are in bed together. That way, he cannot complain that I am a bad wife and my life with him will be good. That's what she said."

The three of them looked at each other in dead earnest. None of them knew anything about sex, so this information was a revelation to them. Josie finally said, "My parents have been happily married for a long time, so I guess my mother knows what she's talking about. Oh, and she said something else: Good Italian girls do not get divorced."

"Divorced!" the two friends spoke the word in unison. No one in the town knew anyone who was divorced. Only celebrities in the newspapers got divorced.

"Now, help me finish packing, you two!"

"You must promise you'll write to us and tell us about your journey! And about married life, too. We *have* to know, Josie!"

"I will, I will. I promise! I can't believe this is happening to me!" There was a pause filled with heaviness. " I'll miss you both so much . . ." The tears started to flow and for a brief moment, Josic's resolve wavered as a touch of regret crept into her heart. She recovered in an instant, hugged her friends in a long embrace, and they said their last goodbyes.

The following morning dawned overcast and chilly as the Mattola household prepared for the leaving. Josie's mother had dark bags under her eyes, which were lately moist and red from crying. Her father looked worried, for he wasn't at all sure this was such a good idea. Even though the man was vetted by the Bishop, he couldn't read him and had the natural protective instincts of a father towards an unknown man after his daughter. What bothered him most, though, was his daughter moving so far away that he could not easily step in to help her if she needed him. No one in *Citta St. Angelo* could afford a trip to

America except the Bishop. The new husband also seemed a little rough around the edges for his daughter. But there was nothing to be done about it now.

As dawn became day, the trunk and the suitcase were moved to the front step of the house in which Josie had spent almost her entire life. A few of the neighbors came to say their goodbyes as they heard the goings-on next door. Soon the neighborhood kids ran to the family to tell them a horse and wagon were coming up the main street with two men in it. "That must be Giacomo," Josie thought. "He's quite the punctual one, isn't he?" She stood in the new morning in her most comfortable dress and shoes, a scarf around her head, and her lovely winter coat, holding hands with her mother, listening for the sounds of the horse's hooves on the cobblestones.

At the last minute, she broke free and went back into the house for a last look alone. She walked into the living room, up to the new sewing machine that had been her mechanical partner over the past few months and touched it one last time. 'I'll get one just like you in America,' she promised herself.

Giacomo and his brother pulled the wagon up to the house at about 7:30. He climbed down, shook Signor Mattola's hand, kissed Signora Mattola on each cheek, and kissed Josie hello. Not much was said as the men loaded the trunk and the suitcase into the back of the wagon, leaving room for the newlyweds to sit. Josie smiled at her new husband with tears in her eyes, trying to put on a brave face and be a grown-up. He smiled back, tipped his hat to the Mattolas, helped her into the wagon and gave her the blanket to cover up with, and climbed in himself.

The driver urged the horse to turn the wagon around, and they were off, bumping their way over the cobblestones. For a few minutes, Josie could see her parents waving to them as they drew further away, her mother crying in her father's shoulder, and her heart hurt so badly. She leaned into Giacomo for comfort. All her bravery left her that moment and she started to sob like a baby. Giacomo patted her on the back lightly and leaned into her, lost in his own feelings. He simply said, "That's all right, my girl. It will be all right."

With all of his strength, he fervently wished it was to be true, but somehow he suspected that they had a long, rough road ahead of them.

Chapter 14   The Train

By the time they got to the train station at Pescara, they were both stiff and sore from the long wagon ride over Abruzzo's rough roads. They had to catch a noon train to Rome, transfer to another train to take them to Naples, and meet the ship that would take them to America on the very next day. It was a tight schedule that allowed for little margin of error. The Bishop had given Giacomo a generous stipend for traveling in addition to the passage tickets, which were well-guarded in his breast pocket. Neither was prepared for the emotional stress of the trip.

His brother drove the horse at a decent clip most of the way and when they finally arrived at the station, they had some time to spare. Giacomo's brother gave the horse a rest and some water while they waited for the train and the men smoked cigarettes before saying their goodbyes. By this time, Josie had regained her composure and was in the full spirit of the adventure.

The train arrived only a few minutes late and before long, the couple was on their way. Josie watched out the window incredulously as the train slowly climbed into the Appenine Mountains. She had peered at those mountains in the distance through her bedroom window for so many years, and now she was surrounded by their snow-covered peaks that glistened in the winter sun. Small towns just like *Citta St. Angelo* perched atop high hills that were surrounded by ancient walls passed by in a blur. As they crossed the divide, she began to notice that the towns they passed seemed to be larger and had bigger houses in them. The closer they got to Rome, the more automobiles they saw on the roadways, and by the time they entered the city limits, there were only a few horse-drawn wagons.

Before they disembarked, Giacomo told her to stay very close to him and not to wander away. He knew she had never been out of the small town they had left behind and feared she would get lost or accosted by pickpockets or worse. Josie was surprised at this sudden lecture, for Giacomo had slept soundly for most of the train ride. She wondered how he could sleep when all of the world going by the train was so fascinating to her, then she remembered that he had been this way before so these things weren't new to him. She remembered what her mother had said, that he was the boss. She realized she was totally dependent on him. It occurred to her that she carried no money, no food and no papers; if they were separated, it would be almost impossible to find each other in the huge city. Giacomo would make sure she didn't leave his side.

Since they had to change trains at the station, it was necessary to leave Josie with the trunk and the luggage so that Giacomo could purchase the tickets and find the track from which that the next train would leave. They carted their belongings to a waiting room with seats where Josie could stay until he returned. The noise was deafening and the crowds of people intimidated Josie a little. Before he left, he cautioned her, "Don't speak to anyone, and don't leave the luggage! I'll be back soon" and he disappeared into the crowd.

Josie took some crackers and sausage out of the trunk and started making some lunch. No one paid any attention to her, although there were many children, men and women passing by and milling around her luggage. She took her scarf off her head and tied her long hair back with it at the base of her neck. Suddenly she looked up and saw a man staring at her from across the room. Lowering her eyes, she continued to eat and turned away from his gaze. The next thing she knew, the same man was behind her hovering over her shoulder. She turned and looked up at him and he said, "Are you traveling alone, *Signorina*?" She was shocked at the nerve of this man, wondering if he was going to steal something from her, then she was

95

confused about what to do. Giacomo had said not to speak to anyone, but surely he would want her to protect their belongings. The man spoke again, "*Scusi, Signorina*, can I offer my assistance?"

She stood up and looked him straight in the eye, for she was rather tall for her age. "Go away! Leave me alone! My husband will be back shortly, " she exclaimed as she gestured with her fingers like she was sweeping him off.

The next thing she knew Giacomo appeared, telling her to sit down. She could see he was angry. He threw her a disapproving look as he sidled very close to the man and sneered in his face, "Get lost, or you'll be sorry, pal!" The man was taken aback and didn't move right away. Giacomo, springing like a cat, pushed him in the chest and yelled, "Beat it! NOW!" The man stumbled, lost his balance, went down on one knee and started to mumble an apology with his hand raised. Giacomo stood above him fuming with fists cocked as the people surrounding them moved off, expecting a fight. Josie jumped up and implored Giacomo to let the man leave, trying to divert his attention and calm him down. The man took off, melting quickly into the crowd amid the comments of the onlookers.

Giacomo was not pleased. He turned to Josie, still red in the face and breathing hard, ready for the fight, and launched into her.

"I told you not to speak to anyone! Is this how you listen to me? What's wrong with you? You better straighten out or I'm going to . . . " his voice trailed off when he realized that he was yelling and people were staring at him. He took a deep breath, tried to compose himself, and lowered his voice. He stopped pacing and sat down next to her. "Josie, listen to me," he was almost pleading. "You have to pay attention to what I say. You're too young to know the things I know. Traveling can be dangerous, very dangerous. You never know what people are up to. So don't talk to anybody unless I talk to them first. You hear me?"

"Yes, I hear you," she said meekly. He frightened her. She would've said anything to calm him down.

"Now we have to get to track 7 so you take the suitcases and I'll take the trunk. Let's go." She was amazed when he heaved the trunk onto one shoulder as she followed him through the crowd, towing the two suitcases. They slowly wove their way down some stairs, through a passageway and into a covered railroad yard where the massive trains were arriving and departing. The din of the machines and the smell of oil and exhaust were sickening, but they found track

7, hauled the luggage up into the train and boarded. It wasn't long before the train pulled out for the trip to Naples.

Josie was exhausted but her mind was racing, so sleep was out of the question. Giacomo seemed withdrawn and she sensed that he didn't want to talk to her right then. She didn't know if he blamed her for the incident or if he was just being overprotective. She was flattered that he tried to rescue her but at the same time, she was slightly annoyed that he didn't trust her to take care of the situation herself. Did her mother's words "to obey" her husband mean to obey him in *every* circumstance, like the obedience expected from children? Did she really disobey him by telling the man to go away? Was Giacomo going to be a jealous husband? All of these thoughts raced through her head but produced no answers. The only thing Josie could arrive at was that she had to be more careful. Careful of what, though, wasn't quite clear.

Chapter 15   The Ship

They finally reached Naples, the great port town of the southern Italian peninsula, in the early evening. A mass of travelers, luggage, dockhands, trucks, horses and wagons, and cargo loads on the piers clustered around the great iron hulks of the steamships berthed at the docks. There was movement and noise everywhere. Josie could not believe how large the ships were. She stared wide-eyed from one to another, taking in their massive bulk, and crossed herself at the thought that one of them would be taking them across an entire ocean to their new life in America. She looked up at the top deck, craning as far as her neck would reach, wondering if it was as high as the belltower at the *Catedrale* at *Citta St. Angelo*. Imagine the things one could see from a vantage point that high! People bumped into her as she lugged the two suitcases along because she wasn't always watching where she was going. Giacomo was in front negotiating the path through the crowd, still hauling the trunk on his shoulder and still not saying a word to her. Finally, they stopped at a small shack that had a sign above it that said, "The Hamburg American Line."

Fortunately for them, the ticket agent spoke Italian, although not their dialect, but he and Giacomo soon entered into a discussion of arrangements for their departure the next day. The agent wanted Giacomo to check their trunk and one of the suitcases overnight so that they could be loaded onto the ship early. Giacomo refused. The agent, who no doubt had seen hundreds of emigrants like the couple standing in front of him now, was getting annoyed and flipped his hand dismissively in the air as if to say, "You'll see. . . " He validated their tickets, checked their papers and then gave Giacomo directions to the hotel that had an arrangement with the shipping line to house the passengers until the ship departed. In their case, they would stay only one night. The hotel was only a couple of blocks from the docks, so again they trudged forward, dragging their worldly possessions with them.

Although the hotel was one step up from a flophouse, Josie thought it must be an absolute haven for the weary travelers who filled its halls and rooms. Like them, there were dozens of working-class Italian families, couples and single men just whiling away time in the lobby, outside or in the restaurant next door. They were all dressed like she and Giacomo were, and had the brown skin and rough callouses of people who worked outside with their hands. She observed them carefully as she passed; they looked back knowingly at her and Giacomo, for they all knew that they would be shipmates on the morrow. But she didn't speak to anyone.

At last they were in their room. Josie didn't much care at that point that the bedding was old and a little stained, that the wallpaper was peeling in more than one spot, or that the bathroom was down the hall. She took off her coat and scarf and flopped on the bed, exhausted. She was too tired to think that this dingy room might be their honeymoon suite, since Giacomo hadn't made any advances towards her since they left. She was just too tired to think at all. Giacomo mumbled that he was going to the bathroom to wash up, and by the time he returned, she was fast asleep in her traveling clothes.

She woke up to the sound of a key unlocking the door. For a moment, she was disoriented and jerked upright, not recognizing the unfamiliar surroundings. In walked Giacomo with a cigarette in his hand. She smoothed out her dress and rose to meet him. As she stood up, she felt a little faint, staggered to catch her balance, and fell into his arms.

"What time is it? How long did I sleep?" she asked him. It was dark outside. She was starving.

"About three hours. You must be hungry, eh? Change your clothes and we'll go get something to eat." He sat on the bed watching her as he finished the cigarette.

For the first time, the idea that she was now married struck her with its full impact. She had never undressed in front of a man before. She had never been so far away from home before, either. Up to that point, their time together had been filled with arrangements, preparations, and traveling, the getting from one place to another. This lull took Josie by surprise and she started to get a little nervous. A meal would buy her more time to consider what would come next in their new relationship. She turned away from him and his thirsty eyes and put on a clean dress. She would have to bathe later.

They entered the night arm in arm, walking among the crowds of émigrés marking time until their departure for America. The evening air held the promise of new beginnings and the apprehension of leaving the only world they had ever known, the hopes and the fears of hundreds of people migrating to an unknown destiny, probably never to return. Josie thought these people were all so courageous to embark on such a mission; even Giacomo, her new husband, was full of bravery for taking her on this journey.

They found a small cantina that served food and ordered a meal. Giacomo had two glasses of wine to celebrate their last day in Italy and their new life as

a married couple. As they ate and drank, Josie saw
him loosen up a little and relax, and the coolness
between them diminished as they started to converse.
She wondered out loud how their families were back in
the village, sighing at the thought of the people she had
left behind. She chatted about the size of the ship and
asked how big their room would be; Giacomo just
smiled and gave her an occasional one-word answer.
But at least he was talking to her! They had coffee
after the meal and lingered for awhile at the table,
watching the people walk by. The wine seemed to put
him in a better mood.

They walked back to the hotel past the huge
ship which was lit up like a carnival. People milled
around on the docks and deck hands in their white
uniforms could be seen on the various decks getting
the ship prepared for its departure. Sounds of yelling
and the clanging of machinery punctuated the night as
Josie marveled that there was so much activity at such
a late hour.

Back at the hotel, Josie went to wash up in the
bathroom. When she returned to the room, Giacomo
was lying in his underwear on the bed.

"Well, *cara*, you should show me what a good
wife I married."
She blushed at what would happen next and said a
little prayer to Mother Mary.

She took off her clothes, lay down next to him, closed her eyes and held her breath. He started kissing her slowly, then more urgently, grasping at her breasts and the spot between her legs which had become very tingly all of a sudden. He fumbled with her nightgown while she struggled to remove it over her head. In her nakedness, she lay very still as he rolled on top of her, not touching any part of him, letting him show her the way. He was all over her, kissing and licking her body in a journey of discovery and passion, and when he finally entered her, she experienced an intense stab of pain along with a rush of pleasurable, new sensations that flooded her from head to toe. He reached his peak, then fell down onto her, almost crushing her with his weight, leaving her gasping for air and covered with sweat. He made a few grunting noises that she interpreted as satisfaction, then rolled off her. "You're a good girl," he said to her. Then he lit a cigarette and sat up in bed, smoking it with his head resting on one arm.

So that's what marriage is all about, Josie pondered. She got herself up and cleaned herself with a towel. No fireworks, no symphonies playing, no comets streaking across the heavens, just a lot of heavy breathing, sweating and bodily fluids. It was over in a flash, and she actually enjoyed most of it, or at least she didn't hate it. I guess I can get used to this, she thought; it's not so bad. She turned to look at her new husband and smiled. He actually smiled back at her as he took in her naked body. As she got back into the bed, she was especially happy to see a couple of small spots of blood on the sheet on her side.

Her mother would be pleased. The blood was an auspicious sign. She was no longer a virgin.

PART II: Sicilia 1870

Chapter 16   A Bad Seed

As he rounded a bend in the path, Rocco Di Santi could hear the desperate shrieking of an animal long before he could see anything. It was an "I'm fighting for my life" shriek that made the small hairs on his neck and arms rise. He quietly waited for the next sound, hoping to tell which direction it had come from and possibly be of some assistance. As a child, he had walked this path between his village and the main road so many times that he knew all of its natural features by heart. Most of the village children knew the accessible hideouts among the mountain paths that wound up from the valley and the creek at the bottom of the ravine. As he walked further, he smelled a whiff of smoke, not from a cigarette but from a small campfire. The sound had stopped for now. He thought maybe his senses were playing tricks on him and was about to dismiss the idea but he stopped again, only this time he thought he heard the soft sound of sobbing. He was sure he heard it.

He cautiously stepped along the path until he could smell the smoke from the small fire quite close by. On the upper edge of the path was a group of olive trees and a small clearing where he thought he saw the bushes move a little, so he headed in that direction. The sobbing, never very strong, was more controlled by this time. Rocco parted the bushes and instantly recoiled at the sight, frantically yelling, "Stop! In the name of God, stop right now!"

He was too late. A teenage boy of about fifteen was holding the limp, charred corpse of a kitten with third degree burns up its tail and hind legs. The flesh was black and bloody in some areas and smelled like singed fur and flesh. A thin rope halter had been slung around its front legs and over its back and had been tied to a stick so that the boy could dangle the animal over the fire. The kitten, already beyond any more suffering, lay in the lap of the boy who was cradling it and crying gently over it. He had a black eye, a dirty face and unkempt clothes that were full of mud, ashes and little bits of charred cat fur. Rocco was appalled.

He jumped on the boy, yelling at him and knocking him over, but the boy recovered quickly and looked at him with eyes round and full of fright and surprise. The two stared at each other, one standing and one crouching, before either one spoke.

"What in the world are you doing to that poor animal? Are you sick? How would you like it if I tied you up and put YOU in that fire? Who are you?"

The boy just stared at Rocco with his black eye and said, "Don't hurt me, please."

Rocco couldn't be sure but he thought the boy might be a little slow-witted. He had heard of a family in the next village whose son was mocked and made fun of mercilessly by the kids in the village. "Tell me your name," he demanded.

"Luigi. My name is Luigi. Don't hit me!"

"Get up! How could you do such a thing! You're going to dig a grave for that kitten you just killed. Right now! Put out that fire." The kid got up, laying the body of the cat gently on the ground, and started looking for a stick to dig a hole with. Rocco found one first and handed it to Luigi, then pushed him to get him moving to dig. "Why did you kill that cat? And where did you get the black eye?" he asked, more in control now.

"None of your business . . ."

In an instant, Rocco grabbed the boy's shirt, slammed him up against one of the olive tree trunks, and kicked him in the groin. He did not consider himself a violent person, but something about this kid and the scene he had just witnessed had unnerved him and shaken him to his core. He wanted to hurt the boy

108

as he had hurt the helpless kitten, but it struck him at that moment that more violence was not the best response in this situation. Luigi was doubled over in pain on the ground and did not fight back. He just repeated, "Don't hit me, don't hit me" over and over again and started to cry. Rocco leaned over him and ordered, "Get up and dig!"

Twenty minutes later, a respectable hole was dug in the loose dirt and Rocco made Luigi take off his undershirt and wrap the kitten's body in it. He laid it gently in the hole and covered it up with dirt. Then he said, "Let us pray," looking sideways at Luigi to make sure he was participating in the ritual. He asked God to take the soul of the tortured baby straight to heaven and to forgive the boy who had committed this horrible act. When he was done, he looked straight at Luigi and said, "Now, it's your turn to ask for forgiveness. Tell God you're sorry."

The boy shuffled his feet and looked down at the grave. He seemed somewhat detached from the small funeral ritual, as if he had just happened upon the scene. Rocco lowered his voice and said, "Go on. God will forgive you."

Luigi didn't speak for several moments. Then he squeaked out, "I'm sorry for killing the kitten. Please forgive me." He started to sob again. Rocco thought, well, at least he feels some remorse, that's good. He put his hand on Luigi's shoulder and said, "Now stop crying and tell me how you got the black eye."

Luigi wiped his eyes on his sleeve and sat down on the ground. "My old man." There was a short pause. "What do you care?"

Rocco was only a few years older than this boy, but he could see that he already had a troubled life. He didn't want to get involved, but he also didn't want to encounter another scene in the bushes like the one he had just experienced. He felt responsible for this human being who was crying out for some kind of intervention in his miserable life. What harm would it do to talk to him? "Is that why you were torturing the cat?"

Luigi just sat there looking at the ground.

"You can't go around hurting and killing weaker, helpless beings, Luigi. God expects better than that from his children. Will you promise me you won't do anything like this again, Luigi? What do you say—promise?"

A glint of emotion crept into Luigi's eyes and Rocco felt for a split second that he had reached the boy. He had stopped crying and seemed to have pulled himself together a little. However, he was wrong. Luigi pulled his hands out of his pockets and put them

110

on his hips, striking a defiant pose. His eyes narrowed as he backed away from Rocco.

"What are you, some kind of a priest, *Padre*?" he said sarcastically, mocking Rocco.

He turned on his worn-out heel and took off into the underbrush, laughing as his voice faded in the distance. Rocco could hear him chanting in the sing-song fashion of children through the ages "Pa-drey, Pa-drey, Padrey . . . ha ha ha!"

Chapter 17 The Funeral

Father Rocco smiled benignly at the mourners dressed in black as they filed slowly into the church. No one spoke a word as each one made the sign of the cross at the entrance to their pew and sat down. When they were all in place, he left the church's entrance foyer and made his way down the nave's center aisle to the altar, gathering up the altar boys as he passed. Signora Longo had a lot of friends and admirers in this town, he thought.

Although Father Rocco was the priest at the church in the village of Piaso five miles from this village, he had been asked to officiate at Signora Longo's funeral because the regular priest was in the hospital. He didn't mind. It did him good to serve other congregations and broaden his spiritual reach among the people in his home region. Life could get pretty routine in these mountain villages. He suspected that the people attending the funeral might be happy to see a different face for a change.

In this part of Sicily, almost everyone was a farmer and almost everyone was poor. Mrs. Longo was an exception; her late husband had been in business and when he died years ago, he had left her relatively well off so she never had to work. This apparently caused some envy among the hard-working women in the town. Her only son, and as Father Rocco expected, her heir, was grown and as rumors had it, didn't work either. He hadn't met the son, only a few of the other relatives.

The mass started with the familiar "*Dominus vobiscum et cum Spirito tuo*" that always made Father Rocco's heart beat a little faster. The congregants responded in one voice: "Amen." The words calmed and empowered him at the same time as he felt the spirit of the Lord rise up in his soul. He wanted everyone in the audience to feel that same passion, the same love of God that it seemed he had always had. Even as a boy, Rocco had felt the calling to be a priest and to minister to the spiritual needs of the people around him. In the late nineteenth century in Sicily, the priesthood was an admirable vocation, one that promised a secure livelihood with room for advancement. He was especially attracted to the part about advancement; he considered himself a leader of men who deserved to rise in the ranks of the Catholic clergy and who knew? Perhaps one day he might serve the Holy See in Rome. If he planned his career carefully, anything could happen. Today he wanted to make an especially good impression because he knew that he was being evaluated and people in small towns had nothing to do but talk.

As he continued the requiem, he noticed a young man in a black suit standing in the back of the church. He had a couple of companions with him but they weren't dressed as well as he --Father Rocco couldn't make out their faces. The man in the black suit gestured to the other two to wait for him outside and he entered the church alone, trying not to draw attention to himself. It was too late for that. People had heard them, some turned and stared at him and started to whisper to each other disapprovingly. He sat down in the back of the church away from the others.

Father Rocco was so accustomed to performing the rituals of the service that he could do them automatically, but he made a mental note of the scene. He thought he recognized this man. He looked so familiar to him, like a playmate that he knew as a child whom he met in later years as a grown-up. Was he related to the deceased? He would find out after the mass was over.

The recessional came and he followed the altar boys holding the church's precious relics as they marched down the nave past the weeping mourners. The young man in black was the last person he passed and as their eyes met, he saw a glint of recognition cross his face. Rocco knew him from somewhere, but where? He had recognized him too. As the service came to an end, the mourners passed by Father Rocco

114

one by one, thanking him, commenting on his service and making small talk about Signora Longo. He looked up again and saw that the young man in black had disappeared.

Alone now, Rocco walked back to the church's altar and entered a side room where the vestments and other church regalia were kept and started to undress. The altar boys were cleaning up the altar, putting away the chalice and plates that were used in the service. Rocco wondered who he could ask to move the casket out of the aisle and into one of the side rooms, waiting for the carriage hearse that would take it to the cemetery after the mass. He had to discuss the details with the family but at the moment, they weren't available.

The altar boys came into the changing room and politely said goodbye to Father Rocco. He remembered when he was so young and rosy-cheeked, filled with the Holy Spirit and devotion for his God. Then one of them said, "Father, there's a man in the church who is standing by the coffin—don't forget to check on him before you leave! *Ciao*!" and off they ran.

Rocco heard him before he saw him. He was rocking back and forth on his feet and crying quietly, repeating "Mama, Mama" to the woman in the open coffin. Ah, he thought, so *this* is her son. No wonder the mourners were whispering about him; how disrespectful to be late to your own mother's funeral! He held back awhile out of sight, half eavesdropping and half unwilling to break the man's moment of grief. After a respectful length of time had passed, Rocco stepped around the corner to introduce himself and was repulsed at what he saw.

The man was holding his dead mother's left hand as he tried to wrest a ring with a very large stone from her finger. The ring would not slide off, so he spit on it to give it some lubrication and was moving it back and forth, round and round, trying not to disturb the clothing or the position of the body. He was becoming increasingly frustrated and swore at the ring under his breath. He dropped the rigid hand and kicked the casket base in anger and was pacing back and forth with his hands in his pockets when he turned to see Father Rocco glaring at him.

"Can I help you?" Father Rocco asked sternly. "Who are you, may I ask?"

The two men stared at each other face-to-face as Rocco stifled the urge to throw the man out of the church. "Are you related to the deceased?" he pushed.

"*Si*, Father, I'm her son. Her only son. My name is Luigi, Luigi Longo." He paused and looked at Rocco hard. " Don't I know you? " he squinted his eyes trying to remember.

A flood of recognition washed over Rocco as he was finally able to place the man. He had found him torturing a cat in the woods outside of Piaso seven years ago. The revulsion of that episode returned with a vengeance to meet and mix with the disgust he now felt for the son who tried to steal a ring from his dead mother's finger. Rocco fought hard to control his feelings and remain calm.

"I meet many people in my line of work, my son. We may have met before, I don't exactly remember." Rocco wanted to keep the upper hand with this unstable man. " But you seem agitated. Have you come to say goodbye to your mother?"

"My mother?" He seemed flustered and off balance. "My mother is dead." He looked at the coffin again and his eyes settled on the ring. "She's dead and now I . . . want to get what belongs to me. What rightfully belongs to me." He looked again at Rocco to see if he would stand in his way.

Rocco offered his arm to herd Luigi away from the casket and murmured, "I'm sure your mother left her estate in good order and you'll be receiving your inheritance very soon. Have you seen your relatives? They are probably waiting for you outside where the hearse is supposed to come to pick up the casket. We shall wait together and I'll be right here with you if you need me. I want to make sure your mother gets her proper burial." He smiled sweetly.

"Huh, thank you, Father. A proper burial for Mama, *si*." Luigi was being guided to the side exit of the church where Rocco was sure there would be some people milling about, waiting for the carriage to arrive. Through the door, the sun was already hot in contrast to the cool interior of the church. The walk to the cemetery would be long and sweaty. Several people gathered around Luigi and started admonishing him for being late to the service and asking questions about his whereabouts. Rocco eased away from the group when he was satisfied that Luigi was in their good hands. He didn't have much time.

That bastard would probably try to defile the dead again if he got the chance, Rocco surmised. He saw in him a dark, lost soul who was capable of incredible evil. Did he have the guts to try to save his mortal soul? He didn't think he was up for that fight. Although the little he knew about this man disgusted him, for a moment he felt pity for him as he asked God for forgiveness. That didn't mean he had to trust him, however. Rocco didn't want anything to go wrong with the funeral or burial of such a high-profile citizen of this backwater town, and he couldn't shake the sense that Luigi would probably try to steal the ring from his mother's hand again. He had to act quickly and asked God for forgiveness again for what he was about to do.

The carriage came a short while later and Luigi and the pall bearers loaded up the closed casket into the back compartment. Rocco kept an eye on Luigi during the entire trip to the graveyard as they walked slowly behind the carriage, trudging through the dust as the women sobbed and wailed. During the burial service, Longo stayed in the rear, behind the crowd as Rocco offered condolences and advice. As the funeral cortege marched slowly back to the village after the burial, Father Rocco Di Santi and Luigi Longo trailed behind, walking almost side by side. No one would have suspected as they made their way on the dusty, rocky road back to town that, under his cassock, a flawless, 3-carat white diamond ring was buried deep in the pocket of Father Rocco's trousers.

Chapter 18   The Magistrate

Father Rocco couldn't remember a time when
he didn't want to be a priest. It seemed to him that he
had always known he would serve in the priesthood,
even when he was a little boy. His aunt would take
him to the *catedrale* in Sicily's largest city, Palermo,
when he was growing up and she told him that his
mother and father, who had both died of cholera when
he was a toddler, were angels and they were hovering
over him inside the huge church. He could never see
them, but his t*zia* assured him they were there
nonetheless and that they were living in the rafters of
the church. Any time he wanted to talk to his parents,
all he had to do was to go to church and visit them, she
said. So he did. Often.
     When he was young, this was of great comfort
to him. He missed his parents so much that he was in
the church every other day, trying vainly to remember
them. He grew to love the liturgy, the décor of the
church, even the music calmed him and made him feel
close to his parents, and by association, close to God.
As he grew older, his recollections of his parents faded
a little each time he visited the church to keep their
memory alive. But life went on and his ability to recall
them disappeared, so he would go simply to light a

candle and pray for them to watch over him. There were many times in his life that he felt his prayers were answered by his God, who continued to be a real and living entity in his soul.

Rocco was a good student and thrived in the big city, a place where intellect and scholarly pursuits were encouraged. He studied the history of Italy, the great leaders who from Roman times had led the western world in commerce and law, philosophy and art. He grew to believe that the Roman Catholic Church, for all its excesses and fallibilities, was still the greatest institution in Europe. It was, he believed, the church's birthright to be the repository for the world's greatest works of art, literature, architecture and music. He saw no irreconcilable differences between the great scientists of the past and present and the Catholic Church's spiritual teachings; indeed, he felt that all learning and creativity was divinely inspired and was welcomed in God's kingdom. Even the latest technology of his era—the steam engines, trains, even a machine that allowed two people to talk to each other over great distances—were ordained by the Holy Spirit to carry on the great work of the Mother Church.

This day Father Rocco walked down the aisle of his own little church in the Sicilian mountains and he wondered what was going on in Palermo. It wasn't that he disliked his parish of St. Lucia. The people here were the salt of the earth, simple folk who farmed the land and raised sheep and lived and died in the same village, eking out a living from the rocky and rugged countryside. They were poor and faithful. Most of them aspired to no greater position in society and were satisfied with—or resigned to —their destiny. Father Rocco didn't even mind the poverty much; but truth be told, it was the grinding sameness of life in a small village that every so often came to unsettle him. No matter how often he reminded himself that it was a sin to be prideful, his youth and ambition made him ever so impatient to be moving ahead in his career. Today he was having those same thoughts. He was wondering whether the events of the past week would have repercussions that would affect his potential for advancement within the Church hierarchy when his musings were interrupted by staccato hoofbeats in the distance heading towards the center of the village.

He stepped outside into the warm sunshine and watched a man trot a sweaty horse up to the small piazza in front of the church. The man dismounted and led his tired horse over to the fountain in the middle of the square and let him have a long drink. He loosened his saddle and found a shade tree to tie the animal to. A few of the townspeople glanced curiously at the stranger, then went on with their business, trying not to appear obvious. Strange people did not often come to this part of Sicily. They usually brought bad news.

Father Rocco walked across the piazza to greet the man. "*Buon giorno, Signor,*" he said warmly, holding out his hand. "What brings you to Piaso, my friend?"

The man took Rocco's hand in a strong grip and smiled. "Are you Father Rocco Di Santi?" he asked as Rocco nodded. "You're just the person I'm looking for, Father."

The two men walked side by side into the church. Rocco asked the housekeeper to bring a cold drink and they sat in the colonnade out of the sun. The man introduced himself as a magistrate of the circuit court of the county who had come to see Father Rocco on a matter of some urgency. It involved a desecration of a grave in a nearby village, he explained. Last week. He didn't have to elaborate about how shocked the family and the townspeople were. A high-profile family, he added. A very well-connected family involved in some very illegal activities.

Rocco suspected what was coming next. "Whose grave was desecrated, Signor?" A desecrated grave was a very serious matter that required immediate attention.

"It was the fresh grave of Signora Longo, a wealthy widow. Only two days after her burial. Two days!" He crossed himself and bowed his head.

"The grave was dug up and the casket was broken into and ransacked in the middle of the night. Whoever it was just left it like that to be found the next day, open, with the body turned on its side. I understand you officiated at the funeral, Father. I'm told there were a great many people who attended, *e vero*? Is it possible that you remembered someone there who acted strangely, who might have had a grudge against the deceased or the family, someone unhappy or angry at the funeral? Did you notice anything unusual that might shed light on our investigation?" The man looked straight into Father Rocco's eyes, looking for a reaction.

"Was the body damaged in any way? Was anything taken?" Rocco tried to look shocked, all the while hating the position he was in and, worse, not having enough time to think things through. He didn't want to lie but the alternative might be much worse.

"No, it didn't appear that robbery was the motive. Nothing seemed to be missing from the body. Father, as you can imagine, things like this just don't happen here. It is very unusual for such a senseless, malicious act of destruction to occur. It's almost as though it was an act of revenge. Who would want to take revenge on a corpse?"

Father Rocco maintained his composure, putting on his best face of sympathy. "What a terrible sin! Someone must be in great pain to commit such an abomination. I will pray for the criminal to repent and come forward."

Inside, he was in a state of quiet turmoil. He was in a spot. Did anyone see him remove Mrs. Longo's ring? What else would someone be looking for if not that ring? Everyone at the funeral saw it on her finger. It was precisely the public appearance of the ring that made the grave desecration all the more understandable, yet despicable at the same time. Still, the magistrate did not seem to think robbery was behind the deed. But one didn't really know to what lengths magistrates would go to solve a crime. The man took another leisurely sip of his drink and did not seem to be in any hurry.

"Signor, I believe the Longo family had requested that she wear a large diamond ring when she was buried. I think I remember that she had a ring on in the church during the funeral mass. I'm sure many people there saw it. The pall bearers came after the mass and secured the casket, then loaded it into the carriage hearse to go to the cemetery. I was cleaning up after the mass with the altar boys, of course, you know that I was filling in for Father Anselmo . . . I didn't know where things were to be put away, so it took me a little while to straighten up. When I was done, the family was ready to go to the cemetery so we all walked there and the body was buried." Rocco thought he was saying too much.

"And did you notice Signora Longo's son during the mass, Father? His name is Luigi."

Rocco blinked. "Yes, of course. I met the whole family. I remember Luigi especially well because he was late for the service. The rest of the family seemed upset at him. . ." his voice trailed off. He thought it was a good thing he didn't lie very often for he made a lousy liar.

Would the magistrate notice his discomfort? Who wouldn't believe a priest?

"And is there anything else suspicious that you can think of, Father?"

Rocco dropped his head and put his hand over his eyes as if to remember. Forgive me, Dear Lord, for the lies I am telling, he prayed from the bottom of his heart.

"No, nothing that I can think of. I do hope you find the one who did this."

The magistrate smiled and nodded. "We will try, Father. Thank you for your time and for the drink. I must be getting back. If you remember anything else, would you write me at my office?" He passed a small piece of paper with an address on it to the priest.

"Certainly. Go with God, my friend."

The man gathered up his horse, mounted and turned toward the mountain path, the same path where years earlier Rocco had caught Luigi torturing the cat. Rocco waved at the man as he walked out of sight down the dusty street.

Luigi. Rocco had underestimated him. He could see now that Luigi would be trouble, big trouble. He had to be careful. Extremely careful.

He went into the church, knelt in front of the altar and prayed for forgiveness. And he prayed extra hard for protection.

Chapter 19   The Summons

Several weeks after the magistrate's visit, Father Rocco was watering his garden and pondering the likelihood of anyone finding out about the lie he told the magistrate about Signora Longo's ring. His conscience was heavy with guilt and he was suffering like a man unfamiliar with the consequences of a dishonest way of life. As uncomfortable as that may be, he told himself, he had better get used to it since there was no going back now; to confess his collusion would mean the end of his career as a priest and he felt he was not suited for, nor did he desire, any other line of work. He prayed daily for forgiveness to assuage the burden, but it did not seem to lessen. As he considered how long this mental state might last, the mail was delivered to the church office and among the parcels and letters, he was surprised to see a cream-colored envelope emblazoned with the seal of the Holy See on the front in red and gold print. It was from the Vatican, addressed to *him*.

Oh, my God, he anguished. He stared at the envelope, his hands began to sweat and he anxiously paced the floor of his office. Had the archbishops and monsignors in Rome somehow found out about his perfidy? How could that be? He was certain no one knew . . . or did they? He ripped open the envelope in a panic and tore its contents out.

23 Mai 1887

The Holy Father Pope Leo requests your presence at a private meeting in his office to discuss the prospects of your future in his Holy Church and your desire to consider a promotion and relocation. Please respond immediately to arrange for an appointment.

Secretariat of State Gaetano De Lai
Office of the Roman Curia, Vatican City, Italia

Father Rocco was struck dumb. His relief washed over him as he slumped in his chair. Not only had they not found him out, he was being considered for a promotion! What kind of a promotion, he wondered? Would they make him a bishop? His prayers for forgiveness seemed to be answered in a most unexpected way and it appeared that he was off the hook, for the moment at least. What blessed irony this is, he thought! His head was spinning in a mixture of confusion, guilt and gratitude. Pull yourself together! he reminded himself. Now he had to make travel plans as quickly as possible so he dashed off a response and started to arrange for a trip to Rome.

Two weeks later, Father Rocco di Santo disembarked from the second-class cabin of the train that had been his home for two days to find himself directly in front of the gates of Vatican City in Rome. Awestruck, he peered down the boulevard that bisected the tiny municipality. The street broadened into the massive square of St. Peter built by Bernini, enclosed by a forest of stone columns that held up a covered portico graced by the statues of saints and church dignitaries on its roof. They seemed to watch protectively over the faithful who were ever-present in the huge piazza. At the far end he could see the mighty basilica of St. Peter's Cathedral with its indomitable Renaissance dome designed by the master, Michelangelo. This was not Father Rocco's first trip to Rome, but each time he visited he had the same reaction—God in His glory had inspired the greatest artists, sculptors and architects in history to proclaim His kingdom on earth through their works at St. Peter's Church. It was only fitting, he thought, that such a great church should show the world its earthly presence in this way. After all, if not for the Church, much of the art of the western world would have been lost in the passage of time, for the hoards of the heathen did not appreciate fine art.

He entered a building that contained the offices of the Roman Church's Curia.

After he registered his presence, he sat down to wait and rest. Soon a clerical assistant came to show him to his room, a Spartan cell with just a few pieces of furniture and the most basic of necessities. A large crucifix was the only decoration. He felt sure that the rooms for the higher clergy were much more accommodating, but he was not ungrateful; he was, after all, only a priest and at least he didn't have to pay for a hotel room. He was consumed by the anticipation of the upcoming meeting with the Secretariat—should he be humble, should he be assertive, how could he represent his few achievements in their best light? He knew he was not very adept at playing politics and felt a little awkward among the sophisticated clergymen he saw at work in the offices. They seemed so . . . *worldly*. He washed up and brushed the road dust off of his cassock and pants as best he could and settled down for a nap.

No sooner had he drifted off to sleep than a sharp rap on the door woke him. He was being summoned for dinner. The aide took him to a dining room where several clergymen were already seated around a huge carved oak table. The room was decorated with religiously-themed frescoes and the windows were curtained with heavy tapestry drapes. He could tell by the men's clothes that they were important-each was impeccably dressed in their ecclesiastical garments according to their rank in the Church. Introductions were made and by the time he was introduced to the man seated at the head of the table, Father Rocco realized that this was a "business lunch." The man was Gaetano De Lai.

"Father Rocco, you are no doubt pleased to be in Rome?"

"Yes, of course, your Excellency." Am I already perspiring? Rocco thought.

"Please relax and enjoy your meal, Father. The pasta is homemade and is especially good, thanks to Father Guillaume." Rocco shook his head in assent and after they said grace, everyone began to eat. They chatted congenially with each other, talking about local issues and trying to impress each other on the finer points of church law. No one included Father Rocco and he was beginning to feel very out of place. He had not expected this to be a group interview over dinner.

The plates were cleared and some sherry was brought out. All they are missing are the cigars, thought Rocco, as unseemly as that would be for priests. A couple of the younger men left to return to work, Rocco presumed, and only he, Gaetano and two other men remained. They were the Archbishop Gianini Provenzano and Archbishop Luc de Boisson.

De Lai began to speak. "Father Rocco, we have asked you to come here to discuss your future in our

132

Holy Church. We would like to ask you some questions to see if you may be suited for a transfer of position. Is that something you might be interested in?"

"Yes, your Excellency, of course. I would be humbled to serve in any capacity where I am needed."

"Ah, yes. Well, be careful in Rome when you say that. You could wind up in the janitorial service!" The other two men laughed heartily and looked knowingly at each other, then looked at Rocco for his reaction. Rocco smiled back smoothly but he feared his nervousness was beginning to show in spite of his best efforts to remain unrattled.

"Please tell us about your work in Piaso. What sort of a parish is it?"

Rocco told the men about the church's operation, how many parishioners he had, how many staff members, the annual income of the church and its expenses, and the type of people in the congregation. He tried to focus on the aspects of the church's operation that he thought might impress these administrators. He also tried to downplay how poor the congregation was.

"When I first came to the parish, there was no training program for acolytes and the choir was a mess. I was able to start a training and recruitment program which now consists of six of the local boys. The choir is improving every service as well. Also I've increased donations to the church by five percent in the last two years. I am often asked to substitute for the region's other priests who are called away on an emergency to perform their functions, and I have become somewhat well known in the area."

De Lai was listening carefully. "Is that how you came to officiate at the funeral of Signora Longo?"

Rocco was taken aback. He wasn't expecting the question. "I . . .ah, yes. That's correct. Their priest had to go to hospital." Again he smiled nervously. Would he be caught in the lie? He was a terrible liar. *Forgive me, Lord. I am such a sinner . . .*

"Relax, Father. This is not the Inquisition!" There was no deceit in his voice. "The Holy Father received a very impressive letter from the Longo family singing your praises and telling what a wonderful job you did with the mass and internment ceremony. They were so impressed that they made a rather large donation to the Church of St. Peter in your honor. This is what first brought you to our attention. We wanted to bring you here to thank you personally."

This news quite amazed him and Rocco breathed a sigh of relief. "You're welcome, Excellency."

"Now to the matter at hand. There is an opening in a parish in the province of Abruzzo on the

Adriatic Sea, directly east of Rome. It is a larger parish than the one you are currently serving, and it is a hilltop village a lot like Piaso. The bishop has retired because of poor health and we are looking for someone to revitalize the parish, institute some changes and infuse some new blood into the cathedral's staff . . . "

Did he say "Bishop? Cathedral?" He was stunned. Is this the promotion?

". . . and so we are here to discuss your thoughts about becoming the new bishop of the Cathedrale de Sant'Angelo in Citta St. Angelo, Abruzzo. What do you think, Father Rocco?"

Rocco was floored. Gather your wits about you, man! He recovered in an instant. Don't say yes right away, he thought. Ask more questions to show them that you're thorough and a man who considers serious proposals carefully. Apparently, the pause was longer than he intended.

De Lai leaned over the table and smiled again, indulgently.

"Of course, you can have some time to consider this if you need to . . . " he leaned back into his upholstered chair and looked slightly bored.

"Oh, no, Excellency, I mean, no, I don't need more time. I'm very flattered that you would consider me for this position. I . . . I hope that I am worthy of your confidence." He looked at the other two men. It was happening too fast, he thought again. So fast . . . am I ready to become a bishop? Why not? Yes! Confirmation of his decision came to him in a flash of faith in answer to his silent prayer of thanksgiving. "Yes, I accept!"

De Lai stood up, smoothed his clothing, and signaled that the meeting was over. He seemed pleased as he shook hands with Father Rocco, then the other two men, who had been silent the whole time, also shook his hand and congratulated him. "We will be in touch with the details, but it is important that you go back to Piaso and prepare to leave within two weeks. A replacement for you will be sent so that you can prepare him to take over before you leave. You will be installed in the St. Angelo *Catedrale* in one month. I will see you then. But before you go, the Holy Father would like to meet you."

The Holy Father himself! Pope Leo wanted to meet him. That must have been some donation, Rocco mused. The Longo family bought him a promotion. A nice promotion! He had the deepening sense that there was much more to this deal than what was being presented to him. Would he ever be able to find out the real reason? Probably not. Maneuverings among the rich and the powerful were always discreet. He didn't really much care, the acknowledgement was enough for him and his career in the clergy was now launched. He was going to become a bishop!

"The Holy Father will see you now. The attendant will take you to meet with His Holiness. Enjoy your stay in Rome!" De Lai nodded cordially as he left.

Rocco was whisked away by the same young man who had escorted him there. Apparently, the word was out, for he was surprised when he said, "Congratulations, Father" to him. As he thanked him, he thought, this young man looks up to me. He admires me, sees himself in ten or fifteen years looking for the same thing to happen to him. Rocco nodded at him and thought, all you have to do is steal a diamond ring from a corpse and you too can become a bishop like me.

They walked through a complex of buildings, across St. Peter's Square, crossed to the left through the stone portico and entered the building which housed the Pope's apartments. There were marble statues and paintings and frescoes everywhere. Every major artist of the Renaissance and Late Middle Ages was represented in these galleries. They were very close now to the Sistine Chapel where conclave was held to select new popes and where Michelangelo spent years toiling on the ceiling and the wall above the altar. They climbed a set of stairs and Father

137

Rocco found himself panting lightly from the exertion in front of a large set of ornately carved wooden double doors . The aide rapped gently on the door and another priest opened it. Rocco stepped into the private apartment of *Il Papa* himself.

He waited apprehensively in the outer chamber as the aide announced him. He could hear some muffled comments spoken and then some footsteps behind another door. In a moment the door opened and in walked Pope Leo. He was a man of about 70 with a slow, serious manner about him. He shook Father Rocco's hand in introduction and said, "Welcome to the Vatican, my son, Have they taken good care of you?"

"*Si, Si*, holy Father, I am quite comfortable."

"Come, sit and pray with me. I understand you are to become the new bishop of the *Catedrale* of Sant' Angelo in Abruzzo." Rocco nodded his assent.

"Then we must pray for God's guidance in your new position."

He gestured to a small altar at the other side of the room. Above the midsection of the outer wall stretching to the ceiling was a gigantic mural, a fresco he knew well. It was Raphael's *School of Athens*, where all of the western world's most famous humanists were depicted in one place as if they were giving a lecture to a group of youthful college students.

Plato and Aristotle were there, and Copernicus, Leonardo da Vinci, several popes and saints as well as vignettes of Michelangelo and Raphael himself. It was a collegial and symbolic, if not physically possible, gathering of the greatest minds in the world. With what great skill Raphael had painted the faces of all these men, he thought. Rocco looked up penitently at the figures and they all seemed to be looking down at him and smiling.

Then Pope Leo said, "Let us pray."

Chapter 20   Embarcation

Early the next morning of January 3, 1924 all of the passengers departing for America from the port of Naples gathered in the hotel lobby with their luggage and were briefed about the trans-Atlantic passage that they were about to embark upon. Every size, age and shape of immigrant was in this particular group but the predominant travelers were young couples like Josie and Giacomo Constanza. Several babies were among the travelers, with older children and even some ancient *nonnis* dressed all in black who never said a word except to bark orders at the children.

Three representatives from the ship line were there to explain things to the immigrants. They were all given paperwork to fill out written in Italian, stating their name, address and other biographical and occupational information. The representatives made it clear that they were not to lie on the forms and to remember what they wrote down. The representatives also had to verify any documents of importance that they had such as a marriage license or trade union form. One man told the emigrants that there was absolutely no fighting allowed on board the ship for any reason, so they should not gamble or get impatient with other passengers. Another man in a white coat with a stethoscope around his neck looked like a medical doctor. He told the passengers that he would be vaccinating them and that it wouldn't hurt. They had to sign and date all the forms at the bottom.

Josie began filling out her forms and didn't notice Giacomo sitting there staring at her. She looked up and saw Giacomo watching her, his forms untouched.

"Do you want me to help you?" she inquired. Giacomo just grunted.

It occurred to her at that moment that he couldn't read. She realized that he probably had not had much education, certainly not as much as she had had, but she didn't want to draw attention to his illiteracy in front of the ship representatives. She smiled and without saying a word she finished her forms, then exchanged with him quietly and began to fill his out as well. She had to ask him questions about his date of birth and his service in the military which he answered with one-and-two word responses. He's embarrassed, she thought. When she was done, she asked him to sign his name at the bottom and he put a squiggly shape on the line.

After the forms were collected and the documents were checked, the doctor came around to each group of immigrants and told them to roll up their sleeves. He took a hypodermic needle and quickly scratched the surface of each person's arm, hardly breaking the skin, using the same needle each time, just quickly wiping it off with a not-so-clean towel. He changed needles only once for the entire group of people, about fifty passengers. The children at first screamed when they saw the man in the white coat approaching them with a large needle, but after watching several of their siblings get "scratched," they stopped fussing. *Il dottore* stamped another form as "Vaccinated" for each person he scratched. Then he asked each passenger to roll his or her upper eyelid inside out as he looked for trachoma. No one in the group apparently had the mysterious eye disease and they were all cleared.

The whole process took a couple of hours and people were beginning to get restless. Finally, one of the representatives stood up and announced that every person entering America had to have $20 with them, babies excluded. A few people in the group began huddling with their relatives to count their money and make sure that they had the proper amount. One woman burst into tears as she and her husband realized that they didn't have enough. Her sobs could be heard throughout the lobby but no one came to the couple's assistance.

The group was being herded slowly out of the hotel toward the dock and the children and grown-ups began to queue up, dragging their luggage. Josie looked at the sobbing woman and back to Giacomo, trying to gauge his mood. She said, "Wait here a minute, please. I want to talk to that woman," and she quickly moved to her table before he could say anything.

The woman had her hands in front of her face and had stopped crying. "Excuse me, please, " Josie said. "My name is Josephina Constanza" and she put out her hand. The teary woman took her hand limply and Josie could see that she was a little older than she was. "May I sit down for a minute?"

The woman's husband was not to be seen, and she glanced at Giacomo who was talking to one of the representatives. "Where are you from?"

"Aquila," she said weakly.

"Then we are neighbors! I am from Citta St. Angelo, very close by. My husband and I are traveling to Pennsylvania, Easton, Pennsylvania. What is your name?"

"My name is Sofia. We were supposed to go to a place in Pennsylvania too, I think it was called the town of Allen. Now it doesn't look like we're going anywhere. My husband doesn't have enough money for the two of us. I'll have to go back to Aquila, I guess." Tears welled up in her eyes and she put her head in her hands.

"I know this is none of my business, Sofia, but how much money do you need to continue on?"

"Oh, I don't know, about 500 lira, I think. We're very close but we don't have enough for traveling expenses." She seemed to perk up a little.

"Let me ask my husband if we can loan you the money." Josie said it impulsively, then immediately wondered if she would regret it.

"Oh, my God, you would do that for us? What a wonderful thought!" Her eyes sparkled with hope.

Josie made her way through the crowd back to Giacomo. Would he be angry at her? There was only one way to find out and it was too late to back out now. She sidled up to him and kissed him on the cheek, taking him completely by surprise, for public displays of affection were rare. A cacophony of noise surrounded them as anxious immigrants jostled for position in the line and everyone was talking at once.

She whispered softly in his ear. "I will not ask for much from you, Giacomo, but I would like just this one time to ask you for a favor. The woman I just talked to is named Sofia and she and her husband are just 500 lira short of the money needed for the trip to America. I know we have some extra money from the Bishop. Could we loan them this much so they can continue the trip? Otherwise, she has to go back to Aquila. I know it's unusual but we'd be doing a good thing for them. They are traveling in steerage and are also headed to Pennsylvania." She had no idea how large Pennsylvania was but it seemed like such a coincidence that they were going to the same state. "Please, Giacomo?"

Giacomo looked at her like she was a lunatic. What kind of girl did I marry? he thought. Giving money to total strangers? Five hundred lira was not a lot of money, only about five American dollars, but the whole idea was preposterous. He frowned back at her and was ready to say no when she said, "If you were in the same situation, wouldn't you help out your neighbor? They are our neighbors, Giacomo, and our countrymen. *Paisanos* must stick together, right?" She was dead serious.

"Well, let's meet these people, then I'll see," he equivocated.

They both pushed their way through the crowd to Sofia's table where her husband had joined her. They were in animated conversation but they stopped as Giacomo and Josie approached. Introductions were quickly made and as Giacomo sized up the man he was about to make a loan to, the women held each other's hands, waiting for the verdict.

Giacomo seemed to like the husband, whose name was Nicholas Abbondanza. They moved off together to speak a few words and shook hands in the middle of the crowd. A few of the passengers picked up on what was going on and smiled their approval, but the women were so excited that they hugged each other and jumped up and down in place. Giacomo looked at Josie disapprovingly but said nothing.

"*Now* we can get on the ship!" Nicholas' relief was evident in his face and Sofia was dabbing at the remainder of her tears. They walked out into the morning sunshine together, the men carrying their steamer trunks on their shoulders and the women toting two suitcases apiece. They soon blended into the crowd of immigrants moving inexorably up the wide, steep gangplank into the belly of the ship that would bring them to America.

At the top of the gangplank, ship employees were directing people to their accommodations. Josie found it difficult to comprehend that such a large structure could float across an ocean. They went down narrow corridors, up stairs, down more stairs, carting their luggage and maneuvering around the hundreds of passengers already on the ship. Finally they were directed to the ship's level just above the steerage compartments, in second class passage, to their tiny room not much larger than a closet. When they dumped their luggage, they were quite cramped. The twin bed looked small and mildly threatening to Josie as she thought of the nights she would be pressed up tightly against her new husband. Giacomo was sweating with the effort of carrying the trunk and had taken off his coat and shoes and was sitting on the bed. *He'd* think the room was elegant! Josie thought as she sat on the steamer trunk. In the shuffle they had lost the Abbondanzas but she knew they were somewhere just below them in the lowest level of accommodations, the cavernous area called steerage because it was close to the steering mechanism of the huge ship.

About an hour and a half later, they heard a long, deep, ear-piercing whistle that was so loud it rumbled through the walls of the entire ship. Giacomo said that they should go out on deck and take a last look at their homeland. They joined hundreds of other passengers at the railings hollering to those left behind on the dock, waving handkerchiefs, laughing and crying as the behemoth moved imperceptibly, gathering momentum, separating from the dock as it crept slowly toward the open ocean nudged by tiny tugboats.

They held hands as they said goodbye to the land of their birth, *Italia*. Josie was overcome with emotion and began to cry softly. Her heart was beating rapidly and she experienced a sensation she had never felt before, like she was drowning but in a cloud. She thought about her parents and the friends whom she was leaving behind and for the first time since this adventure began, she had second thoughts. Would she ever see them again? She looked at Giacomo, who was unusually staid and immutable, keeping his thoughts to himself. They looked down at the deck immediately below them and saw the heads of Sofia and Nicholas Abbondanza, who turned and looked up at them at almost the same time. They waved and smiled at each other—Sofia was crying too. When Josie saw them, she didn't feel so alone and was reassured. She clutched Giacomo's arm as an undeniable reassurance passed over her, carrying with it the promise of a future of abundance and hope for them all. Yet it was all mixed together with the sweetest sadness she could possibly imagine as she lingered at the railing, savoring her last look at the country that would always be home. Most of them knew they would never be back.

Chapter 21   At Sea

Three weeks at sea. Twenty-one days. For most of the passengers on the steamship *Queen of Italia*, this was their first trip outside of their native village, let alone their native country. Although they put on a brave face, most of them were shell-shocked at the prospect of going so far away from home to an unknown place where they would be at the mercy of complete strangers. Not speaking the language. Unfamiliar customs. Strangers everywhere. Only the promise of a better life for their children drove them to commit such an insane act. Even the reassurances of relatives and friends who had gone before them were only half-believed. The most convincing argument was the trickle of money that came back to their villages from those transplanted countrymen —who obviously were working enough to send money home. This voyage was truly a leap of faith for most of the passengers.

It was an enormous leap of faith for those in the steerage compartment, like Sophia and Nicholas Abbondanza. The conditions in steerage were the roughest accommodations on this floating city; they were not exactly inhumane, but very trying. Passengers had little privacy, with families, children and single men and women crowded into the bowels of the ship where the constant rumble of the engines never ceased. Wooden bunk beds with questionable mattresses were the norm and curtains separating the space between the beds offered the only barriers. One or two bathrooms served twenty to thirty people. The food, provided twice a day, was a sort of oatmeal in the morning and a cross between gruel and stew at night with a chunk of bread. Water to drink, however, was plentiful, but baths or showers were not permitted, only washing up, so by the middle of the voyage the smell of humans became ever stronger in the lower holds.

Another restriction was that steerage passengers were not allowed on the upper decks. This regulation was less based on prejudice than on practicality; mixing men of varying social classes was sure to cause friction and fighting was strictly forbidden on board. Steerage passengers could go outside on their own covered deck to take the air, exercise and socialize but they were not allowed to move around the ship vertically. Crew members who caught someone from steerage trying to climb to an upper deck immediately turned the person back, sometimes using physical force. But there was one major advantage of the steerage compartments— passengers in steerage were less likely to be seasick than those on the higher decks. And the perpetual hum of the engines meant that they were always moving toward their destination.

Josie was one of those passengers who fell prey to the motion of the ship early on. Second class passengers had slightly better accommodations on the next higher level of the ship than steerage. The food served was more substantial and of better quality. Most of them had brought their own food with them as well. Josie and Giacomo had brought some food, but as soon as they hit the open sea, Josie couldn't keep anything down. Bread and water was the only thing she could manage to eat in very small portions.

"Josie, try and eat something," Giacomo pleaded. "You have to eat or you'll be too weak to pass the medical exam when we get to America. Please!"

Josie just turned her head away most of the time. The nausea made her dizzy and she *was* getting weak. She just couldn't help herself. Giacomo wanted to make love every night but most of the time she was too busy throwing up to participate. After a week, she was a mess, and Giacomo was so concerned that he took her to the ship's doctor.

Il dottore listened to her heart and lungs, said she was fine and told her to eat.

"She keeps throwing up, Doctor! What should I do?" Giacomo was confounded by the doctor's lack of empathy, then remembered that the doctor probably saw fifty people a day with the same complaint.

"Bring her to the lowest deck of the ship once a day, feed her some crackers, and don't let her look at the horizon. That's all I can recommend," he prescribed. "It should help a little."

The next morning he helped Josie down the steep iron steps that led to the steerage deck, clasping the permission slip he had obtained from the doctor, and there in the dawn was Sophia, staring out at the ocean. She turned to see Josie leaning heavily on Giacomo, her skin looked almost gray, her hair unwashed and large bags sagged under her eyes.

"What in God's name happened to her?" she cried.

Giacomo looked at Sophia and said matter-of-factly, "She can't hold anything down. The doctor said to come down here and not to let her look at the sea. Can you help me feed her some crackers?"

Sophia took Josie to her and guided her to a chair. "You poor thing, you poor thing," she repeated as she stroked her hair. Josie just melted into her arms, too weak to say anything. Giacomo gave Sophia some crackers and black coffee as she waved him to leave them alone. He disappeared up the stairs as the sun rose above the farthest reaches of the eastern sea.

Sophia made Josie face the inside of the ship so that she couldn't detect as much movement. At that level the ship's pitching was minimal and the sea was calm; some time passed and Josie seemed to perk up a little so Sophia gave her a bite of a cracker and a sip of coffee. That seemed to revive her some. She was able to keep it down, so a little while later, Sophia gave her some more. Within an hour, Josie was looking more alert and the dizziness and nausea had abated. They tried walking a few steps together with some success. For the first time in a week, Josie could stand up without vomiting. She was overjoyed!

Sophia was just as grateful that she could repay the kindness that Giacomo had shown in lending them the money to continue the voyage. She wanted to know more about their benefactors but didn't want to appear nosy. They were an odd couple—this attractive, young girl with the older man, quiet and mysterious, not at all a likely pairing of people yet not all that unusual. Sophia made note of the ring on Josie's finger and wondered how they had gotten together. Josie must have been reading her mind.

"I am so happy to be here with you," she exclaimed tentatively. "Thank you for helping me.

I've been so sick . . . Giacomo isn't very . . . " her voice trailed off.

"Josie, please don't think I'm prying, but how long have you two been married?" Sophia couldn't get the words out fast enough.

Josie took a deep breath. "Only a couple of weeks. This is sort of our honeymoon—some honeymoon with me throwing up all the time. I've never been on a ship—I didn't know I'd be so sick. He's probably really mad at me."

"Being seasick can happen to anyone, *cara*. I doubt that he's mad at you. He seemed very worried about you when he brought you down here. He's worried enough to take you to the doctor. So he can't be THAT mad."

"It's really important that I get better so I can pass the medical exam when we land in America. I *can't* fail that exam, Sophia. I *have* to go with him to Pennsylvania. I can't go back to Citta St. Angelo. I can't!" She was getting excited so Sophia took her hands and held them in hers.

"Now, now, take it easy. Try to relax, close your eyes and rest." Sophia's curiosity was on high alert. She could see this girl had a secret—what was it that made her so anxious? Now she was dying to know more.

"Tell me about your hometown. What did you do there and how did you meet Giacomo?"

"Well, I was a student and he worked for the Bishop. We met . . . at church. At first I didn't even like him, I thought he was too old for me. And he was a farmer . . . not that there's anything wrong with that, but he had been in a war and I didn't think he'd be interested in me. But the Bishop sponsored him to go to America and he wanted to marry me and go with him so that's what we did. We got married and here we are, on a ship headed to Pennsylvania." A wistful look haunted her face as Josie told her story.

"Would you mind if I asked how old you are?"

"No, Sophia! I just turned 17. But now I've told you, you must tell me! How old are *you?*"

"I'm 21, and I've been married for two years to Nicholas."

"And do you love him?" Josie was intent on the answer.

"Yes, very much. We're like two birds that mate for life. I can't imagine life without him, and I'm sure he feels the same about me." Sophia's face lit up as she spoke. Josie became quiet again.

"Have some more to eat, Josie. Let's see if this stays down," Sophia broke off another piece of cracker which Josie took automatically.

"I guess I don't know much about love," she said almost to herself. "It's so strange being married but not being sure if you're in love . . . "

Sophia looked at her squarely and in her most reassuring tone said, "These things have a way of working out, you'll see. Right now you need to get stronger and not worry about the rest of your life! You must come down here every morning, early, before the babies start to cry and the people get up and we'll eat something together. How does that sound? "

"Oh, yes, I'd like that. Very much. Thank you so much, Sophia. I really need a friend right now."

"We'll always be friends, Josie. We'll be friends for life."

They shook hands on it.

Giacomo came looking for Josie later on and found them talking animatedly as Sophia fed Josie crackers. He was at once relieved and if he let himself admit it, a little jealous of Sophia's attention to his wife. Josie did seem to feel better, even as people were beginning to stir and walk out on the deck to get some fresh air. The two women seemed oblivious to the commotion around them and just kept on talking. Women—they just talk too much, he thought.

Sophia was happy to see him, pleased that her nursing skills had resulted in such a speedy recovery. As Giacomo thanked her, he thought Josie looked disappointed that she had to leave to go back up to the second-class deck with him. She made him promise to bring Josie back down each day until she had recovered fully. Giacomo grudgingly agreed, thinking that it would only take a few days until his wife would be herself again. He wanted her to himself, not making friends all over the ship. The next thing she'd want is to loan everybody money! Or have him meet a bunch of strangers they would never see again. No, she needed to stay close to him. He needed to keep an eye on her.

As they began to climb the stairs, Josie turned and waved at Sophia, smiling and happy for the first time in a week. Giacomo pulled her back toward him and with his hand placed firmly in the small of her back, moved her in front of him and up the stairs.

"Let's go," he ordered.

Josie followed him begrudgingly. How could she make him understand that she craved the attention and social interaction of other women? She didn't care for him any less, but to be together all the time with a person who hardly talked to her and who seemed to be in a world of his own was a tremendous change for her. She had been an only child and her parents doted on her! She had many girlfriends in her town and her teachers liked her as well. She felt so cut off from her world that she regretted making this life-altering decision. She took some comfort in Sophia's words that it would all work out, but she was beginning to lose her faith. At least she was feeling a little better. She was heartened when Giacomo asked her how she felt.

"I'm all right as long as I don't look at the sea, I think." He grunted. She looked thin to him.

"Do you have enough strength to get washed and change into some clean clothes?"

"Yes, I think so."

"Well, get to it, then. We're going to the dining room tonight."

Chapter 22   The Dining Room

The two of them entered an already full dining room of passengers from many different walks of life. Most were childless couples who, like them, had managed to secure a second class ticket that allowed them more freedom on board, better accommodations and much better food. The din of clinking glasses and hungry diners met them as they walked inconspicuously to an open table where they sat with a single businessman and a British man and his wife who were already eating when they arrived and sat down. The diners gave them a cursory glance and nod, then continued eating.

Giacomo immediately ordered some wine which Josie refused. Before the waiter came back to take their order, he had drunk both glasses and ordered another. Josie marveled silently how he could drink an entire glass of wine in almost one gulp and not seem to show any effects. He let out a hearty burp which elicited a few disapproving glances from their tablemates. He didn't seem to care.

They proceeded to eat in silence, Josie picking at her food and eating slowly and carefully. She was feeling a lot better but did not want to overindulge. She knew she had to get her strength up and hopefully put on the weight she lost before they landed in less than two weeks. She was bored and tired most of the time, feeling the effects of being in the limbo between two major phases of her life. Giacomo was aloof as usual, but he did seem to dote on her when she was sickly. Normally quite independent, she found being ill very difficult and shameful.

By his third glass of wine, Giacomo seemed to loosen up a bit. He looked around at his tablemates and introduced himself and Josie. Niceties were exchanged. The British man and woman did not speak Italian but the businessman did so they began to chat, ignoring Josie. The man came from Naples and was a salesman for a large manufacturer of farm equipment on his way to the United States on business. He and Giacomo proceeded to get drunk after deciding to go in on a bottle or two of wine. Josie sat and watched them, happy that Giacomo finally seemed to be enjoying himself and hoping that he would sleep so well that night that he wouldn't want to have sex.

The evening dragged as Josie became more and more tired. The British couple had already left. The *Napolitano* and Giacomo were acting like they'd known each other for years. Several times she interrupted politely to ask Giacomo to take her back to their room so she could go to sleep but he dismissed her with "in a minute. . . " or "just a little longer . . . "

She tried her best to stay awake and be pleasant but it became harder and harder and finally . . .

Giacomo's drinking pal looked over at her and said, "Hey, what's wrong with your wife?" Giacomo turned to see Josie fast asleep with her head laying on the dinner table on the napkin next to the unfinished plate of food. He jumped up, grabbed Josie by the sleeve of her dress and shook her. "What's the matter with you?!" he shouted. A few diners close to their table had turned to look at them. Giacomo, embarrassed and tipsy, smiled back and pantomimed, "It's OK, no problem" using the thumb-to-forefinger circle that was so favored by the Americans. As Josie came to, she realized where she was and she knew things were *not* OK. One look at Giacomo's beet-red face told her he was drunk and she was in trouble.

"Giacomo, please just take me back to the room," she pleaded softly.

He glared at her in anger and intoxication, said goodnight to the salesman and grabbed Josie by the arm. He pulled her away from the table roughly and started half-walking, half-dragging her to the dining room exit. He stumbled on a chair and hit another table as the two of them tried to catch their balance and a stream of curses flowed from his mouth. "You tripped me, you bitch!" he swore at her as everyone in the dining room looked at them in earnest. Josie was mortified. She tried to talk to him but he snapped "Shut up!" They were almost to the door.

Somehow she managed to hold him up without antagonizing him further as they tottered across the deck and down the stairs to the lower level where their cabin was located. Giacomo insisted on knocking on the door of a room two doors down from theirs in spite of Josie's entreaties that it wasn't the right cabin. When he heard a male voice from inside that said "Go away!" he agreed to move on. As they approached the room, Josie became more and more nervous about what would happen once they got inside. She was shocked at how Giacomo was acting.

They were now in the tiny cabin and Giacomo, stumbling, pulled her towards him and started to kiss her roughly. She didn't resist, wary of doing anything that might make him madder. He breathed in her ear, " You think you're tired now, just wait . . . " as she pulled away from him.

"You've had too much to drink, Giacomo. Let's just go to bed. I'll help you get undressed. Come on, let's just . . ."

He wasn't listening to her as he grabbed her and threw her on the bed. He pulled up her skirt and ripped off her bloomers, leaving her nylons in place. Before she could protest, he had his pants off and was on top of her. He grabbed her chin and pushed her head to the side so she couldn't look at him directly. She felt him fumbling with something between her legs and realized that his manhood was not cooperating, although surprisingly, her body was ready. He cursed again and again, getting more and more frustrated, losing his balance on one knee, then regaining it. Finally he was ready and thrust his penis into her so hard that her whole body moved up towards the top of the bed. He thrust into her several times more and exploded like a broken wine bottle. Then he collapsed.

Josie thought at first that he was dead. His unconscious weight was beginning to restrict her breathing and he smelled terrible. She wriggled her way out from under him, moving his limp arms here and there until she extricated herself and her clothing from the bed coverings. She had seen drunken men before and knew that they often didn't remember the next day what went on the night before. But she knew and she would remember. As she stared down at Giacomo's passed-out frame, she wondered where exactly she was going to sleep, since moving him would be a chore and she didn't want to risk waking him up for a repeat performance. She quietly got her toilet articles and went to the bathroom to clean up.

The next morning she woke up on the floor wrapped in a blanket on a pillow she had stolen from their bed. Giacomo was still passed out and was snoring. How many nights would she find herself sleeping on the floor, she asked herself. The nausea started again and she lay back down and closed her eyes.

Chapter 23   Steerage

The next morning crept cold and grey over the passengers in steerage as the women woke up to start the day and attend to their children. Sophia knew that Josie would soon be coming to the stairway where they always met at 7 o'clock for breakfast. There was no way anyone could sleep in steerage after 6 or 6:30 anyway; there was too much activity. The heavy cloth dividers between sleeping areas offered the minimum amount of privacy and no noise reduction at all. Everyone seemed to need to use the bathroom when they woke up, so there was always an exodus to the toilets at daybreak. The path to the bathrooms wound through a mass of humanity—mothers breast-feeding hungry babies, children getting dressed, fathers and mothers trying their best not to disturb their neighbors with little success. Couples who tried to sneak in some intimacy were heard throughout the area and were usually met with good-natured comments later like "Sounds like YOU had a good time last night!" Occasionally tempers flared and words were exchanged but everyone to a man was literally "in the same boat."   Sophia had confided in Josie that mornings were the most humiliating part of the trip which required the utmost self-control on her part.

Even though most of the passengers were Italian and lower or working class people who generally came from large families and were used to much privation, the mornings strained even the strongest fabric of social conventions. They were like rats in an overcrowded maze. No wonder the ship's management strictly forbade drinking liquor and fighting among steerage passengers!

This morning Josie had quietly left the cabin with Giacomo still hard asleep. Her mind was racing. She was more disturbed than ever after the events of the night before. Should she say anything to Sophia? She so looked forward to their meetings but didn't know how much she should divulge of her most private moments with Giacomo to a stranger, even a friendly one. I am so confused, she thought. Why would he treat me like that? I'm his wife! In her seventeen years she had never seen a man act that way in public to his wife or to any woman. Maybe it was just an isolated situation since he *was* under a lot of pressure, she rationalized. It was a huge responsibility he had undertaken—the trip to America, a new wife, starting over in a strange country—it was a lot to deal with. She decided not to say anything to either Sophia or Giacomo and to pretend that everything was fine.

Sophia met her with her usual warm smile at the bottom of the steel stairway on the ship's steerage level. They found a spot out of the wind where they could get some fresh air and not look at the horizon. Josie wore her lovely coat and a matching hat and Sophia commented that she looked a little better and stronger as they ate soda crackers and drank some tea. They huddled together for warmth as well as camaraderie, sharing a bond that would remain unbroken through their entire lives. The American Passage, it was called. They had no idea that 18 million others from across the European continent would make the same trip to America over the course of fifty years to become part of the largest peacetime migration of all time.

"*Buona mattina, cara*!" Sophia exclaimed with delight. She loved to see the young girl who was blossoming into a woman right before her eyes, who was learning the ways of the world in a crash course of experience and circumstance. Josie smiled back at her and looked modestly downward, turning her head to the side. An ugly purple bruise was visible under her chin. Wait, what is this? Maybe she was learning the world's ways too fast, Sophia thought.

"How was your dinner last night?" Sophia inquired congenially.

"Oh, it was fine." Josie tried to sound nonchalant. " I was able to eat almost a full meal, thanks to your wonderful care. I *am* feeling a lot better and I think I put on a pound or two. Giacomo is pleased, I think. It's hard to tell with him, you know; he's not a big talker."

"I noticed. What did you two do after dinner?"

There was a pause in the conversation. Josie hesitated, began to blush. Sophia waited patiently. She watched as Josie struggled to hide her agitation. Josie wanted so much to confide in Sophia about the turmoil that was inside her and ask for her advice and counsel, yet something was holding her back. Was it fear? She was indebted to Sophia for helping her during her illness yet she didn't know exactly how much she could trust her to keep a secret. If Giacomo found out that she was talking to Sophia about their private life, he would be furious. Finally, Josie said, "Nothing. We went right to bed."

Sophia leaned back and murmured, "It must be nice to have your own cabin where people aren't breathing down your backs every minute." She sighed. "We're so grateful to be on this ship going to America, it's like a dream come true for us. But it is very uncomfortable and hard on our marriage. You're very lucky, Josie, you and Giacomo. I would love to just see a second class room once before this trip is over!"

"I know," said Josie, although at the moment she wasn't feeling particularly fortunate.

"Sophia, I have an idea. Let's do something really sneaky! Tomorrow when Giacomo is gone from the cabin, I'll meet you down here and we can try to sneak past the guard upstairs and you can come to see our cabin. We have to be careful, you know, but what would they do to two women if they catch us? They'll just send you back down to steerage and me to my room. What do you say, Sophia?" Josie's eyes were twinkling with the idea of an adventure.

"Yes! Why don't we go up there now?" wondered Sophia.

Again, that shadow crossed Josie's face, subtle and nuanced. Sophia could see Josie trying to hide it again, whatever "it" was.

"No, today's not a good time. Because, you know, I . . . ah. . . saw that big, mean guard patrolling our floor on my way here. I know that tomorrow the nice guard is on duty, so we should wait. How about tomorrow, then? What do you say?" Josie was beginning to become an excellent storyteller.

"Yes, tomorrow! I'll be ready. We'll meet right here. Nine o'clock."

The two of them giggled with anticipation. Josie wanted so much to return the help that Sophia had provided by showing her where she was staying.

"I'd better go back up before Giacomo . . . misses me. Thanks, Sophia. I can't wait until tomorrow!" She clasped her hand and squeezed it. "*Ciao*!"

"Good bye, my friend. Be careful."

Josie shot her a serious look and started up the stairs. She knows, she thought. She knows.

Chapter 24   Busted!

Josie was so excited to have a visitor to her cabin that she tossed and turned all night. She woke up early and began straightening up and organizing the little room, folding and hanging up clothes and tucking shoes under the bed. When Giacomo woke up, he wondered out loud why the room looked so neat and Josie said that she felt well enough to do some house chores, to which he assented with a nod. Josie was feeling better, without a doubt. She seemed to have gotten her "sea legs" about two weeks into the journey, she was eating more and gaining weight. She no longer looked so thin and gaunt. Both she and Giacomo were very grateful for this, because the medical examiners could deny any immigrant entry into the United States on the mere suspicion of ill health.

The cabin was spotless.

Giacomo got washed and dressed, wondering where his shoes were. Josie smiled at him and brought him his shoes and a pair of clean socks.

"Are you meeting Sophia for breakfast again?" he asked as he tucked in his shirt.

"*Si*. It's so much easier to eat below deck. There's less movement of the ship and I can keep the crackers down better. Are you going out too?" she asked sweetly.

"In a bit." He lay back down on the bed and closed his eyes. She sat in the chair and quietly worked on some crocheting. She was waiting for him to leave—hurry up, she thought— I'm getting hungry! Of all days for him to hang around. Finally, he jumped up, grabbed his jacket and key and left without saying a word.

Josie immediately got her shawl and key, peeked out the door to make sure he was gone, and headed to the stairway down to steerage. She could not see Sophia but knew she'd be there. She also looked for any of the guards that occasionally patrolled the hallways, but there were no guards either. A guard could usually be found in steerage in the mornings, but not today. Clutching her package of crackers and the ever-present note from the doctor, she slowly descended the stairs, sweeping the hallway with her gaze. Sophia was not in sight. She waited at the bottom of the stairs as the steerage passengers moved past her, back and forth, on their way to the bathrooms, to the outer deck or to meet other passengers. No one paid her any attention since they were used to seeing her and Sophia together.

Sophia came a few moments later. As they kissed each other on each cheek, Josie noticed her face was flush with excitement.

"Let's go!" she exclaimed. The two interlocked arms and walked as casually as possible up the stairs and into the world of second class. At the landing at the top of the stairwell they paused, pretending small talk, so they could look around again for any guards. Again they saw no one.

Nothing would have distinguished either woman as a second-class or steerage passenger. Sophia was dressed especially nicely and was trying to act primly and properly to play the part, but she honestly didn't know what might mark her as either level of passenger. Neither woman was rich, even middle class, yet they were equally matched in clothing tastes and knew how to speak properly for their station in life. Walking down the hall arm in arm, they eventually came to the hallway where Josie's and Giacomo's cabin was.

Josie inserted the key and quickly opened the door. The two slipped in without being seen. Sophia caught her breath when she saw the tiny room, so neatly organized with every earthly possession they owned in its place.

"Oh, my God, it's lovely!" Sophia exclaimed. There wasn't much room to move around so Josie offered her the only chair and she sat on the bed. Josie showed her the well-used little cubicles and drawers that were built into the walls and showed her the tiny closet. The furnishings were old and worn and the wallpaper was peeling in a few places, but it still was a nice cabin. "Would you like a cracker?" Josie unwrapped the package and they started to snack on the morsels. "So what do you think?"

Sophia couldn't believe her friend's good fortune. "It's so quiet—and private! You must be able to sleep really well!"

"Most of the time, yes. The bed is pretty small and I'm always on the inside. The bathrooms are down the hall so I don't get up often during the night." If Sophia really knew what went on in that bed, she would cringe.

"It's still like heaven compared to where I sleep. The babies sometimes cry all night and no one gets any sleep. I guess you can stand anything for a short time, but I'm about to go crazy in steerage."

Josie nodded in sympathy. "We're almost to New York, you know; it won't be long now. Only eight more days, if the weather holds, they told Giacomo. Eight more days!" They both popped a cracker into their mouths.

Suddenly, the sound of a key rattled in the door and in walked Giacomo. Startled, all three looked at each other to see what the next one would say. There was hardly room for three people in the cabin, so Giacomo couldn't move much, so he just stood there. "Hello, Sophia," he said slowly, looking at Josie. "What're you doing here?" The mood instantly changed.

"We thought we'd have breakfast inside the cabin this morning. Sophia was interested to see what the rooms looked like and I wanted to show her ours." Josie tried to act like this was the most natural thing in the world.

"Does Nicholas know you're here?"

"Well, no, not exactly." Sophia wondered why that would make a difference.

"You know you're not supposed to go outside of steerage, right?"

"Yes, but –"

"Then I think you should go back. Come on, I'll take you."

Josie stood up. "Giacomo! She's my guest! Can't she stay for awhile longer? We're not hurting anybody. Please!"

"Suit yourself. But if you get caught, don't look for me to help you. You women—always making trouble. You'd better get back soon, Sophia." He slammed the door and left.

"I'm so sorry, Sophia. I don't know what gets into him. He's usually not so rude. I guess I should've asked him if you could come, but if I had, he probably wouldn't have let you come anyway."

"That's all right, he's just looking out for you. Come on, I should leave before he comes back. Come to the stairway with me." They were both so disappointed.

They stepped out into the hall, locked the door and headed toward the stairwell. As they rounded the corner, they spied the guard that Josie had hoped was not on shift. There he was with his back to the girls, a large, burly, greasy-haired man in a wrinkled uniform. He turned to see the two of them staring at him halfway up the hall.

"Hey, you two, come here!" he commanded. The two of them walked toward the guard, heads held high. They knew they were busted!

Josie spoke first. "Good morning, sir. I am Mrs. Constanza in cabin 247 and this is my friend Sophia. . ."

"Yeah, I know her. She's from steerage. What are *you* doing up here?" he growled and made a phlegmatic sound in his nasal passages. The women wondered how he knew she was a steerage passenger. Before they could say anything more, he moved closer to them and leaned into their faces.

"You know, I could make a lot of trouble for you, both of you."

"What kind of trouble?" Josie asked feigning innocence. Sophia wasn't saying a thing and kept a poker face.

"Since you broke one of the main rules of transport on this ship, that is, no fraternizing with the passengers outside your ticket level, I'm obliged to report you to the authorities. They don't like it when people try to mingle with the steerage riff raff." He looked directly at Sophia when he said the last part. Then he leaned one arm against the wall blocking their path to the stairway and managed to look rather menacing. No one else was in the corridor. "I'll have to report you to the authorities and they'll definitely tell the immigration officer that you broke the rules . . . "

The two women looked at each other. This wasn't happening . . .

"So . . . what happens if you report us to the authorities?" Josie asked tentatively.

"You could get sent back to your crummy little village, that's what. Is that what you want? Your husbands—you *are* married, aren't you two?—they could get sent back too. They'll just *love* that. I've seen it happen before. Yeah, you're in some big trouble, girls." He wiped his greasy nose on his sleeve and leered at them. He seemed to be enjoying the harassment.

Josie wasn't going to let this lout talk to her like that. "Sir, we're passengers on this ship, no matter what ticket level we hold. Just because we—"

"OK, girls, come with me. You're under house restriction until we get this sorted out." He grabbed Sophia's arm and began to lead her away. Sophia looked pleadingly at Josie.

"Wait! You can't just take us away like this!" Josie said indignantly.

"I can't? Watch me!" He grabbed Josie's hair and pulled. "Let's go, ladies." Josie squealed with rage and pain, but mostly humiliation.

"Hey! Look, wait a minute! Maybe we can work something out here." Sophia yanked her arm out of the guard's grip and backed away from him. She had no idea what they could do in this situation but she wanted to buy some time. Maybe he'd take a bribe. Then she remembered that neither of them had any money. They'd have to think of something else. But what? And where were the people who normally were present in the hallways almost every day?

Josie's hair was still firmly in the grip of the man who now was pulling her towards him backwards, reeling her in like a fish. Her neck was bent back in an extremely uncomfortable position as she stepped back to keep from falling. Suddenly, the guard released his grip on her hair, spun her around and grabbed her by the waist. He pulled her into him and pressed his mouth full onto hers as she struggled to avoid him, letting out a muffled expletive that got lost when it encountered his tongue. Her arms were flailing about as Josie felt one of his huge hands engulf her breast and squeeze it hard. As he hunched over her, Sophia started pummeling him in the back, annoying him but not really hurting him. She kicked him several times in the leg, yelling "Leave her alone! Stop, you monster! Stop!"

Just then he finished the kiss, pushed Josie away from him like discarded trash and she fell onto the floor in a heap. Sophia ran to help her and as she picked her up, the guard wiped his mouth, pointed his index finger at them and said, "Now, we're even. Just remember, I'm watching you two. You better keep quiet—think about immigration." He chortled a beefy laugh.

The girls stood immobilized in the hall watching the guard as he walked away. He turned one more time to look at them and said to Sophia, "Get back to steerage, you whore."

His final words to them were, "I'm watching you. . ."

Both women collapsed, crying onto each other's shoulder. Tears of relief, anger and helplessness turned to tears of rage at the assault and threats by one of the ship's own employees. They both knew how lucky they were to have gotten off with just a kiss and a grope. They could've gotten raped. He could've pulled Josie's beautiful hair out! Besides, the man was dead serious about turning them in to the immigration authorities for what was actually a relatively mild infraction onboard ship, but they didn't know that. How awful it would have been to have been denied entry to America because of a creep like this guard.

"We can't tell our husbands about this, Sophia," Josie looked at her earnestly. "Promise you won't say anything. Promise!" She was insistent.

They both agreed on silence. Josie could not bear to hear Giacomo berate her for getting caught breaking the ship's rules after he had found Sophie in the cabin. He'd never let her live it down.

They decided not to see each other for a day or so to let things calm down.

Chapter 25 English

Josie walked Sophia to the stairwell and they said their goodbyes. They agreed to meet at 7 o'clock on the same stairwell in two days' time.

The days crawled by for Josie, who had very little to do except eat and rest. Giacomo wasn't around most of the day, spending his time on deck with the other men where he could smoke and gamble a little playing cards. She knew no one in second class and probably wouldn't be "allowed" to talk to them anyway, since Giacomo seemed to be upset by new people who she let into their life together. She did have one pastime: someone had given her a basic English textbook, old and worn, and she had been quietly studying a few words of English here and there so she could communicate at a rudimentary level with people in America.   She had actually memorized about 50 words or phrases by this time and was hungry to learn more. Unfortunately, she had no one to listen to so she wasn't sure about the pronunciation or the flow of the spoken word but she guessed as best she could. She remembered Giacomo's discomfort when she learned he could not read and she suspected he'd be even more intimidated if he knew she was studying English.

"Escusa may." It sounded more Italian than English. She tried again. "Escuse me." Better, she thought. "Escuse me," she repeated several times.

She was walking up and down the hallway the next day and brushed against an older woman who rather indignantly said, "Pardon me!" in English. Josie haltingly asked her if she spoke English and she said, "Who vants to know?" This led to an introduction and a short conversation in the hall in a mixture of English, Italian and pantomime. The woman quickly warmed up to Josie and they decided to go out on deck where Josie leaned against the railing with her back against the sea facing the inside of the ship to avoid getting seasick.

The woman was traveling alone to meet her husband who was already in the United States. They were from somewhere in Germany and she had picked up English during the war when she was assigned to work with British and American prisoners. Her name was Gilda and she was a tall, large woman of about 40 with blonde hair and green eyes. She was stocky but carried her weight well and Josie thought that she must've been athletic in her younger years because she was in such good shape. The two made an odd pair on the ship's deck.

Gilda didn't speak Italian and Josie barely spoke English but with the little she had learned, she was quickly able to pick up the gist of their conversation, although at a simple level. Gilda seemed happy to oblige her lack of knowledge. Josie thought, she must be as bored as I am! They spoke about their homelands and families and hopes for their lives in the new and wonderful land of America. Josie wanted to write some of the words down so she would remember them later so Gilda dug a pencil and piece of paper out of her purse to show Josie the written words. Gilda seemed agreeable to meeting again the next day when they could continue and they set up a rendezvous spot. They walked back to the cabin and before leaving her, Gilda gave her some advice.

"Vhen you need assistance or you are in trouble, you say 'Help!' in English. Can you say that? hellllllllppp," she repeated it very slowly, making funny shapes with her mouth.

Josie parroted, "Elp." Gilda smiled and made an "h" sound—"huh, huh, huh-elp."

Josie smiled back at her when she finally got the pronunciation correct. "Help. Help."

Gilda held up her index finger and wagged it at Josie. "You say only dis vord vhen you have big trouble. BIG trouble!" she gestured holding her hands out wide to both sides of her ample body and emphasized the word BIG. Josie smiled and nodded her head in assent.

Later in the cabin, when Giacomo came back but before they went to the mess hall for dinner, she was reviewing her lesson. She was engrossed in reading her notes and pronouncing her newly-acquired words when he suddenly grabbed the paper from her hands and demanded, "What's this?"

Josie remained calm. She was beginning to learn that an emotional response often escalated things and made him defensive.

"I am learning a few words in English, Giacomo. It will help us to know some English in America, don't you think?"

He scowled at her. He didn't think wives should be smarter than their husbands and this one was already smarter than he was because she had gone to school.

"We're not even there yet and you have to learn English?" he snorted.

"Is there anything wrong with that? I thought it would be helpful," she kept her voice low so as not to sound like she was challenging him, looked directly at him and smiled.

He walked up and down the length of the tiny room with the paper, not reading it but clutching it in his hand like it was going to bite him. Josie wondered at this man's strength and apparent inability to control his anger and feelings of frustration. What a volatile combination! The more time she spent with him, the more often she would see him wrestling with some sort of inner demon as he became disproportionately annoyed at the smallest things. At first she thought he was just being protective on this great journey, but as time passed on the ship, his actions and moods seemed to become more erratic. He was never a big talker; now if he said ten words to her all day, that was a lot. Only when he had a glass of wine or two at dinner was he in a better mood.

She was bothered by the idea that he objected to her learning the language of their adopted home. What harm could that possibly cause?! She would've thought that he would be happy since she would then become his translator and they wouldn't have to depend on outsiders. Did he really think that everyone spoke Italian, and their dialect even, in America? But Giacomo seemed to work on an intuitive level, not a rational one sometimes, a level she didn't know well or understand. She still had much to learn about the world of adults, who were mostly mysterious to her back in her little village.

Giacomo stopped pacing and stood in front of her seated on the bed. He looked agitated, red in the face, and was breathing harder than usual. It seemed as though he was working up to something.

185

He looked down at Josie and said measuredly, "I don't want you studying English."

Josie hardened her face muscles into her best poker face. She was raging inside. She knew that two raging people were not going to leave the room without a huge argument. Somehow she felt that if she gave in on this, she would lose the small advantage she had in this strange relationship, the advantage of her new status as wife. She stood up slowly, moved toward him and embraced him gently, smoothing his hair and running her hand across the back of her neck. Mustering up her greatest reserve of self-control, she whispered, "Why not?'

He seemed to relax a little. A few seconds passed with no sound. Then the explosion.

" I don't have to give you a reason!" he yelled at the top of his voice. He threw his hands up in the air and wheeled around, throwing the sheet of paper onto the cabin floor. His fist raised, he was one impulse away from striking Josie, when he pivoted several degrees on his feet and with that momentum, slammed his hand hard into the cabin wall. Josie let out a startled yell and as Giacomo removed his hand from the wall, she saw the blood.

"You're bleeding! Oh my God, you're bleeding! Why did you do that, Giacomo? Why?"

He let out a stream of curses as he walked over to the trunk, opened the lid and grabbed the first piece of cloth he could find. It was her slip. He wrapped his hand in it to staunch the bleeding coming from his skinned knuckles and went out into the hall, still fuming and cursing, but at himself now, not at Josie.

She followed him, concerned about him and wary of him at the same time. She could see a spot of blood seeping through the slip fabric. What should she do? She peeked at him from the doorway and he snarled, "Leave me alone!" She went back in and closed the door.

This can't go on, she mused. Every time she did something to improve herself, make a friend, or tried to include Giacomo in an activity as a couple, he went crazy. Since they left Italy, she was anxious and living on edge all of the time, trying to please him and anticipate his moods, trying to get to know this enigmatic and implacable man. For over three weeks she felt she had been a model wife, keeping quiet and following his lead. What had she done to make him so angry? She didn't understand why he acted this way. Had she made a mistake marrying him and agreeing to move to America with him? She knew it wasn't going to be easy, but she at least thought that they'd be together, working as a unit, as husband and wife. Not as slave and master!

Josie crept to the cabin door and slowly, silently opened it and peered into the hall. Giacomo was gone. Good, she thought, maybe he went to the doctor's. Not that the doctor would do much-- most of the passengers suspected he wasn't a real doctor anyway.

When he came back, she vowed, she would have a long talk with him and find out what was making him so upset. Meanwhile, she waited and studied some more English.

It was a little past midnight when she was awakened by the sound of a key in the door of the cabin. The lights were out and she smelled Giacomo before she could make him out in the dim light from the hallway. He smelled like a winery. He had obviously been drinking again. A lot. He staggered around in the small room bumping into furniture as he tried to take off his clothes in the dark. Josie didn't move and pretended to be asleep. Eventually he found his way to the bed and flopped down into it.

The next thing she knew he grabbed her and started kissing her, saying something that was mostly incoherent. He ran his hands up and down her body, under her nightgown and then found the spot between her legs. She obliged him dutifully and it wasn't long before he climbed on top of her, breathing heavily, and began to have sex with her. She lay there very still so as not to provoke him, unsure of whether he had forgotten about their conversation earlier or not. She just let him ride her for awhile, moving with his body rhythmically but silently, knowing her role and not trying to get in the way.

He seemed to be slowing down and all of a sudden, she noticed he stopped. His body seemed to relax but she couldn't see anything so she wasn't sure. His full weight sank down on her as he slowly fell unconscious. She couldn't believe it—he had passed out! Now he was fully on top of her and breathing deeply in a sound sleep. He soon began to snore. She tried to wiggle around him but he was too heavy. What was she supposed to do now? It was getting harder and harder to breathe, not to mention that his breath was almost making her gag. He was so heavy— his short but muscular frame weighed much more than he looked when he stood upright. Don't panic, she thought. She could wait a little while longer.

In a few minutes, she felt him try to shift his weight. This is it! she thought. With a supreme effort of will, she slid one arm out from under him and pulled herself upright, giving herself more leverage. She gently placed one of her knees against his hip and pushed slightly; he responded by moving away from her and rolling off her enough that she could move completely out from under him. He took up most of the bed though, only leaving her with a narrow space between him and the wall. But at least he was facing the other way and breathing in the other direction. His body was no longer crushing hers and for that she was thankful.

She collected some of the covers and made a little nest for herself to stay warm. He would probably not feel the chill until the morning when he woke up only halfway covered. Josie fell asleep with more troubled thoughts on her mind. As she drifted off, the words that Gilda had coached her on earlier were the last things she remembered.

"Escuse me. Helllllppp. Huh-huh-huh-ellllppppp."

Chapter 26   The Guard

Giacomo's hand really hurt. He was used to pain from being in the Army and he was not a complainer, since nobody listened anyway. He unwrapped the slip that was by now half soaked with blood and studied his shredded skin. He thought that he might have broken some of the small bones in his hand. Maybe he should go to see the ship's doctor— what could the doctor do for him anyway? The ship offered minimal medical attention unless a passenger was bleeding to death. He would just have to tough it out until they landed in New York in less than a week.

Even more troubling to him, though, was the wife he had left back in the cabin. Imagine her trying to learn English! Who did she think she was anyway? Was she trying to show him up? She obviously wasn't used to listening to a male authority figure. Thank her weakling father for that! He needed to put her in her place and if hitting her was necessary, he would have to do it. After all, a man had to assert control over his own wife or he received no respect from the other men, or the other women, for that matter. The next time she displeased him or talked back to him, he would let her have it and that would show her who was boss in this family. She was old enough to be hit now and then.

Something else was bothering him about his wife, though.

He tossed it around in his head. She was raised differently than he. She didn't grow up on a farm, where wives were frequently hit by their husbands and daughters were treated like third class citizens in the family, less important than the boys because they weren't as strong, and often less important than the cows or other livestock. Giacomo had seen enough of town life to know that men usually didn't hit their wives for minor infractions and generally town wives were still obedient and deferential to their husbands anyway. She was so young—he had to keep reminding himself of that, young and inexperienced as well. What did she know of the ways of men? Had she ever had a brother? A boyfriend? No! And she was very pretty . . . his thoughts drifted to their marriage bed. She was a willing partner—so far. Maybe he should give her the benefit of the doubt. He did promise her father that he would take care of her. A promise was a promise. Yet she did have a sharp tongue. What could be done about that? He shook his head in confusion.

He wandered to the doctor's office, not knowing whether it would be open or closed. His hand was swollen and bruises were beginning to appear and it hurt like hell. He found the doctor's office but the doctor was gone. His luck . . . He probably needed to wash it and remove the debris from the hole in the wall that might still be stuck in the wound. Then he should douse it with some wine or alcohol to sterilize it. The only place that had wine was the mess hall and he realized then how hungry he was. *She* would be hungry, too, he surmised. He had half a mind to let her starve. Should he go back and get her or go to eat alone? He decided to walk around the ship a little longer. He didn't want to see her just now. He was too angry.

As he made his way to the dining hall, Giacomo passed other passengers on the deck, some of whom he already knew, he just didn't feel like talking to anyone. He really wanted a drink. I have to figure out how to get Josie to listen to me, he thought. But how? As he mulled over his dilemma, he walked around the corner of the hallway on the way to the dining hall and ran right into a large, overweight guard, one of the ship's employees who were on duty to provide "security" on the deck, mostly keeping people in line and breaking up fights. The man towered over Giacomo and was almost twice as wide as he was. Startled, both men swore at each other and then Giacomo realized the guard spoke Italian.

"*Scuzi, signor, mi dispiace.* I should've been looking where I was going." He kept walking.

The guard grunted, then studying Giacomo's features, made after him.

"Hey, you, where is your wife?!" he threw Giacomo the bait.

My wife, he thought. What does he know of my wife?

"Why do you want to know about my wife?" Giacomo asked suspiciously.

"No reason, just concerned about my passengers. We wouldn't want anything to happen to our passengers, now would we?" He sneered at the last part of the statement.

Giacomo wasn't convinced. He got closer to the man and looked him right in the eye.

"Are you saying something might happen to my wife?"

"Eh, you never know, these women, a big ship, people everywhere in close quarters down here. Things happen sometimes. We see a lot of things . . ."

"Oh yeah, like what? What did you see? Did you see something about my wife?"

The guard could see he was getting to Giacomo. This little man with big muscles was already jealous. "Well, we have to keep control over these people so there's no fighting or breaking the rules on the ship. We report every infraction to the Captain who records them for the Immigration people

194

at Ellis Island in New York." That should get a rise out of him.

Giacomo realized then that man was up to something. He obviously knew something about Josie and he was making Giacomo work to find it out. How could he get him to part with the information without fighting with him? He had to try another way.

"You know, my wife is very young. She's a bit of a wild one, that girl." He softened his tone slightly. "Sometimes it's good. . . " He winked at the guard suggestively. "And sometimes it's not so good. I have to keep an eye on her all the time. It gets tiring . . . " He was close enough to the guard to feint a congenial jab in the ribs. Would he fall for it?

The guard took a few steps away from Giacomo and looked up and down the hallway as if resuming his security duties. He had a self-satisfied look on his face as he returned.

"I know what you mean about your wife. She seems to, let me say, take liberties when you're not around."

"Really? What kind of liberties?" Giacomo acted like he was only mildly interested, offered the man a smoke and lit one for himself. He couldn't wait to hear the response, but he was exercising as much self-control as he could muster. All kinds of thoughts filled his head—was she being unfaithful? Was she

195

making a cuckhold out of him? And what did this sleazy man hope to gain from this conversation?

"You know, there are rules on this ship and if I report infractions to the Captain and he tells the Immigration staff, people can be denied entrance to America. So sometimes it's worth it to stay on the good side of the guards, especially the guards who have some damaging information about wives who might have broken some important rules. Rules that could get them deported before they even get to the United States. Rules like the one your wife may have broken. See what I'm saying?"

So that's it. He wants a bribe, Giacomo surmised. I wonder what rule Josie is supposed to have broken? Giacomo did not look surprised or shocked. He just stood there and stared down the guard.

"How much?" he proposed.

"Uh, I don't know what you mean, signor." The guard was trying to play coy but wasn't very good at it.

"How much?" Giacomo repeated.

"I think that twenty American dollars would be a fair amount to pay for some 'immigration insurance.' I don't suppose you have that kind of money, do you?"

"Not with me right now I don't, but I can get it. How do I know you won't turn her in anyway? We're almost to New York. I have to have some reassurances."

"Hmm, reassurances. If you keep your wife locked up and out of trouble, you won't need any reassurances. Because there won't be any more trouble, will there? " The guard was almost salivating at the thought of making some easy money.

"I'll get back to you tonight. Where will I find you?"

The guard smiled broadly. "I'm a security guard. *I'll* find *you*. At about 8 o'clock, *si*?"

"Eight o'clock. Oh, and what is this infraction that you are accusing my wife of? I think I should know how much of a bad girl she's been for $20."

"Why don't you ask her yourself? Ask her and that other woman from steerage where they were a few days ago, where they weren't supposed to be," he laughed and snorted at the same time. "Eight o'clock then."

Giacomo nodded. Now he knew exactly what to do.

Chapter 27   Land

For two days after the incident with the guard, Josie spent little time outside of the cabin. She felt like an exile in her own little world. Now she understood what prisoners felt like. As time crawled by, she kept a low profile so as not to aggravate Giacomo or run into that nasty security guard. She had to laugh at the irony of the use of the term "security" when she thought of the disgusting kiss and groping of her breast, which was sore for two days afterward. Come to think of it, he wasn't all that much more disgusting than Giacomo, her own husband, after his "performance" the nights he got so drunk. Giacomo seemed not to remember the next day and their life together went on as usual—with minimum conversation and interaction. Were all men pigs or morons?

The brief time she spent in the mornings with Sophia eating breakfast in steerage was now cut even shorter. They were both still wary of the guard making trouble for them, but he didn't seem to be on either of their decks in the days before they arrived in New York. Neither women told their husbands about the incident and as time passed, they thought it was forgotten. Their anticipation was high as the days passed, counting down like minutes on a huge, cosmic clock. Soon they would be in America! The land of promise, where freedom and opportunity awaited anyone who wanted it. They were not naïve enough to believe that the streets were literally paved in gold; they knew that was a fairy tale. Yet every single immigrant on that ship knew the magnitude of the journey they had undertaken in crossing the Atlantic and how life-changing it could be for them and their families. Most of them never knew that they were part of such a huge wave of humanity that would help to build the United States into the greatest nation in the world.

The morning after their biggest argument, Josie hadn't gone out at all. She only had a few crackers in the cabin and was starving. Giacomo hadn't been around all day and she wondered if he was going to come for her so that they could eat in the dining hall that evening. Just as she was about to go by herself, he opened the door and walked into the cabin, grunting a greeting. She was actually happy to see him and rose to kiss him hello when he said gruffly, "Sit down. I have to talk to you."

Her stomach churned as she took her seat. Giacomo looked very troubled but not threatening as before. As was his custom, he launched right into the subject.

"What were you and Sophia doing up here in the cabin?"

Josie started. The question was unexpected; she had thought Giacomo had forgotten the incident.

"We weren't doing anything except eating some crackers. Why?"

"Did anyone see you come into the cabin?"

Hmmm, Josie thought. Technically no, she was pretty sure no one had seen them go *into* the cabin. What happened later was another story.

"I don't think so. Giacomo, what is this all about? Sophia left right after you came back to the cabin. I've hardly seen her since."

Giacomo was silent. He was trying to weigh the credibility of the guard against his wife's story. Should he believe him or her? He wanted to believe Josie, but there were so many doubts . . . He paced back and forth in the little cabin deep in thought. Was she lying?

"You know, Josie, it would be best if you told me the truth. Our whole future in America depends on your telling me the truth." He said this as gently as he could manage.

Josie's heart was moved by his apparent concern and unusual tenderness, a side of him she rarely saw. Her heart waned to connect with his effort to protect them both. Which was better, to keep the secret from her jealous husband or to tell him the truth and bear the consequences? She paused for a moment of contemplation, then decided to tell him the truth, or most of the truth, anyway. She took a deep breath.

"All right." There was a long pause.

"After you left the cabin, I walked Sophia down to the stairwell and we ran into a guard who spoke Italian. He recognized Sophia as a passenger from steerage—I don't know how, but he did. Nobody was around and he started to give us a hard time, threatening to report us and to tell our husbands. He had grabbed me by the hair and was pulling on it very hard, so Sophia tried to negotiate with him to let me go and not to report us to the Immigration authorities. He finally let me go . . . "

"What did this guard look like?" Giacomo seemed uncharacteristically calm.

"He was very big, tall and heavy-set, with greasy skin and black hair. He had a bad complexion and looked kind of dirty, unkempt. He made a strange snorting noise too."

Giacomo pressed her for more information. "Did he do anything else?"

Josie looked down at the floor. If she said no, he'd know she was lying.

"He forced me to kiss him."

"Is that it?" Giacomo now looked like he was about to blow a fuse.

"Yes. What are you going to do, Giacomo? It really meant nothing, then he let go of my hair and we left. I haven't seen him since then, and Sophia's been staying below too. Shouldn't we just forget about it? Can he really get us in that much trouble? I'm so sorry I invited Sophia to come to our cabin to visit . . ."

Giacomo was showing an inordinate amount of self-control, Josie thought. She expected a huge blow-up, with accusations that she had provoked the incident and that somehow she had deserved that kind of treatment. But he seemed to be lost in his thoughts and not particularly worried about her. Not at all the reaction she expected. She was, to be honest, waiting for a punch or a smack across the head. Yet there was nothing. Would she ever get to know this man?

"What are you going to do, Giacomo? Giacomo?" Suddenly she realized how famished she was. He was still deep in his own thoughts. She moved towards him and touched his arm. "Giacomo?" She faltered and nearly fainted.

He caught her just as she was going down. He gently helped her up onto the bed.

"Stay here and I'll bring you something to eat. Don't leave the cabin. *Capische*?"

He immediately got up and left, leaving Josie stupefied. What is going on? she wondered. She ate a few more crackers to stave off the hunger in her stomach and lay down on the bed to rest . . . and wait. Again.

An hour and a half passed and there was no Giacomo and no food. She was a nervous wreck, a hungry, nervous wreck. Where is he? Is he in trouble? Did he go after the guard? The questions mounted but there were no answers to be had. Her stomach growled and she had a headache from not eating. It was beginning to turn from dusk to dark outside and soon the dining hall would be closed for the night. She didn't know which was worse, the waiting or not knowing anything. She couldn't stand it any longer.

She put on her beautiful coat and wrapped a scarf around her head, opened the door and made her way cautiously down the hall to the outer deck. No one was about and the hallway was empty. They were probably all eating dinner! The sun had set but there was still some light on the horizon and the ever-present wind created by the moving ship hit her hard in the face as she closed the hall door behind her and walked out onto the deck. It was very cold there but she didn't seem to mind the discomfort; she bowed her head and said a prayer to St. Michael to watch over Giacomo. It was very quiet except for the sound of the engines driving the huge ship and the metal sides cutting through the water. She could only stay a minute.

As she lifted her head up, the last bit of light faded in the west, leaving an orange stripe in the sky where it met the horizon. She blinked once or twice and looked again at the horizon to the west, something that she had trained herself not to do during this trip to avoid the nausea. What was that she thought she saw? A thin black line was clearly visible against the fading orange sky. It looked like trees! The jagged outline of trees far away in the distance!

It was land. She was looking at land. Very far away but there was no mistaking it—she saw land. In the fading light, there it was, silhouetted against the evening sky. Was it America? At that very moment, the ship's horn let out a long, thunderous bellow that sent vibrations throughout the entire structure and even the air surrounding it. To Josie, it seemed as if it was saying hello to the entire continent. She could feel the vibrations move through her whole body, they were so strong. She clasped onto the railing and reveled in the feeling for a moment with her eyes closed, then as she opened them, the last rays of the sun before it fell below the horizon framed the tiny treeline in a riot of backlit color. How incredibly beautiful, she thought. It must be a sign from heaven, an omen to welcome her and Giacomo to the new land. A sign from the

Archangel himself! An intense aura of peace overcame her, she felt like a blessing had been given and she was humbled and grateful. She forgot completely about her hunger. In another moment, the sight was gone, the ship was again quiet and the journey continued.

She fell onto her knees on the deck and sobbed in gratitude.   Then she noticed with a mixture of gratitude and curiosity that she was not in the least bit seasick.

Chapter 28   Confrontation

Giacomo left the cabin at 7:30 and headed for the dining room. He had to get some food for Josie or she might pass out and become sick. Being so close to New York, that would not bode well for their entry into the United States. She had to be healthy and in good spirits to pass the physical exam at Ellis Island, that was a fact. He also had to get the situation with the guard resolved tonight. But right now Josie came first. The dining room closed at 9 so he still had some time.

As he entered the dining room, he looked for the guard but he wasn't there. He flagged down a waiter and ordered some beef stew. There was no such thing as "take out" on the ship; passengers were supposed to eat their meals in the dining hall, but everyone brought food back to their rooms. He wasn't sure how he would disappear with a bowl of stew but he had no time to order anything else. Josie was in no shape to accompany him to the dining room and they didn't have enough time to eat a sit-down meal anyway. Giacomo had to be there at eight to meet the guard.

The stew came and he pretended to sit down and eat. As soon as the waiter disappeared and the people around him were preoccupied, he slipped out the side door with the bowl of stew tucked under his jacket. He cradled it like a baby, leaving one arm free and started walking back to the cabin, which was quite a distance away. The steam and heat from the stew were beginning to warm him through his clothes. He was hungry too; the smell was intoxicating. He walked at a brisk clip down the hall and turned the corner by the bathrooms when he saw the guard standing in the hallway with his back towards him.

Now what should I do with this stew, he thought.

The guard must have smelled the stew for he turned abruptly and faced Giacomo. "Hey, *paisano*, you're early. What's that smell?" he snorted his odd nasal sound and ran his fingers through his greasy hair.

Crap, Giacomo thought. I'm not ready to deal with him right now.

He held up his free hand as if to say "stand back!" and fidgeted around on his feet. "I have to use the men's room, it's urgent! I'll be right back! Why don't you wait for me down the hall? I have to go to the cabin first, eh?"

He ducked inside the bathroom, hoping the guard would not follow him. He waited a respectable amount of time, nibbling on some of the stew in the meanwhile. When he walked out of the bathroom, the guard was not in sight. He headed to the cabin with the half-cold stew still tucked in his jacket against his chest. Even though it had congealed a little, some of the tasty sauce had splattered on his shirt and looked a little like blood. But he was sure Josie would be happy to finally have something to eat. He unlocked the door.

She wasn't there. That bitch wasn't there! He *told* her not to leave and she went out anyway. What the hell! This girl didn't listen for anything! He had even brought her dinner like he said he would. He was so mad at her right then that he didn't care whether she ever ate again. She could live the rest of her life eating crackers, he didn't give a damn. Let her starve! When they got to Pennsylvania, things would be different, he vowed. Very different. They just had to get there first. He put the stew bowl down on the night table with the cold stew in it and left, slamming the door behind him. Now *he* was boiling.

Giacomo knew he had to cool down a bit before he went to deal with the guard, otherwise there would surely be a fight. He had half a mind to let the guard turn Josie in, then he might be able to enter the U.S. without her. There's a thought! He mulled it over, but decided the plan would not work; they were married, and they would probably both get deported back to Italy if one of them did. He went out on the deck to smoke a cigarette and calm down his agitation. His watch said 8:05.

He headed back in the direction of the bathrooms and decided to wait there for the guard to find him. He had twenty American dollars in his money belt if necessary, but he had no intention of giving it to the guard. The slimy man didn't deserve to be rewarded for treating women like that. If he did it to Josie and Sophia, he could bet he'd done the same thing before, and more than once. He waited.

The guard appeared a few minutes later with a Cheshire cat grin on his face. He sauntered up to Giacomo and asked sarcastically, "What took you so long?"

"None of your business," Giacomo shot back.

The guard raised up both of his hands in mock protest and raised his eyebrows. "Whatever you say! Now let's get down to business!" He still had that same smirk on his face. Giacomo thought, what a cocky bastard he is. Not for long, though.

"Before I give you the money, I want to hear again what happened with my wife and the woman from steerage. Go over it one more time for me, eh?"

The guard stopped smiling. He looked around him, taking note of the people in the hallway. No one was paying any attention to them, except for a casual glance here and there. Nonetheless, the guard moved into a small alcove where they wouldn't be overheard. Giacomo looked around too, pausing for a moment, scratched his forehead, then followed the guard, being careful to be on the outside, not letting the guard box him in.

"Well, like I said, your wife and her little friend were in your cabin together a few days ago. That's a clear breach of the rules, you know. Second class passengers and steerage passengers are strictly forbidden to mix with each other, for their own safety. I saw the woman from steerage leave the cabin with your wife and I followed them. To make sure they were safe, of course."

"Of course," now it was Giacomo's turn to be sarcastic. "And did you stop them?" he asked.

The guard straightened up and sucked in his gut. "I ask the questions here, *paisano.*"

"If you want your money, then you'll answer mine," Giacomo countered. "What happened next?" he demanded. The guard shifted his weight uncomfortably.

"I stopped them to talk to them to tell them that the one from steerage wasn't allowed to be on this deck and that she couldn't come back up here again."

"That's it? That's all that happened?"

"Well, yeah, sure, I sent her back down to steerage and that was it. Now if you don't want any more trouble, you'll keep your wife under control and keep that other one downstairs until we get to New York. I can make your stay at Ellis Island extremely difficult, you know. All I have to do is . . ."

Giacomo cut him off. "I don't think you're telling me the whole story, *paisano.*" He punctuated the last word syllable by syllable.

"Whad'ya mean? You weren't there, what do you know?" There was that snort again.

"Here's what *I* know." Giacomo moved right up to the man's chest and lowered his voice. He poked a finger lightly at his uniform as he spoke. "*I* think you decided to take some liberties with the ladies, especially my wife. *I* think you grabbed her by the hair and pulled some of it out! *I* think you decided it was all right to squeeze her breast until it was black and blue, *pai-sa-no*. And *I* think you're a lousy extortionist dressed up like a guard and that this isn't the first time you've intimidated women passengers for money. I think you have a little side business going on here that your captain would be interested to know about. What do you think he'd do if I told him, eh, *paisano*? He might not believe the women, but he will definitely believe the *husbands*."

"Husbands?" The guard didn't look so cocky at that moment.

211

Suddenly from around the side of the alcove, a tall figure appeared and joined the two men. He was as tall as the guard but much younger, and in much better physical shape.

"*Paisano*, this is Nicholas, the husband of Sophia, who was with my wife in our cabin. Both of our wives told us the same story. It was a little different from your version, wasn't it, Nicky?"

"Yeah, especially the part about when you kissed his wife while you had her neck twisted back by her hair. Did you forget that part?" Nicholas moved in closer so no one else would hear their conversation. Giacomo had brought him in on the meeting quietly to have a witness and to confirm the story. When Giacomo had scratched his forehead, that was their pre-arranged signal for him to move in. Nicholas had heard the whole conversation from the start while he stood out of sight behind the alcove.

The guard looked around furtively and noticed that now several people were staring at the group of men. He began to understand that his ploy for some easy money was not going to materialize with these two peasants and he was embarrassed at being out-maneuvered by the little one. He hadn't planned on the steerage husband messing up his little scam. He was beat and he knew it.

Giacomo knew they had him cornered but he needed to make sure there would be no more problems before they disembarked in New York. He took out a pencil and a scrap of paper and leaned up towards the guard's chest. On his lapel was a badge with his employee number on it. Even though Giacomo couldn't read, he could write numbers and he proceeded to write down the guard's badge numbers while Nicholas was speaking to him. We may be peasants, he thought, but we're not stupid peasants. He tucked the piece of paper into his pocket.

Nicholas was wrapping up with, "Now we don't expect any more 'security' from the likes of you, you understand? You leave us alone, all of us, until we leave this ship and nobody will make any reports about anybody, got that? You got it?" he looked him straight in the eye.

The guard grunted and began to back away from the two husbands.

All of a sudden a scream down the hall interrupted their discussion. Passengers turned to look toward the noise and the guard began moving to investigate, but Nicholas and Giacomo barred his way. A crowd started to gather around the men, all looking in the direction of the noise.

It was Josie. She had come in from the deck to find the guard, Giacomo and Nicholas huddled together in a taut, hostile group. This was no friendly conversation, she was sure of that. What were they saying? The combination of her hunger and her surprise at seeing the three men together made her scream. Even though she didn't know what was going on, she saw the guard and her revulsion for him was immediate and complete. And on Giacomo's shirt was what appeared to be a spot of blood! She strode rapidly towards them with fire in her belly and indignation in her soul, fists clenched, not having any control over her passion, acting on pure emotion.

The crowd parted to let her pass as she marched right up past the two husbands to the guard. He towered above her, his jaw drooped and he seemed confused. She put all of her weight and what little energy she had left into the upward sweep of her right arm and with her palm open, she smacked the guard directly across the face. There was a distinct crack of flesh hitting flesh as her palm connected with his greasy skin. SMACK! The folks in the crowd gasped.

"That's for touching me, *bastardo*!" she said.

Josie turned and kissed Giacomo and Nicholas on both cheeks in the European way, and with her head held high, she walked back through the astonished crowd. With a palm-sized red mark on his face, the guard disappeared into the group of angry passengers as Giacomo and Nicholas followed Josie to the cabin.

When they opened the door, they found her passed out on the floor from hunger. The bowl of cold stew was still on the nightstand.

Part III: America

Chapter 29   New York

Giacomo roused Josie, lifting her up carefully from the floor onto the chair and brought the stew to her. The smell was still pungent enough to grab her famished attention as she tried to orient herself to the scene in the cabin. The last thing she remembered was smacking the guard across the face. Was Giacomo all right? How long was she unconscious?

He began feeding her some of the cold stew which she ate ravenously. Stew had never tasted so good, she decided. He gave her some water to wash it down or else she would have eaten the whole bowl in one gulp. He could see her coming gradually back to life. What a relief!

Josie was finally able to focus on Giacomo. She looked at him gratefully and said softly, "You smell like stew. . . "

"And you gave us a big scare!" He didn't have the heart to start an argument with her just then.

"Where did you go? I brought back the food and you were gone."

"I had to get out. I was so hungry, I thought some fresh air would help me forget the hunger. I thought I was going to pass out! I only thought I'd be gone for a minute but then I saw the sunset and, Giacomo, I actually saw land! And trees! Did you hear the ship's horn? They were saluting the land! It was so beautiful! Then when I came back in I saw you and Nicholas with that bastard guard and I didn't know what to think. It looked like you had blood on you, but you weren't fighting, just talking, and I didn't know what happened to me, I just snapped, I guess. The last thing I remember was smacking him across the face. What happened?"

"Don't worry, don't worry. He won't be bothering us anymore. Let's just say we came to an agreement and leave it at that." Giacomo heaved a sigh of relief. This was the most conversation they had had together since they had gotten married. Giacomo had to admit that she had guts to do what she did to the guard in front of all those people. His admiration for her grew in that moment. She was a spirited one, this wife of his. He smiled to himself when a series of sharp knocks were heard on the door, interrupting them.

"Ship's staff. Open up. News about tomorrow."

TOMORROW? They were going to land!

Giacomo opened the door and two ship employees started to brief them on what was going to happen when the ship reached their destination, New York harbor, in the early dawn of the next day. They both concentrated on the instructions so they wouldn't forget anything.

"You should have all bags packed tonight and gather up your immigration papers. Make sure you don't leave anything behind in the room because you can't come back. Do not take sheets, pillow or towels that belong to the ship line with you. Make sure you have at least twenty American dollars between the two of you. Do not take anything you can't carry. You can be on deck at 7 a.m. when we arrive so you can get a look at the sights. First class passengers disembark first, then second class, then steerage. Be ready." They shook their heads mutely.

They could hear the staff knocking on the neighboring cabins giving the other passengers the same message. Up and down the hall the sound could be heard for an hour, the same message that was conveyed to all of the passengers that night. How excited the immigrants were to know that their voyage was almost over! How anxious they must have felt in anticipation of the examination they would be subjected to before they would be allowed into this wonderful country they had heard so much about! Would they be deemed worthy? There was not a traveler on board that ship who didn't dread the alternative--deportation back to their homeland-- and many, many prayers were sent heavenward in the late hours of that evening.

Josie and Giacomo were so worn out that they both fell into bed after organizing their few belongings and their papers. Their marriage license, their passports, their vaccination records. Josie laid out their clothes on the chair and neatly arranged the rest of their personal items in the trunk that Giacomo would carry. Her satchel was also at the ready. They washed up and as they climbed into bed, Giacomo reached for her, drew her close to him, and instead of making love, he held her spoon-style while they both fell asleep. The last thing she remembered was his breath in her hair.

Long before first light, the sound of people preparing for arrival woke them up—
slamming doors, talk in the halls, men and women jockeying for time in the restrooms. The whole ship was alive with excitement! How soon would we land? Which side of the ship should we be on for the first look at the new land? Some women were so nervous

they were dabbing their eyes in the hallway. A huge shuffle of luggage and muffled voices inside the cabins could be heard down the corridor of their deck. Giacomo and Josie rose, freshened up and got dressed immediately so they could be out on the deck as the sun rose to experience their entrance into America. They were in great spirits as the memory of the previous evening faded and the threat of extortion was gone. They made their way to the dining hall and fought the crowds to have a quick breakfast. Leaving their bags in the cabin, they joined the hundreds of other passengers on the second-class deck on the starboard side of the ship.

It was cold and sunny that day as the winter sun appeared on the eastern horizon. The huge ship chugged doggedly through the Verrazano Narrows straight past the low hills of Staten Island in the west. The vast harbor opened up to them with outstretched arms of land in a gesture of welcome; the rising sun crept between the skyscrapers in Manhattan to the east and they saw maritime businesses with dock workers by the hundreds lining the shores of lower Manhattan. Smaller ships traveled in all directions and tugs pushing barges filled with rocks and coal were passing each other going up and down the Hudson River. In the distance they could see a short, green statue which grew taller and taller as the ship labored further into the harbor.

It was the Statue of Liberty, the copper lady who had welcomed millions of immigrants just like them to America. She stood stoically watching over the harbor, immune to the rain and heat and freezing cold. The expression on her face was detached from the mundane events of daily life, the dramas of thousands of displaced people who had been floating on the sea for weeks banking on a promise, *her* promise. She held her torch high in a lofty gesture that spoke of justice, opportunity and freedom which she extended to all regardless of their backgrounds. Hundreds of passengers on the deck of the ship waved, cheered, cried and stood in awe as the ship moved silently closer and closer to that green beacon of hope. Grown men could be seen with their hats held over their hearts and tears streaming down their faces. Hope is what those passengers needed right then, for behind the Lady of Liberty, who stood on her own little spit of land in the middle of the harbor, was another island, an island full of anxiety and trepidation, called Ellis. The island of hope and tears. Josie imagined the Lady of the Harbor sending out reassurances of peace and calm to all of those on board. "Welcome. Only one more test and you'll be free. . ."

The ship slowly came to a halt about a half mile from Ellis Island, but it did not go to the dock. Instead, in a few minutes, two smaller steamboats came to carry the immigrants to the processing center. The passengers were instructed to collect their belongings and almost in one body, they moved deck by deck to the loading area and onto the smaller ships. The seas pitched the steamboats about in the wind as Giacomo and Josie went to cross the gangway; Giacomo took her satchel and juggling both the trunk and the satchel in his arms, he told her to hold on to the gangway railing as she crossed. "Don't look down," he told her, and she didn't. "Look straight at my back," he said, and with her heart in her throat, she stared at him as she gingerly crossed into the steamboat, feeling the heavy push of the crowd behind her.

When both tiers of their steamboat were full of first and second class passengers, it left for the immigration center. Another steamboat would be right behind it to take the steerage passengers and anyone else who was disembarking in New York over to the island. Nicholas and Sophia would be on that boat. Giacomo was amazed at how quickly and efficiently the whole process was conducted. He didn't know that the Ellis Island facility was capable of processing up to 2,000 immigrants a day and that 12 million passengers would ultimately pass through its halls before it was closed in 1944, its staff only deporting two percent of that number back to their original home countries. Two percent!

The anxious passengers disembarked after the steamship pulled up to the dock behind a huge complex of buildings, the largest of which looked like a Byzantine cathedral with red and white bricks decorating its façade and spires topped with curious onion-shaped cupolas. The crowd was guided down a boardwalk towards this imposing building and Josie and Giacomo, swept along in the mass of humanity and luggage, walked into the building and took their place in the queues of people snaking their way up to a wide staircase. Tables of officials checked passengers' paperwork as the line crept through the Great Hall towards the stairs. At the top were two lines of stern-looking officials watching them climb the stairs. The group at the top were doctors and immigration officials who were screening the passengers for those who could not walk up the flight to the second floor. Several passengers who became winded or who faltered, limped or stumbled or dropped luggage were asked to step aside when they reached the top. This method was not lost on the passengers below; Josie and Giacomo trudged carefully, relentlessly to the top landing without a mishap and were guided to a huge room with aisles delineated by low partitions like little fences where they took their place in the lines waiting to see a registrar. Noise filled the gigantic Registry Room and bounced off its walls and floors, but they could see that there was order in the seeming chaos as the lines moved steadily through the labyrinth of fenced pathways that fed into the processing area. Within an hour of arrival, the couple was standing in front of a processor who spoke Italian.

The man asked Giacomo for their names and their papers. Everything seemed to be in order so with a quick pound of a stamp on their passports, they were moved to the next phase—the dreaded medical exam. Josie smiled at the man and said, "Thank you" in English, which generated a stern look from Giacomo. The official, surprised at an immigrant who could speak some English, nodded back at them. As they moved toward the area where the medical exams were held, they heard wailing and some arguments as people were pulled aside for further questioning. Josie threw a worried look at Giacomo, who mouthed that it would be all right.

They entered the infirmary section and had to part ways, both going to gender-specific areas where female nurses attended to the women and children and male doctors and officials examined the men. Josie was told to remove all of her clothing as a nurse looked her up and down, then felt her hair and scalp, and ordered her to cough as she listened to her chest with a stethoscope.

"You're pretty skinny . . . , " the nurse commented, but Josie didn't understand what she said. She got dressed again. Following several of the other women, she was ushered into a room with chairs and was told to sit. In a few minutes, a male doctor came in with a small, curved wire tool in his hand which he then laid above and then below the upper and lower eyelids of each of the women, rolling the eyelid up over the tool. It was rather painful and impossible to blink with the "buttonhook" wrapped around Josie's eyelid. Some of the women cried out and wouldn't be still so the doctor asked a nurse to stand behind the chair and hold the immigrant's head from behind while he deftly turned the eyelids up over the hook, looking for trachoma. One woman's daughter was found to have the eye disease, and the two were led out to the hospital for treatment, which meant that the family would have to wait for days before they could enter the United States. The mother started to cry, and the child was already whining, but at least they would be treated—for free—and eventually would be allowed in.

Josie was told she could rejoin Giacomo after more of her papers were stamped. She breathed a sigh of relief. Staff directed her and the women in her group back down another corridor to where the men who had passed their medical exam were waiting. She thought she must've looked quite disheveled at that point as she patted her hair but she didn't really care. She had passed! She was ecstatic. Now if she could just find her husband . . .

She stood alone in a sea of immigrants, yelling for their family members in numerous languages, pushing and shoving luggage before them, holding suitcases over their heads, some crying, some somber, some praying, some smiling. She moved off to the side where an official gestured her to wait and looked through the passing crowd for Giacomo. He wasn't there. She waited and waited, watching family after family be reunited and move on, but Giacomo didn't appear.

What had happened to him? Where was Giacomo?

Chapter 30   Reunited

After about an hour of waiting, Josie guessed
that she was not going to be reunited with Giacomo at
this point in the entry process. It seemed like hundreds
of people had passed by her in that time and she wasn't
even sure whether these people were from her ship. As
she waited, panic was beginning to rise inside her
even though she tried to present an outward
appearance of composure. She tried so hard not to
look worried, as though this was an everyday
occurrence and she was taking it in stride. She
vacillated between breaking down and crying in
frustration and being strong and stoically continuing to
wait. An official-looking man in a uniform eventually
came up to her to tell her to move on when she finally
mustered up the courage to ask him, in her newly-
acquired use of the English language, how she could
find Giacomo.

"Scuzi, signor, I look for my husband. He no
comes of medical room. *Per favore*, you help me?
Thanks you." The man smiled kindly at her funny
English grammar, quietly admiring her charm and
beauty. Most of the immigrants who passed through
these rooms were poor and not very physically
appealing, since most were of the peasant class of their

native country. But this one was a looker. He gestured her to follow him.

They entered another room with several officials sitting at a desk. One of them spoke Italian, so the man guided Josie over to him. "This is Mr. Walters, young lady. He will try to help you. Good luck." She shot him a grateful smile as he thought, your husband must be a lucky man. She sat down next to Mr. Walters at his invitation and he too had a friendly smile for her.

"What seems to be the problem, Miss?" he asked in Italian.

"My husband and I were separated when we were being processed at the medical exam and I waited for him at the exit area but he never showed up. His name is Giacomo Constanza. Can you help me find him?" she said sweetly. She was aware of the other men looking at her talking to Walters. They seemed to be chuckling behind her back.

"I'll call one of the medical examiners to see what happened to your husband. Can you describe him to me, Signora?" Walters asked.

"Well, yes, he's rather short, about 5 foot 7 inches, has black hair, is clean-shaven and has brown eyes. He was wearing a brown corduroy jacket and a white shirt with dark pants." She thought that probably described about half of the men at the facility that day. "Please help me find him. Oh, and he was carrying a small traveling trunk."

"Please just wait here. I'll be right back." He disappeared down the hall.

Josie was aware of the other men staring at her so she tried to ignore them. In fact, she sort of liked the attention they were paying to her, but she never would tell Giacomo that. She had to remind herself that she was married now, and married Italian women had to behave. He would be back any minute.

Mr. Walters came back very soon to tell Josie that he had found Giacomo and that he would take her to him.

"What was taking so long to clear his entry?" she wanted to know.

"There is some sort of problem, but I'm sure it's only minor. You'll be on your way in no time. Follow me, please."

She trailed after him through a labyrinth of halls painted in dull institutional green. With each turn she was aware that she was getting further and further away from the Great Hall, where they had first begun this frightening selection process. Was this Walter guy leading her into a trap? Would he be a gentleman or, like the guard on the ship, would he try to take advantage of her? She was on high alert as she dutifully followed him down some stairs to a lower level. They stopped at a room with a door the top half of which was made of frosted glass. As he opened the door, she could see Giacomo seated inside with his hands in his lap.

"Giacomo!" She ran up to him without regard to decorum or permission. He looked up at her solemnly, saying nothing. He didn't have to; she instantly saw that one of his eyes was red and would soon develop a beautiful shiner. She gasped and put her hand to her mouth.

"What happened to you?!" she exclaimed. Then she looked around and noticed a policeman standing in the other corner of the room. A policeman! This can't be good, she thought.

"Sit down, Miss," the policeman said. "Your boyfriend here is in a heap of trouble." She understood two words: "sit" and "trouble."

Giacomo wasn't talking to her so she just kept quiet. No one said a word for fifteen minutes. Josie's mind raced full of thoughts about being deported, returning to Italy in shame, or worse, being stuck here in America without Giacomo or any money. What would she do then? Suddenly the door opened and a tall man in a suit walked in with the same man who had spoken to her in Italian earlier. Mr. Walters nodded to her imperceptibly. The man in the suit began to speak in English as Walters translated what he was saying into Italian.

The suited man turned to him and said, "Who is this woman?" Walters told him that Josie was his wife. He looked Josie up and down, cleared his throat and continued.

"Mr. Constanza, Statute 28.75, Section 2 of the United States Immigration Law of 1920 states that any person or persons deemed argumentative, hostile or aggressive during the immigration entry process can be denied entry into the United States and can be deported back to his or her home country." He waited for the translator to catch up.

"As you saw fit to argue with the medical examiner's staff when they took your trunk for search during your examination procedure, and since you became aggressive, punching one of the staff in the jaw in reaction to his removal of your trunk, we can only assume that you are a person of low character, a brigand and a ruffian who has no place in our country, and a person of hostile character." Again he waited for the translator to finish.

Josie looked wide-eyed at Giacomo, who continued to look at his hands in his lap. Her worst fears were coming true.   This can't be happening! How could he do something like that today of all days?! What was he thinking? It took every ounce of self-restraint for her to remain silent.

"This is your only opportunity to explain your actions and then we will let you know our determination. What do you have to say?" The translator stopped. All eyes were on a very nervous, contrite Giacomo. He stood up, still holding his hands and addressed the translator.

"Signore, I-uh-I am a very simple man, a farmer and a gardener, who has never been out of my country. I'm not very educated in the ways of the world but I did serve honorably in the Great War. All of this is new to me and to tell you the truth, it's very overwhelming, this whole trip. I'm not a violent man" (with this he looked directly at Josie), "yet when they took my trunk away, I thought they were not going to give it back. I thought your people were stealing it. Inside that trunk are the only reminders of my home, as small as they may seem to you. My tools, our wedding linens, our clothes and some wine and food from Abruzzo. I've carried them on my back this whole trip. We cannot replace them in your new world. I'm sorry I punched the officer but I was trying to defend my possessions, the only ones I have to begin a new life in America. If you send me back, my wife will have to come with me because she can't stay here by herself, and your country will lose two very good workers. America needs people who know how to grow food and take care of plants, does it not? We are not criminals, only hard-working people. You will see. I am asking you to give us a second chance, *per favore*. Just another chance. That's all." He sat down again.

Josie was so moved she started to cry. She had never heard Giacomo speak so eloquently in the short time she had known him. It was a revelation to her to see this side of him, and regardless of what happened next, his little speech touched her heart. If they had to go back, then they would relocate somewhere in Italy to live inconspicuously. She looked at him with tears in her eyes and held his hand, hoping for the best. She said a silent prayer to Jesus and St. Michael Angelo too.

Mr. Walters was just finishing his version of the defendant's speech. He then spoke privately to the official. It seemed to Josie that he was adding some information. Would he speak in their defense? The tall man in the suit left the room with him and they were alone again, except for the guard. She hoped the guard didn't speak Italian.

"Giacomo, I was so worried about you! I was so afraid... Do you think they'll let us stay? What will we do?!" He wrapped his arm around her and gave her a reassuring hug, even though he didn't feel very reassuring at all. Why did he have to hit that man? He may have destroyed their chance at entering the golden land of America. If he had to go back, he'd have some explaining to do to the Bishop. But the worst part was the disappointment he would have to face with Josie.

"It'll be okay, my girl. I'm sorry, I'm sorry for all of this. It'll be okay."

Time seemed to stand still as they sat in the little room awaiting their fate, which was now in the hands of the bureaucratic immigration officials. They had no idea that, although ninety-eight percent of all immigrants entering the United States from Europe at Ellis Island were allowed in during these years, a small portion was not. People with medical conditions like trachoma, mental illness or retardation, obvious diseases or physical malformations, and those thought to be hostile or of ill repute were often sent back home. It was especially heartbreaking to have one member of a family denied entrance, making it necessary to send either the whole family packing or to split the family up. This situation was very common among the rejected immigrants at the port entry of New York. Although Josie and Giacomo could not have known this, they were in good company. All they could do now was wait, as their answer depended on the backlog of the administrative staff assigned to evaluate those immigrants on that particular day.

As it turned out, fate would be with them. There were few immigrant rejections on their particular ship and Giacomo had spoken persuasively on his own behalf. Normally, the Review Board would take a day or two to evaluate an issue like theirs, during which time the Constanzas would be retained as "guests" of the United States on Ellis Island until the dispensation of their case. As they waited tensely in one of the small rooms for the verdict, Mr. Walters talked outside to the tall man in the suit in favor of letting them pass through immigration. They both talked to the guard about the assault and they all agreed that Giacomo's story made sense and that the guard wasn't willing to press formal charges, since he got the best of Giacomo anyway. It was all sorted out in about a half hour without going through the formal review process.

Mr. Walters was asked to go back to the room and release the Constanzas. The trunk had been searched and the wine confiscated, but otherwise they would be allowed to continue. He opened the door to the room to deliver the news.

"Mr. and Mrs. Constanza, you're free to go now. It's been determined that there is insufficient evidence to deny your entry into our country. You must be aware however that you have been very lucky and that behavior like this will not be tolerated in the United States."

Josie jumped up and down like a little kid and hugged Giacomo, then hugged and kissed a very surprised Mr. Walters. He gently put his hands on her shoulders and pushed her away. Giacomo looked tremendously relieved and didn't even get mad at Josie for kissing another man in his presence. He kept repeating "*Grazie, grazie*" over and over again.

"Follow me and we'll retrieve your trunk. Your wine bottle has been confiscated, I'm sorry to report. Let's go!"

In a matter of minutes, the two found themselves on the pier with their trunk and Josie's suitcase and stamped papers allowing them to enter the United States. They held the papers in their hands and stared at them while the sky turned dusk and the lights on the skyline of New York were starting to twinkle. They had never seen such tall buildings reaching up to the sky—and so many of them! Buildings stretched from one horizon to the other across the choppy water in front of them. Whoever had built so many buildings in one place must've had a lot of money and power, they surmised. The sight was so beautiful and so close that Josie wanted to reach out her hand and touch them so see if they were real. Was Easton, Pennsylvania like this too? They would soon find out.

Chapter 31   The Letter

Father Rocco spent a few minutes picking up flower petals in the cathedral after Josie and Giacomo's wedding. It was a simple ceremony, one befitting the station of the couple who had recently played such an intimate part in saving the Bishop's life and career. The whole town seemed to rejoice in the celebration, partly because of the element of surprise but mostly, as he suspected, because of the attractive girl who was chosen like Cinderella to marry and head off to the promised land, *America*. The power of that one word was spellbinding. Of course, Giacomo was no prince, yet he was acceptable enough to play the part since he was willing to leave the only home he had ever known and take a new wife to a strange and wonderful land to forge a better life than the one he faced in Abruzzo. For that alone he had the respect of the townsfolk, for that took more courage than they had. How romantic it seemed to them! No one knew the true reason that the two had been hurriedly betrothed and married, then shipped off to the other side of the world. Only the Bishop knew.

He looked out through the cloister at the fruit tree that had recently been transplanted and noted that it seemed to be thriving. Would anyone suspect that this tree marked the grave of a henchman of the most notorious figure in the Sicilian *Cosa Nostra* organization? The tree certainly didn't seem to mind.

In the passing days, life in Citta St. Angelo regained its normalcy. The rhythms of small town life resumed and one would never have known the recent drama that had unfolded within the old walls of the *catedrale*. Father Rocco wanted to keep it this way. Normal and boring. And unsuspicious. He wondered how long it would be before the messenger was missed.

Two days after the Constanzas left for America, Father Rocco took pen to paper and wrote a brief letter to his counterpart and friend at the Church of the Annunciation in Easton, Pennsylvania. Years before, he had gone to seminary with Father Giancarlo Philippi; they had kept in touch and followed each other's careers over the years. He knew that Josie and Giacomo would need help getting set up in a foreign country, especially since they didn't speak the language. They would need to find a place to rent and a job for Giacomo—as quickly as possible before their money ran out. They had no furniture or household goods either. There was so much involved when starting from scratch!

Ciao and Blessings to you, my old friend—

I hope this letter finds you well and not bearing the curse of your arthritis over the winter in America. May God keep your knees warm and the aches at bay. We recently had a special wedding here in Citta St. Angelo: the marriage of my gardener to a lovely young lady who attended our Parish school. His name is Giacomo Constanza and hers is Josephina. They have had the good fortune to save enough money to emigrate to America and at my suggestion, they wish to settle in Easton and perhaps become your parishioners. . .

Father Rocco stroked his chin thoughtfully and wondered how likely that scenario might actually be. Not very, knowing Giacomo's dislike of organized religion.

In friendship, I am hoping you might give them whatever assistance that you can provide initially to help them get set up in your wonderful country. Giacomo, albeit a man of few words, is very strong and can make anything grow. He is also an excellent tradesman and carpenter and can build most anything. Josephina is delightful and well-educated. She has a gift for sewing and designing clothing; in fact, she created a whole new outfit for the statue of our patron saint, Michel Angelo, in the catedrale here. They are

239

honest and hard-working people whom I can vouch for on my life.

Truer words were never said, he swore.

They should be arriving towards the end of the month. Please let me know when they arrive and if you can manage it, help them to find work and a decent place to stay. I am certain that with the proper guidance, they will become productive and loyal citizens. Let me know if there is any way I can help; I bear a special interest in their success.

Faithfully yours,

Rocco

He found an envelope and carefully sealed the letter inside. He used his hopelessly out-of-date but still effective seal and a drop of hot wax to imprint the back of the envelope. Before he put the letter in the post, he made the sign of the Cross over it to bless it in its voyage across the sea. As an afterthought, he put on extra postage so it would be sent via the new-fangled method called airmail. Imagine—a letter flying across the ocean in an airplane! He wanted to make sure it was in Father Philippi's hands before they got there and he knew this was the fastest way possible.

Father Rocco slept like a baby that night for the first time since the "accident."

Chapter 32   The New World

Father Giancarlo Philippi was not surprised one cold January afternoon to see two very tired, bedraggled people, a man and a young woman, trudging hesitantly up the steps of his church. The man, who looked to be about 30, short and of stocky build, was carrying a trunk on his shoulder. The woman, younger than him with flowing chestnut hair covered partially by a scarf, straggled a few steps behind him. Her complexion was wan, her shoulders somewhat stooped for one so young, yet she wore a handsome wool coat that stood out from their out-of-date garments in its craftsmanship and style. He was pretty certain that this was the couple from the Italian province of Abruzzo that his friend, Father Rocco, had written him about. He was expecting them.

It had been good to hear from his old friend Rocco. Over the years they had kept in touch by letter but as time passed and their duties increased, it seemed there was less and less time to communicate. He always looked forward to his friend's letters; they bore news of the old country and of his *paisanos* in the Church in Italy. A smile came to his face every time he received a letter with the wax stamp of the Bishop sealing the envelope's flap. How quaint a custom in this modern-day society! He felt a twinge of one-upmanship when his friend's seal appeared on each letter, gently reminding him that Rocco was a Bishop now and he was still just a priest. But he didn't mind, really. It did seem a little strange, though, that his most recent letter had arrived with the seal broken and the letter in wrinkled condition. There was writing on the envelope explaining that it had been damaged in handling during its trip across the ocean and Father Philippi thought that such transport by air would surely wreak havoc with a fragile letter such as this one. The seal had been taped back together and the envelope's contents were intact. He thought nothing more about it.

He walked towards the couple and met them halfway up the steps. The man immediately dropped the trunk onto the landing.

"*Buon giorno, bienvenito*, my friends. You must be the Constanzas. Welcome to Easton and to the Church of the Annunciation. I am Father Giancarlo Philippi." He extended his hand in greeting.

Giacomo took the priest's hand in a hearty handshake. "I'm Giacomo Constanza and this is my wife, Josephina. We call her Josie."

He nodded and smiled at Josie. "You look exhausted. It's such a long trip! But now you're here safe and sound so please come in and we'll get you settled. Come! Tell me all about your trip."

They followed Father Giancarlo like sheep into the church. The priest had called for a couple of boys to carry the trunk and Josie's satchel. He led them to the rectory where there was a meal waiting for them. They didn't even say grace--they dove right in. Neither of them had tasted anything so good in a long time! They ate like condemned prisoners eating their last meal.

After awhile, Giacomo and Josie noticed that a few people had gathered in the kitchen and were quietly observing them as they gobbled down their food.   They paused and looked around suspiciously as several people came up to them, introduced themselves, and in their native dialect, began to ask them questions about Citta St. Angelo and people who lived there or in the surrounding areas. Giacomo knew a few of them but Josie didn't know anyone. Still, it made her feel welcomed and she was relieved to be able to speak to people in her own tongue. Using her small vocabulary of English words during her trip was very trying and frustrating. She imagined it was twice as bad for Giacomo, who didn't know any English at all. The people thanked Giacomo profusely for the small bits of information he could give them and wished them good fortune in their adopted town.

After they finished eating, Father Giancarlo guided the couple to a sparsely-furnished room with a small bed in it. "It's not much but you're welcome to stay here until you get settled," he explained. "The bathroom is down the hall on the left. I'll leave you two to rest now. If you need anything, just ask for me."

They both thanked the kind man. In less than five minutes, they were undressed and passed out, tucked tightly together in the little bed. No matter. To them, it felt like a mattress sent from heaven.

They both awoke the next morning, having slept straight through the night. Again, they were famished so after getting dressed, they went in search of the priest. They didn't have to go very far; the housekeeper let Father Philippi know they were up and he met them in the rectory hallway.

Giacomo immediately took the priest's hand. "*Buona mattina*, Father."

"Did you sleep well, my friends?" he looked at them both, but especially at Josie, who looked very exhausted the day before. She seemed to be more rested today. "Yes, thank you, Father, " she said. The priest noted that her whole face lit up when she smiled.

"Signore, " Giacomo was saying in Italian, "I—we—want to thank you for your good hospitality but I really need your help. I need to find a job right away, some kind of work, anything will do. Do you know anyone who would hire me as a laborer? I have good carpentry skills and am always on time for work. I'm very strong! We don't have much money left . . . Can you help me, Father? I know I don't speak any English but I understand pretty good . . . "

"Slow down, Giacomo. All in good time, all in good time. I know someone who can always use a good worker, and I have some work that needs to be done here on the church. You say you're a carpenter? That's just what I need. So come have some breakfast and we'll talk a little more. Then I must go to work."

Josie had tears in her eyes. She wondered if the other immigrants on the ship during the Atlantic passage were having the same good luck that she and Giacomo were. She could hardly believe their good fortune, and wondered to what extent the Bishop had influenced their arrival. It would be naïve to think that this was all a wonderful twist of fate. She knew that forces beyond her control were at work, she just didn't know to what extent. It was probably better that she didn't know.

She was also amazed at Giacomo's ability to converse with men. He hardly said a word to her, but when a man was around, he sure could talk! She wished he would talk to her like he talked to his male counterparts. She never could seem to find a good time to talk to him during the voyage, really talk to him. Try to get to know him a little better . . .

"Father?" Josie timidly interjected when there was a pause in the two men's conversation.

"Yes, Josie?"

"I haven't been in touch with my parents for almost a month. Is it possible that I could write them a letter from here? I think we have enough money for a stamp."

"Of course, my dear, of course. You can just ask my housekeeper for anything you need. Her name is Mafalda."

"Thank you, Father, thank you so much. I really miss my parents . . ."

Josie really missed everyone—her parents, her friends, her cat, even her teachers at school. This trip had shown her one thing. The world is such a big place, she pondered. Maybe too big for her? Would she be able to fit in?

At that, Giacomo cast her a look of displeasure. How could she be worried about a letter to her parents at a time like this? he wondered. There were so many more important things that had to be done. He had to find a job and a place to live--they couldn't live in the church for very long! What a stupid girl! He grabbed her arm in annoyance and hurried her along to the kitchen.

"There'll be plenty of time for writing letters," he said to her under his breath.

Father Giancarlo caught a whiff of dissention between them but decided not to intervene. Before he and Giacomo left, Father Philippi called for Mafalda.

Chapter 33   Easton

Mafalda was a giant of a woman in all respects. She was as wide as she was tall. One could tell just by looking at her that she loved to cook and she loved to eat. At the age of forty, she had lost two husbands and all of her children were grown. She had seen a steady number of immigrants just like the Constanzas in her time at the church; they got off the boat in New York, took a train to Easton and walked the rest of the way to the Church of the Annunciation. They were greeted with food and a warm bed, and they quickly joined the ranks of the region's labor pool that was comprised of waves of immigrants from Italy and Eastern Europe during those years. Italians, Poles, Russians, Armenians, Slovaks, Romanians—she had fed them all. Easton was a thriving mill town with textile mills and factories that worked night and day producing goods for export. There were plenty of jobs in Easton.

There was something about the young girl sitting at the table in front of her that drew Mafalda in and made her stand out from the countless immigrant women she had encountered. Most of the women were older than their years and looked overworked and perpetually tired. Very few had had any kind of medical treatment during their lives. They produced many children, some of whom died in infancy or didn't make it to adulthood. These women were used to grinding poverty and domineering husbands who often drank and gambled their paychecks away. Some were beaten by their husbands. They all shared the same look. Resignation.

But this Josie was different. They were an unusual couple, it was true. She was twelve years his junior, maybe more. She looked as though she hadn't worked hard at all in her young life; in fact, Mafalda at first thought she might be a student at university. And that coat! Where did she ever get it? It was so unique. Mafalda had lots of questions for this young lady.

"Signora, how did you sleep last night?" she began in the Abruzzese dialect. It was a good place to start.

"Oh, very well, thank you. We were so tired. It seems like we've been traveling for a year." Josie said politely, resting her chin on her hands. She sighed.

While she cooked some breakfast for the girl, Mafalda peppered her with questions. Where was she from? How old was she? Who were her parents? How did she meet Giacomo? Josie was attracted to Mafalda's motherly nature and warmth, something she hadn't had for awhile. The story of their courtship and voyage came pouring out of her. The only thing she left out was the altercation in the *catedrale*. No one would ever know about that.

"I was a student at the cathedral school and Giacomo worked there for the Bishop. I never paid any attention to him! He was so much older than I was and I thought he already had a family. One day he came up to me and told me how much he admired my new coat. You see, my father had bought my mother and me a new treadle sewing machine and he had given me the wool fabric and lining, which was enough to make a coat. Then the Bishop asked me to make a new suit of clothes for the statue of the Saint Michael Angelo in the *catedrale*, and Giacomo had to build a scaffold so I could climb up to reach the statue and that's how we met. I thought he was nice and before I knew it, he asked me to marry him and come here to America with him. It all happened very fast and the next thing I knew, I was married and on a ship headed to the United States. The Bishop helped us—he was our sponsor, I guess you'd call it, and he married us right before we left—and off we went! I was a little sick on the ship coming over and we got separated at the Immigration Station but we got back together again and here we are!"

Mafalda sat down next to the girl and watched as she again wolfed down another meal. It seemed to her that Josie had an unusually large appetite. She was flattered that Josie liked her cooking. She tried to make some sense out of the story she had just heard. This one had a lot of spunk!

"I know you'd like to write a letter to your parents. That means you are able to read and write, no? I can bring you pen and paper and you can write to your heart's content. Let them know you arrived safely. Afterwards, if you want to, we can take a walk and I can show you around Easton. Introduce you to the town."

"Oh, I'd love that!" Josie exclaimed. "Can we do that now? Then I can write my parents about it later!" She jumped up and impulsively gave Mafalda a hug. It was a little like hugging a bear but without the fur. Mafalda laughed at this woman-child and her great sense of adventure.

A few minutes later, they were off on a walking tour of Easton, Pennsylvania.

The town of Easton rests on the Delaware River on the western border with New Jersey about two hours north of Philadelphia. It lies in the foothills of the Pocono Mountains, part of the Allegheny chain of the Appalachians. They are old mountains, the Appalachians, full of rounded peaks and lush, stream-fed valleys with creeks and rivers, and many waterfalls. Easton lies at the confluence of the Lehigh River and the Delaware River, two substantial bodies of water with the Lehigh being the lesser of the two. Just before the Lehigh reaches the Delaware, there is a man-made waterfall that slows the water's path into the larger stream and prevents boat traffic from going up the Lehigh from the Delaware. A promontory overlooking this waterfall soars fifty feet above the alluvial rocks that millennia ago have traveled down one or the other river, pushed and pulled by glaciers, and had found a home at its base. As the Lehigh's waters join the Delaware's, there is a mad, swirling crash of forces that create spinning eddies and furious pockets of whitewater when the water is high in the spring, especially after the snow melts. A memorial park sits on this promontory with a cannon honoring fallen soldiers of some long-ago battle. The cannon points at the exact spot where the two rivers meet and is a favorite climbing challenge for local children.

An iron bridge connects the town of Easton to its New Jersey neighbor, Phillipsburg, across the Delaware just north of the confluence of the two rivers. About a half mile further south of the rivers' meeting point is a high railroad trestle that crosses from New Jersey into Pennsylvania. One can sit in the park on the promontory and watch vehicle traffic creep over the iron bridge to the north and then observe trains carefully negotiate the railroad bridge to the south, the rushing waters of the rivers tumbling underneath.

The city itself is built on several hills, similar to a little Rome, with winding streets that challenge vehicles to climb them slowly and brake hard coming back down. Downtown, a large circle, or roundabout, is made from four major streets converging and blending into a crossroads, and inside the circle is another park, a small one, whose centerpiece is a large bronze statue of a Union soldier commemorating the War between the States. He stands with rifle at the ready high on a pedestal, as if guarding the town. Old buildings with stores on the first floor line the shopping district that spreads outwards from the circle. Throughout the town old mills, a few dating from colonial times, operate on lesser creeks that find their way into the Delaware. Street after street of neat row homes connected to each other at their common walls house the workers who labor at the mills. On the top of one of the most prominent hills in the city lies City Hall, a Grecian temple of a building that houses government offices, for Easton is the county seat of Northampton County, Pennsylvania.

Another distinguishing feature of the town is a large hill on its north side that serves a dual purpose: it is where the wealthiest neighborhood in the city is located and it is also the site of the campus of Lafayette College, an exclusive liberal-arts school. Interspersed among the homes of the rich are the fraternity and sorority houses of the well-to-do students who attend the college, and the homes of the professors who teach there. The toniest address in all of Easton is "College Hill."

Mafalda explained all of this to Josie as they walked along a street near the church that offered panoramic views of the city. She pointed out the rivers and the hills, City Hall and the college campus. Josie was surprised to hear of the different classes of neighborhoods, just as it had been in Citta St. Angelo except on a much smaller scale. She wondered if the *palacios* of her home town were like the wealthy folks' homes up on College Hill. Some day she would get Giacomo to take her there to see.

"Mafalda, where do the Italians live in Easton? Where do *you* live? Is your house beautiful?" Josie asked, with that engaging smile.

"Well, the new Italians, the ones who come here right off the ships, they live in a part of town down by the circle but behind the shops. After they work for awhile and save up some money, sometimes they can rent a nicer house in a better neighborhood. Sometimes they can even buy a home. It all depends on what kind of job the husband can get." She didn't tell Josie where *she* lived.

Josie tossed that idea round for a minute. BUY a home? In Italy, people lived in their ancestral homes for generations. The only way someone obtained a home was generally through inheritance. She hadn't much thought about their future together, hers and Giacomo's. Now that she was learning what America was all about, it scared her a little. Suppose he couldn't get a job? Where would they live?

"But don't you worry about that now," Mafalda was saying. "Everything will be fine for you. Giacomo looks like a hard worker and Father will get him a job somewhere. Don't you worry." She hugged her around the shoulders. She'd seen a lot worse than Giacomo in her years serving Father Giancarlo. A lot worse.

"Now let's go write that letter, eh?"

Josie wished she could be so confident in her future. She sat at the kitchen table and stared at the blank sheet of paper. What could she tell her parents? How could she describe the vastness of the ocean, the massive ship, the people she had met so far, the promise of this huge country, America? And what could she say about her enigmatic new husband and their strange relationship? Josie tapped the pen on the table nervously, not knowing where to begin. Words eluded her; she was just a jumble of feelings and impressions. She looked at Mafalda cleaning up the kitchen and when the older woman turned and smiled encouragingly at her, she felt reassured.

"Dearest Mother and Father . . . "

Chapter 34 News

The mail was late that day as Josie's father checked the box at the post office on his way home from work. He decided to wait a minute more as he saw the clerk getting ready to sort the letters and packages into each resident's mailbox. Although Citta St. Angelo was not a very large village, there were still about 200 mailboxes to fill and Mr. Mattola thought, this might take longer than I expected . . . The clerk saw him lingering, waiting for word from his daughter and new son-in-law from America—everybody knew the story by now—and he took pity on him. Finding the letter was easy—it was the only foreign piece of mail in the whole batch.

"Eh, Mattola, here's what you've been waiting for!"

Signor Mattola took the envelope that seemed to be covered in stamps, turning it round and round in his hands. A tear came to his eyes. "*Molto grazia*, Paolo," he mumbled gratefully.

He did not open the letter right away but waited until he got home so he and his wife could share the contents together. He walked briskly in the cold February evening air so that by the time he got to his house, he was breathing hard. When he walked through the door, his wife could tell right away that there was news.

"Aiiieee, take your coat off and open it!" They sat together on the worn sofa and

began to read.

Cara Mama e Papa,

We have finally arrived at the Church of the Annunciation in Easton, Pennsylvania after a very long trip. The priest, Father Philippi, is very kind and is letting us stay in the rectory until Giacomo can find work and we can get a room. Easton is so big and is a very busy town so we expect that it won't take very long for him to find employment. I met a couple from Abruzzo on the ship named Nicholas and Sophia who are living in a town very near to us called Allentown. I have also made friends with Father Philippi's housekeeper, an older woman named Mafalda, who is also from our region. They have made us feel at home in this unfamiliar place. For now I am helping with the chores around the church to earn our keep and hope we can become self-reliant pretty soon.

Giacomo is well and was very good to me during the crossing when I became seasick. I wasn't able to eat much without vomiting so I lost a little weight. I'm fine now though. Mafalda is feeding me a lot!

I miss everyone so much and hope that you'll say hello to Father Rocco, Gina, Cecelia and all of my friends and tell them that America is very beautiful, at least where we are. Also tell them that New York is huge and looks like a fairy tale city at night with millions of lights everywhere, like stars in the sky. I love you so much—

Josephina

They were a little disappointed that the letter was so short, yet it gave them the news that they craved to hear: they had arrived safely. Mrs. Mattola cried quietly and offered up a prayer, like every mother around the world, that she would ever see her daughter again in her lifetime. Mr. Mattola was satisfied to hear that Giacomo was taking care of his daughter, at least up to this point. The grave doubts he had had about Giacomo as a suitor were on hold—for now. Maybe he was wrong about Giacomo.

"Let's go share the good news with Father Rocco!" Mrs. Mattola suggested, her face bright with happiness.

"Why don't we go after dinner?" Papa countered. "I'm starving!" His wife served up his dinner immediately and they ate in relieved silence.

In a small Italian village, it was not unusual to pay an evening visit to the local priest of one's own parish, since he lived on premises and was often found in the church giving confessions, special masses or just cleaning up the sanctuary. Father Rocco was nowhere in the church, however, when the Mattolas arrived with the letter in hand. Mrs. Mattola lingered a moment as she often did these days to study the clothing on the statue of Saint Michel Angelo that her daughter had sewn for the Church, each time noticing a new seam or pleat that she hadn't seen before. In an inexplicable way, gazing at the garments kept her emotionally close to Josie over the thousands of miles that separated them now, the only real connection she had to fill the huge void in her being. She couldn't help but think how regal the clothes made the statue look. The transformation was amazing! It was as if the statue had come to life with its new wardrobe. He seemed even more protective of the Church than ever before. As she crossed herself at the end of her supplication, she couldn't have suspected that there was a secret pocket known only to Josie and Father Rocco hidden deep in the folds of his cape.

Signor Mattola was vaguely aware of how quiet the *catedrale* was, cold and silent. He thought to himself, this is what a church is like when no one is worshipping in it. His wife was deep in contemplation at the base of the statue of St. Michel Angelo, where she usually spent most of her time these days. He missed their daughter too, so much. Being in the church gave them both solace. But they had come to see Father Rocco. Where was he? Maybe he was out.

He called his wife and they walked out of the sanctuary into the courtyard passing under the cloister's covered portico where there was protection from the wind. The garden's plants were mostly dormant now, bare and dead. Even the fruit trees were skeletons of naked branches. How glorious they will look in the springtime, he thought. The Bishop will be hard pressed to find another gardener as good as Giacomo, though.

Signora Mattola wandered over to the eastern edge of the cloister which, unlike the other three sides that were attached to the walls of the various buildings of the cathedral complex, opened to a stunning view of the Adriatic Sea in the distance. The edge of the cloister was built centuries ago on the brink of the hillside facing the sea with the dual purpose of adding a beautiful view to the garden and serving as a defensive lookout. The sky was just turning dark on the horizon in the east as the light faded and the building's shadows cast long, dark uneven streaks over the tall grass growing on the hillside below the cloister lookout. Signora Mattola loved to look at the view from this spot and couldn't remember ever being there at that time of day.

Suddenly she tripped over an object on the ground right next to the wall. It was a man's shoe. How odd, she thought. Who lost his shoe?

Her husband had just joined her and she turned to him, holding up the shoe. "Whose shoe do you suppose this is?"

They looked around, calling for Father Rocco. Still no answer. Maybe he was in the rectory. They were about to head in that direction when Signora Mattola cried, "Wait! Look over here!"

They both peered over the edge of the wall down the hillside into the grass mottled with shadows. At first they could see nothing, but as the wind blew again and the grass swayed, she thought she could see a black piece of fabric move ever so slightly. When the wind moved the grass in another direction, she was sure.

"Look, there! Is that a man in the grass? Oh my God!" She crossed herself fervently and looked aghast at her husband. As the light faded, it was difficult to make out the patchy area in the grass but as their eyes became accustomed to the dimness, a motionless body could be seen lying face down on the hillside. His head was further down the slope so they couldn't see who it was, but his feet were on the upside of the slope closer to them. He was missing a shoe.

"We have to go to the police. I pray that's not Father Rocco."

Chapter 35   Married Life

Giacomo and Josie finally found a tiny apartment where they could afford to live. With the help of the Church, they rented a small second-floor apartment near Easton's downtown section in an alley behind some of the retail stores. It was run-down and dingy but had enough space for the two of them and it even had a tiny backyard where Giacomo could grow some vegetables. Members of the Church had donated a few pieces of furniture—a table, an old mattress and a ratty sofa—to help them get set up. They had found a discarded dresser and rug in the trash and had hauled them back to the apartment together and carried them up the stairs. Josie attacked cleaning up the apartment with a vengeance. Even though they couldn't afford new paint, at least it would be clean.

Mafalda cried for a half hour when she found out that Josie would be leaving the rectory and made her promise to come to see her at least once a week. It was only six blocks away! Josie exclaimed, then she figured that six blocks was quite a distance for the large woman to walk. Mafalda gave Josie a number of chipped dishes and a few pots and pans that she didn't need any longer to help get her kitchen started. She was grateful for any donations. People were so kind to them; it was hard to imagine that complete strangers could be so helpful. America was turning out to be a wonderful place. Josie looked forward to the future in this, her new starter home.

True to his word, Father Philippi had gotten Giacomo a job. Giacomo went to work every morning, clutching the meager lunch Josie had made for him, walking to the assigned checkpoint where a crew truck would pick him up along with several other laborers. They would drive to a jobsite where they toiled for the day, digging ditches for water drainage, pulling up asphalt on a roadbed, or clearing brush from an overgrown construction site. It was brute labor but Giacomo liked it. He didn't have to think about anything, he just followed directions and at the end of the week, he got a paycheck that, although small for America, would've been generous by all accounts in Italy. The crew foreman liked him because he was reliable and very strong and never gave him any trouble. They were used to immigrants joining their crew and laughed at Giacomo's attempts at speaking English-- fortunately, there were a couple of Italian crewmen who could translate back and forth so that everyone knew their job assignments. The Italians would make fun of his accent, the tongue of peasants, but he still didn't mind. Giacomo would come home at night exhausted but satisfied that he had done a decent day's work for a decent day's pay.

At night the two of them would look at each other after dinner, tired and worn out from working all day, and talk about what their day was like. Rather, Josie would talk and Giacomo would listen. She would describe how she connived a reduced price on a box of baking soda from the grocer up the street because it was damaged a little, and where the barber shop was located so that Giacomo could get a cheap haircut from some *paisans* who were originally from Abruzzo. She had found out where she could buy fabric that had defects in it for a fraction of its original cost to make some clothes for them, if she ever got another sewing machine. Giacomo marveled at her resourcefulness. She was like a one-woman public relations firm. Within a month, almost all of the merchants within a mile radius knew the new girl with the red highlights in her dark hair who had settled in town from Citta St. Angelo.

She also talked to Giacomo about the need for them to take classes in English and to study for their citizenship papers. Mafalda had told her that becoming a citizen was extremely important for her family's future. She found out where the classes met and that they were free for immigrants like them. Josie speculated that Giacomo would be a less-than-enthusiastic student, but she knew it was something he had to do to fit into their adopted country.

She would faithfully go to visit Mafalda twice a week as promised, once on Sunday to attend Mass and once during the week, where she helped the woman in the kitchen. Giacomo would walk with her to the church on Sundays but would not attend the service; he would wait outside on the corner smoking cigarettes until she came out. He watched the people go by in their cars and Sunday clothes and wondered at the prosperity this city provided for its residents. Was *everybody* rich in America?! They were the only poor people he knew of, except for the few colored families that lived down the alley from their apartment. Of course, they didn't socialize with the Negro families, they only nodded to them in passing, but they were all aware that they were living in the poorest part of Easton. Not for long, Giacomo vowed, not for long.

At night, Giacomo lay next to his beautiful wife and couldn't resist the urge to make love to her. He couldn't believe that this young, vibrant girl was married to him. She was passionate and compliant and seemed to enjoy his advances, at least she never complained out loud as so many older women were known to do. He recognized that she tried to please him in their lovemaking, even if she was a little inexperienced. How long could he keep her interested? She was so full of energy and optimism. He had to stifle his tendency to be jealous of her; so far, she had not given him any inclination of dissatisfaction or desire for another man. Would that last, he asked himself? Was he enough for her? Would she get tired of being poor and find a man with more money? These thoughts worked through his consciousness every day, but every day he fought them back. At night, when the landlord turned off the heat and the apartment was cold, they snuggled together for warmth and he could feel her heat.

It wasn't long before Josie began to feel a little funny. She was tired a lot, and her breasts began to be tender. Then she missed her period again. That had never happened to her before, so she marched up to see Mafalda and asked her what she thought it meant. Was she sick? Should she see the doctor? Mafalda just laughed and hugged her very hard—that same bear hug that she had given her the first day they were introduced—and she had tears in her eyes.

"What's so funny? Why are you laughing at me, Mafalda?" Josie was miffed.

"Eh, Josie, you peasant girls are all the same! You're so naïve! Didn't your mother tell you about the birds and the bees before you got married?" she laughed heartily.

"The birds and the bees? What do you mean? Of course she talked to me about marriage. And I've followed all of her instructions. So why do you think I'm so naïve?" she retorted.

"*Cara*, you are expecting. Pregnant! A bambino in nine months! Praise God!" Mafalda made the shape of a big belly over her own, crossed herself and Josie for good luck.

"PREGNANT?" Josie exclaimed, aghast. "How can I be pregnant?"

"My dear, you have been enjoying your husband in your bed at night, *e vero*? Well, that's how you get pregnant." Mafalda was amazed at how uneducated young women were from the Old Country. "You should go home and tell Giacomo right away. And then you should go to see the doctor. I'll give you the name of a doctor that can deliver babies. And start saving your money!"

Josie was in shock. This turn of events was the last thing she expected. Pregnant! She couldn't decide if she was happy or angry or . . . it didn't really matter, though, she thought. The deed was done. What would Giacomo think? What would her parents think? My God, she thought, I'm going to be a mother! I'm too young! I just got here! I can't be pregnant . . . maybe Mafalda's wrong. She's probably right, though. Another missed period . . .

She walked home through the overcast day in a mental fog. It looked like it was about to snow and she had nothing for dinner. She stopped at the grocer's and bought some vegetables. Her thoughts were so scattered that she was having trouble focusing on the smallest tasks. When she got back to the apartment, she fell on the bed and took a nap. She was chilly after her walk so she huddled under the quilt her mother had made for her for her hope chest, the one that had traveled with her across the ocean to this unfamiliar place, carried in the trunk by Giacomo the whole way. How fitting that it should cover them both in their new home. She covered her head and soon drifted off to sleep. Before she nodded off, she counted nine months ahead to see when this baby would make his or her entrance into their lives. September. It would be born sometime in September.

Her dreams were unsettled and nonsensical. She saw the statue of Michel Angelo in Citta St. Angelo carrying a baby in one hand and his raised sword in the other. Then she was out in the rain in Easton with no coat on, getting drenched as she stood there rubbing her huge stomach. She saw Giacomo and Father Rocco making a deal and then jumping over a wall. What did it all mean? She woke up with a start and crossed herself.

She heard Giacomo's slow ascent up the back stairs, recognizing his footsteps on the wooden steps. He always walked very slowly after work. She heard him fumbling with the key in the door lock and jumped up to help him open it. When she did, she looked into his tired face and smelled the unmistakable scent of wine mixed with cigarette smoke.

"Giacomo, we have to talk."

Chapter 36   Expectations

Josie was so relieved. Giacomo was actually pleased by the news of her pregnancy. At first he was as shocked as she was, then he had another glass of wine, then another, and as the idea settled in, he became more and more proud of himself. *He* was responsible for making this new life! He took Josie in his arms, lifted her off the floor and swung her around.

"Whoa, Giacomo! Be careful! I don't want to fall!" she chided him. Josie had never seen him express so much emotion so openly. He always seemed so tightly controlled—this was a new side to him and she was excited to see him so happy.

"On Saturday, I'm taking you for a ride," he promised her. "We're going to take the bus all the way to the end and turn around and come back. You'll see as much of Easton as anybody can from that bus. Whaddya think?"

"Yes, I'd like that. I can't wait, Giacomo." Her smiling eyes glistened with anticipation.

Saturday morning came cold and windy, yet the two of them stood dressed in their winter clothes at the bus stop waiting patiently for the bus to come. It was warm inside the bus, full of people going and coming with groceries and packages, some with children dressed like little Eskimos in their overcoats and boots. The bus seemed to stop at every corner on its route, discharging passengers and picking up more. Many of them were Italians, and since Giacomo knew a few of them from work, he introduced them to his wife. He didn't hesitate to tell them that they were expecting.

"Eh, *buona fortuna*, Signora! I hope the baby looks like you and not this ugly fellow!" one of them blustered, slapping Giacomo on the back.

Another one chimed in, "How did you get such a pretty young wife, you old dog! You must've paid a good price for her!" They all laughed at the ribbing except Giacomo, who turned a bright red in the face. Josie blushed a few shades of scarlet too--she wasn't used to the crude talk of the men. Soon the men got off, shouting bawdy comments to Giacomo about his manhood and prowess and generally embarrassing themselves. By then, everyone on the bus knew that Josie was expecting her first child and the women smiled knowingly at her.

The bus lumbered on in the cold, bright morning. They passed through industrial parts of the town with large factories spewing smoke and cinders from their stacks. Several of them were set along a wide, fast-flowing creek. Josie wondered why factories always seemed to be located near a body of water. The trees were bare and at each stop, they could see for a couple of blocks in either direction; row after row of narrow brick houses three stories high attached at their common walls lined the streets in the residential parts of the town. Row houses just like in her town in Italy! Smoke drifted gently from their chimneys. The bus chugged up and down the hills of Easton like a pack animal who knew its way blindfolded. At each stop, the driver would announce the name of the street in a sing-song voice: "Ferry Street" or "Palmer Township line." In about an hour they reached the end of the route, where everyone got off and the driver settled in for a smoke break.

Close by there was a small restaurant where they stopped for some lunch. Josie had never eaten a hot dog before, so Giacomo bought her one with all the fixings. She bit into this new food with trepidation, then immediately decided that it was some kind of specialty treat because it was so delicious!

"Giacomo, this must be food made for rich people to eat," she said seriously.

"Bah, it's not for rich people, it's for everybody! It's American ingenuity at work in the kitchen!" Giacomo explained patiently. "Come on now, we'll miss the bus back home." They walked arm in arm in the cold with the taste of hot dogs in their bellies.

On the return route, the bus turned north and crossed the same creek with the factories they had seen on the outbound trip. Soon they were climbing a steeper hill with sharper curves that was lined with trees and neat sidewalks. At the top, the bus leveled out, stopping here and there as they both marveled at the view—they were in the neighborhood of the most exclusive section of Easton called College Hill. The homes were large, expensive and well-kept, the lawns manicured with sculpted shrubbery and cobblestone driveways. Each home was built in a slightly different style but there was no doubt that the owners shared two things: generous incomes and the desire to show off their homes. Josie looked from one home to another in awe. How could so many rich people live in one place? She noticed the black maids who answered the doors and the shiny cars parked in the immaculate driveways. Sometimes she noticed a couple with their kids getting in or out of the cars. They all look so . . . content, she mused.

"Oh, Giacomo. Look at that house—and that one over there. It has two cars in the driveway! Who can drive two cars? Isn't one enough?" she said incredulously.

"Some of the women know how to drive, you know? They're like men. And some of these people have chauffeurs to drive the cars for them. The guys at work told me," he confided.

Josie just shook her head and sighed.

The sight of this opulence, which really was nothing more than the comfortable upper-middle class existence of the occupants of these residences, was a sobering experience for Giacomo and Josie. They sat in silence as the bus rumbled through the neighborhood, lost in thoughts about their future. The bus did not seem to make as many stops on College Hill. It was not lost on them that the news of Josie's pregnancy would postpone any hopes of economic improvement for their near future.

"Maybe our child will live in a house like one of these some day, Giacomo." Josie was starting to tire, so she rested her head against her husband's shoulder.

"Hmmm" was his only response.

The final stop on the College Hill route was at the entrance to Lafayette College, after which this section of town was named. Lafayette was a small, exclusive liberal arts college that catered to well-to-do sons of eastern Pennsylvania families. The neighborhood through which the bus had just passed was filled with homes of professors and administrators who worked at the college and their families. Spread out among the campus were similar homes that had been purchased by Greek fraternities that housed the students pledged to the brotherhood. Old buildings in which classes were held were scattered around the campus amidst office buildings, laboratories and the library. Lafayette wasn't an Ivy League school but it was close to one in reputation.

Josie had never seen a college campus before. Neither had Giacomo, for that matter. They took in the sights grudgingly, feeling like outsiders looking into a lifestyle where they would never belong. They would be lucky to work at one of the homes of these people, they realized. As the bus passed the stop, they saw a few students bundled up against the weather talking to one another. Would their child go to college one day? Who could tell? The idea was not so far-fetched. This was America, after all. Land of dreams. And this was a very big dream.

Later, the bus dropped them off at the stop closest to their rickety apartment building and they walked the final few blocks in silence. Suddenly the weight of a new world was on their shoulders. Josie couldn't read Giacomo's face but she suspected he felt at least close to what she was feeling. The crush of responsibility. Their world was about to change dramatically. Again.

Giacomo poured himself a glass of wine and Josie made a cup of tea. This took awhile since all they had was one old hot plate to boil water. Josie had been thinking about an idea since they first got to Easton. She skewed up her courage and presented her proposal.

"Do you think I could get a job, Giacomo? I have seven months, maybe more to go before the baby comes. I could work a little to help us save some money."

Giacomo looked her up and down. The wine was starting to take effect, she could tell, because his eyes were glazing. "Let me think about it," he said brusquely.

Josie pressed on. "I could get some work as a seamstress, I'm sure. I did have that job making the clothes for Santo Michel Angelo back home, that was something. And I made my coat. I could ask the tailor up on Fourth Street if he has anything for me to do . . . "

Giacomo just stared at her. They certainly could use more money now. But did he want his pretty wife out working among strangers in a strange city? While she was carrying his child?

"Please?" she pleaded, stretching her hand across the table to touch his.

He put his head in his hands and leaned his elbows on the table. The bus trip had had the unintended consequence of showing them both what money could buy and by corollary, what they were missing out on. He knew his salary paid their immediate expenses but there was nothing left over, and the money the Bishop had given him was long gone. They weren't citizens and could not count on help from the American government or the folks back home. The clock was ticking to the birth of their first child and they had just arrived in a new country. If either of them got sick, where would the money come from for medical care? How would they pay the birth expenses? And another mouth to feed . . . he knew babies weren't cheap. Giacomo was feeling the pressure of making a decision but he was conflicted, partly about losing face with his new-found friends but mostly about letting Josie get a taste of freedom. For money meant freedom. Women in Italy did not work outside the home. Would that be good enough in America? Would staying home satisfy Josie?

She was waiting for an answer. He looked up at her.

"I'll let you know tomorrow. Now why don't you lie down and take a nap?"

Chapter 37   The Job Search

Josie tossed and turned all night, wondering what Giacomo would decide about her going to work. She was bored and lonely. She longed for more interaction with her new home outside of Mafalda at the church. She knew she could bring in some money, she just wasn't sure how. Being pregnant made her physically unsuitable to be a maid or to clean houses, although she wasn't very far along. No one would hire her if they knew she would leave when her child was born. And she wasn't a very good cook. She could cook all of the native dishes of Abruzzo quite well, but outside of that, she was clueless.

The one thing she was good at and had a proven track record for was sewing. That's where her passion was—she loved everything about it, the feel of the fabric, the challenge of putting together pieces of a pattern, matching the print of the material to the design of the article of clothing, and especially sewing on the new machines. That was the problem. She didn't have a machine. It was impossible to afford one on Giacomo's meager salary so that was out of the question. She vowed that if she was allowed to go to work, she would save her money religiously to buy a sewing machine.

When the first sign of light filtered through the window, she was up getting breakfast ready for her husband. She made him a scrambled egg and some fresh coffee, even found a half a slice of bread that she could warm in the pan for him. Soon she heard him in the bathroom and she smoothed her hair to look nice.

"*Buon giorno*," she said happily as he sat down.

No response. She poured him some coffee and put the rest in his thermos.

"Did you sleep alright?" Was she being too obvious?

He looked at her suspiciously. Her belly had started to show a growing "baby bump" that was an ever-present reminder of the arrival of their new family member. He felt her tossing all night long next to him, restless in her anticipation. She has no idea what it's like to work for 50 years, he thought, or she wouldn't be so anxious to get a job.

"What do you want?" he growled, knowing exactly what she was after.

"I want to know if you've decided whether I can start to look for work, Giacomo."

"No, I haven't decided. Don't bug me about it! I'll let you know. I have to catch the bus." He grabbed his coat and lunch pail and slammed the door behind him.

Of course she was disappointed, but Josie wasn't surprised. Her new husband was more moody than usual. She had to admit she was almost getting used to his uncommunicative nature; it was useless to talk to him when he didn't want to talk. The best time to have a discussion with him was when he had had a few glasses of wine. Then he talked a blue streak. Josie thought that she probably should wait to bring the subject up again when he was drinking. He didn't drink during the work week, only on the weekends. She would have to wait until then.

When the sun was up and it was warmer outside, she bundled up and started to walk downtown. She was looking for tailor shops or dress stores that might have need of a seamstress. The sun was bright but the air was crisp and chilly, filled with a brisk wind as she found her stride and covered the four blocks to the downtown circle where the bronze statue of the Civil War soldier stood frozen in time. She strode halfway around the circle and found a small tailoring shop where she was glad to get in out of the wind. A small bell announced her arrival and an old man entered the shop area from an inner room.

"Good morning," she said breathlessly as she patted her hair. "Do you speak Italian?"

"*Sì*, Signorina, I do. What can I do for you today?" he said in an accent not too different from hers.

"Signora, excuse me, sir," she corrected him gently. He had not noticed the ring on her finger, she guessed.

"I am an experienced seamstress looking for some work. My husband and I just moved here from Italy and I wonder if you could use some help in your shop." She stood tall and tried to put on an air of confidence.

"How old are you, Signora?" He flashed a toothy smile and cocked his eyebrow as he asked the question. Josie thought he was being rather impertinent.

"I am old enough to be an excellent worker and old enough to be a married woman, sir. Do you need any help?" she stared him down. This wasn't going to work, she thought.

"Well, now, I'm sure you are. No disrespect intended, my apologies." He bowed his head just a tad as he spoke. "Business is a little slow right now after the holidays but if you can come back in the spring, maybe I'll have something."

"Thank you, sir. Good day." She could feel his eyes on her as she walked out the door. What a creep!

Back on the street, she wasn't quite sure what direction to go in so she headed uptown. A few blocks from the circle on the main street, she saw a large department store called Fineman's. The mannequins in the window were dressed in the latest fashions and were decked out with matching shoes, purses, gloves and coordinated jewelry. They looked so lovely, she thought. This must be a high-class store—just the place for a seamstress like her!

First she decided to walk through the women's department of the store to check out the merchandise. She had never been in a department store before and as she turned corner after corner, the displays of the fine clothes and housewares dazzled her. Everything was so beautiful! It was hard for her to imagine that some women who lived in those great homes on College Hill could come into this store and buy anything they wanted. Some of those women must have ten dresses or more! Lost in thought and wonderment, she didn't see the salesgirl approach until she was right alongside her.

"Can I help you with anything, miss?"

Josie jumped in surprise and, taken off guard, she babbled in Italian, "Oh, no, I mean, yes, uh, I'm sorry. . ." With that, she dropped her handbag and as they both stooped down to pick it up, they knocked their heads together. They were both giggling as they righted themselves and exchanged profuse apologies, and just then Josie noticed that the salesgirl also spoke Italian, although a dialect different from hers. Did everyone in Easton speak Italian?!

"Where are you from?" the salesgirl asked.

"Abruzzo, Citta Saint Angelo. And you?"

"I'm from Calabria, a small town called Septicentano. I married an American man and came over here ten years ago. My name is Viola. I'm pleased to meet you—what is your name?"

"Josie. Josephina Constanza. I've been here just a few months."

"And where did you get that beautiful coat? I don't think I've seen anything like it in the stores around here. Is it Italian-made?" Viola ran her hand up and down the sleeve as she spoke.

"I made it myself. I designed it too. Look, it's even lined."

"Wow, it's peachy! You did a really good job." Viola was clearly impressed.

"Well, that's sort of why I'm here," Josie hesitated. "Does your store have an alterations department that might need a seamstress? I'm looking for some part-time work."

"Ah, I see," Viola gave her a wink. "I have a break in ten minutes. Why don't you look around in the store and when my break comes, I'll take you over to the Ladies Department and see if they're hiring. It won't be long now." She showed Josie a place to sit while she waited, but Josie wanted to look around. Viola worked in the housewares department and she wandered slowly in between the aisles, marveling at the sheer quantity of dishes, pots and pans, silverware, glassware, table linens and floral arrangements that were displayed in this one area of the store. Each item was more beautiful than the next one, and they were all *very* expensive. This must be where the College Hill women shopped!

I'd love to work here, Josie thought. I'll bet a nice clientele must shop here. A clientele with money to spend on beautiful clothes that she will be happy to alter.

Chapter 38   Dealing with Giacomo

Josie trekked home with a huge smile on her face. She had landed a job! The Women's Dresses Department at Fineman's needed an alterations girl part-time, and based on her coat and her enthusiasm, and a word from Viola the salesgirl, she was hired. Of course, it was on a trial basis to make sure she could handle the job, but she was pretty confident that she would be able to make the customers happy. She was so excited walking home that she didn't even notice the snow flurries that started to fall. By the time she got home, she was cold and tired and needed a nap, so she snuggled up under the covers and fell fast asleep. When she woke up, the sky was a steel gray and an inch of snow had accumulated on the streets and sidewalks. Time to start making dinner.

Soon the smells of home cooking, fresh pasta and tomato sauce filled the tiny apartment. Josie tossed around a few strategies about how to tell Giacomo, or whether to tell him at all. Should she wait to see what he said about the issue? He might not bring it up again, though. Knowing it was a sore point with him, she needed to be very careful about how she presented it. She looked in the ice box and saw there was a little bit of red wine left, so she decided to serve some at dinner. Normally they didn't drink during the week and she wasn't drinking alcohol at all now that she was expecting, but she knew a little wine would put Giacomo in a good mood. She had the whole evening planned out.

Soon she heard the sound of tired footsteps climbing up the creaky and now snow-covered back stairs. When Giacomo walked in, he had a layer of snow on his jacket and cap and looked like a snowman in training. Josie went up to him and kissed him on the cheek, then started to brush the snow off before he got too far into the house.

"*Basta*! That's enough!" he waved her away. "What's for dinner?"

"Take your wet clothes off and come and see," Josie was high with expectation. Giacomo washed up in the sink and plopped down to eat. She put a half-full glass of wine in front of him and he grunted, "What's this?"

"Oh, I thought you might be cold, so this will warm you up."

"Humm. . . " was the only response.

They ate in silence as Josie fidgeted around the kitchen and fussed at the food. It was so hard for her to stay calm! She hoped her husband didn't notice anything unusual as she cleared away the plates.

"Ah, that was good. Is there any more wine? Get me some, eh?"

She smiled and poured the rest of the wine into his glass. She studied him as she poured, trying to gauge his mood. He seemed relaxed. It was almost dark outside and the snow was coming down heavier now.

She sat on the side of the little bed, fluffed out her hair and loosened her top so that just the start of her cleavage crack began to show. She wondered if he had noticed

"Giacomo . . ."

He looked up. There was no mistaking her meaning. Immediately he felt his loins stir and he hurriedly took off his shirt, his boots and then his pants. By that time, Josie was flat on the bed and he was on top of her, pulling off her clothes. His lust overpowered him and he pulled her to him, kissing her face and neck, feeling for her hot spot that was already wet and ready, and thrust himself into her like it was their first night together.

Josie moaned with pleasure as he moved inside her, grabbing his buttocks and rocking with his motion. Faster and faster they moved, heated up with hormones and passion, then Giacomo moved her lithely across his body until she was on top of him. He is so muscular, she thought; he could easily crush me if he wanted to . . . but Giacomo had other things on his mind. He climaxed with an arc of his back, pushing himself further into her than he had ever thought possible. She joined him in her climax, pushing her arms against his with heated force. Then they both collapsed in a pile of sweat and body fluids, exhausted.

Neither spoke for a long while. Finally Josie moved close to him and stroked his face and whispered, "I love you" just once in his ear. He suddenly became very still.

Giacomo wasn't used to sharing endearments with anyone; it was difficult for him to show any emotion but anger, which he was all too comfortable with. Would he regret letting his guard down? Should he tell this wildcat wife of his how much he needed her? Wanted her? Every red flag in his psyche rose to warn him to keep his emotions in check. The woman's got the better of me, he thought, and I'm screwed.

Josie rolled away from him, impatient to hear the words she'd waited so long to hear. She feared they were not in his heart, that he really didn't love her and had only married her for convenience and escape, to get to America. She sat up on the side of the bed and waited in the silence for him to say something, anything, but he didn't. She was so hurt that she started to cry. Soon, the sobs became wails and she was crying her soul out to . . . no one, it seemed. She put on her robe and wrapped it tight around her.

Giacomo felt terrible that he was causing his woman so much pain. Never one for words, he was completely out of his element when tears and drama were added to the emotional mix. He thought he should get up and have a cigarette yet that, he knew, was just an avoidance tactic. She was pregnant, after all, and he should cut her some slack since her hormones were out of kilter and she *was* carrying his child. The wailing had stopped now and there were only a few sobs coming from Josie's lungs, actually more like hiccups than sobs. He got up and walked around to her side of the bed and sat next to her. Slipping his hand into hers without looking directly at her, he breathed a deep sigh.

"I'm not like you," he said slowly. "I don't talk about my—feelings. I found out the hard way it wasn't safe, so I just keep my mouth shut." Another hiccup. He paused, looking for more words to say what he couldn't bring himself to admit.

Josie couldn't look at him.

"All I can say is I like you a lot and I'm happy to have you as my wife. Can that be enough for now?" He looked at her little hand and squeezed it for emphasis.

Josie turned and looked at him, tear marks under her red, puffy eyes. She was crushed that her feelings for her husband weren't returned in equal measure. If he didn't love her, what could she do? Nothing. He was right—he probably was incapable of expressing his love. She had to learn to accept that and just—move on. The room was filled with silence.

"Giacomo, I want to get a job until the baby is born," she said flatly.

He put one hand up in defeat. "Okay, Okay." He knew he had lost this round. He shrugged in impatience. It was time for a smoke. If she wanted to work, let her work. She'll see what it's like soon enough.

Josie brooded about her hollow victory as she tried to fall asleep.

Chapter 39   Daily Routine

Josie started her job with gusto. No sooner did Giacomo leave the house than she was washing the breakfast dishes, making the bed and hurrying to get ready. She had at least an eight-block walk to the store, sometimes in windy, cold or rainy weather. She soon found out that the days of lounging around the house in boredom were over. Now every second counted and she had to be productive and focused to get everything done. Giacomo still expected his hot meal when he came home from work, so she found out quickly that it would be easier to pick something up to cook on the way home, adding a few more minutes to her commute. By the end of the day, she was exhausted.

Giacomo didn't have much to say about the new arrangement. At first, he wasn't at all pleased and expected to fight with Josie about things around the house not being done, like the cooking. Typically Italian, he didn't expect to have to do any domestic tasks; they were the work of women. Men ran their outside lives but women ran the life of the home, as Giacomo well knew. Josie was a good housekeeper and he had no doubt that the work at home would be taken care of. He also found that having some extra money at the end of the week was rather nice, though, although he hated to admit it. He decided it wasn't worth a fight with his wife, who seemed to like going out into the world to work.

The new job was a revelation to Josie! She never had worked steadily before and didn't know what to expect. First of all, she didn't have a lot of clothes that were appropriate for work. Each week she took a little money from her small paycheck and went to the local thrift store looking for clothing. She only bought clothes that were tailored and well-made, which she was able to spot right away. One week she bought a new blouse, the next, a slightly used sweater. She found creative ways to combine skirts and tops to accommodate her changing figure and still not look like a peasant. One week she bought a barrette for her hair, another week she found a sturdy pair of shoes that fit her just right. After a few weeks, her wardrobe started to grow, thanks to the kind lady at the thrift shop who let her hold things on layaway. So did her belly.

"Who's the new girl? The one with the baby bump?" Josie heard a saleswoman named Sylvia whisper to Viola on her second day at Fineman's.

"That's Josie. You'll like her, I bet. I do. She's OK, a little green--she hasn't been in the States long. Don't give her a hard time, huh?" Viola was already feeling protective of her new friend.

Josie liked talking to Viola during her breaks. She was the only person whom Josie could talk to in Italian; the others didn't speak the language. It was hard at first not knowing very much English but people in Easton were used to foreigners in their midst who didn't speak the language and they were mostly patient with non-English speakers. At first the girls were a little leery of Josie, who didn't socialize on the job with them, sharing gossip and a cigarette when they had a minute. Josie was all business, so serious and quiet! Josie knew enough of the basics of English to get by with the staff but she was glad she didn't have contact with the customers directly. Her orders came through the salesgirls. Through a combination of pantomime, diagrams and Viola's help with translation, they all found a way to communicate. After about a month, Josie was speaking decent conversational English and started to warm up to the salesgirls, but learning a new language was difficult and tiring. By the time she got home, neither she nor Giacomo had much to say to each other.

It wasn't long before her colleagues began to notice that Josie was expecting. She didn't try to hide it; she just downplayed it with her clothing by not tucking in her tops and de-emphasizing her waist. At the same time, she worked very hard to complete every task she was given quickly and very, very thoroughly, hoping this would help preserve her job. She soon developed a reputation for accuracy and resourcefulness and the salesgirls in the department could depend on her to come through. They liked her ability to size up a job, determine the costs involved and estimate almost to the minute how long it would take to complete. She knew that it would take her a half-hour to hem a pair of pants and almost an hour to raise the sleeves on a jacket. Slowly she earned their respect. They even forgot that she was pregnant. Josie was so busy that some days she even forgot she was pregnant, but when she got home after being on her feet all day, she remembered all too well.

The best part of the job was that Josie got to use the store's sewing machines, fabric, thread and equipment. The first time she sat down to be trained on the company's sewing machines, she had tears in her eyes as she remembered her old treadle machine sitting in her parlor in Citta St. Angelo. It brought back so many memories. . . her heart ached for her family and her friends. She really missed her new machine that she hardly got a chance to use.

On Saturdays she would hike up to the Church of the Annunciation on the hill and visit with Mafalda. She would stop and buy groceries after they visited and haul them home by herself. Mafalda appointed herself to the role of "surrogate mama" to talk to Josie about the changes she would experience throughout her pregnancy and the importance of seeing a doctor.

"Girls don't have their babies at home in America, *cara,* not like in Italy. Girls go to the hospital here! You need to see the doctor before you go have your baby so he will be the same doctor you will have in the hospital. It's very important—tell Giacomo. Make sure you save your money!

"Yes, Mafalda. I'll tell him." Josie was soaking up all of this new information like an encyclopedia.

"If he doesn't listen to you, you tell him Mafalda will come and talk to him." That was truly a threat!

Josie had written her parents as soon as she confirmed that she was expecting, and then again when she had gotten the job. Any day now she was hoping to receive a letter with news of her home. She even had mail delivery now at the apartment and didn't have to rely on the Church to receive her mail.

It was strange to see Mafalda waiting for her at the bottom of the stairway when she got home from work one evening. Mafalda was so heavy it was hard for her to walk from the Church to the apartment, let alone up a flight of stairs; she preferred to wait out in the cold.

"*Buona sera*, Mafalda—what are you doing here!? " Josie blurted out when she saw her friend sitting on the steps.

"Ah, *cara*, bad news came to the Church. I had to come right over and tell you. Can we go inside? I'm half frozen."

Josie helped the large woman up the stairs, hoping she wouldn't lose her balance and fall. There was no way Josie could pick up such a heavy person in her condition. They got inside safely and Josie started to boil water for tea as Mafalda caught her breath from the effort of climbing the stairs.

"Where's Giacomo?" Mafalda panted.

"He's not here right now; I don't know where he is. Why?" Josie was becoming alarmed as she poured the tea.

Mafalda sipped the hot beverage slowly as she regained her breath. "The Church gets a communiqué every month about news within the Catholic community all over the world. It's like a newspaper. Ours came yesterday in the mail. There was an article in it about Father Rocco in Citta St. Angelo."

"Father Rocco?" Josie asked.

"*Si*, they found him dead on the hillside about halfway down . . ." short breaths, " from the cloister overlook at the *catedrale*. The police don't know if he jumped or was thrown over the wall by somebody." Mafalda crossed herself.

Josie gasped and covered her mouth. "Oh, no . . ." she whispered.

"There's more. His body was discovered by a Signor Mattola. Isn't that your given name, Josie Mattola?" Josie slowly shook her head affirmatively as the news sunk in.

She slumped down into the other chair. Father Rocco was dead and her parents found his body? She knew her mother must've been there also, because they always went out together. How can this be? Why would Father Rocco kill himself? That theory was crazy.

Mafalda continued. "The police suspect it was murder. They think he was pushed. An investigation is being conducted."

"How long ago was this, Mafalda? When did you find out?"

"About two weeks ago. It takes awhile for the newspaper to get to us."

"Two weeks. Two weeks," Josie was counting to herself. She had to find Giacomo and tell him. But first she had to get Mafalda to leave.

"Are you okay, Josie?" Mafalda saw the girl turn pale when she delivered the news. There was so much she didn't know about this couple, these two oddly-matched people from the "other side" who on the surface seemed like thousands of other immigrants settling in the Northeast. She couldn't quite put her finger on it but she could feel that these two had a secret, a mystery surrounded them. She was dying to know what it was. It was so coincidental that her parents found the body of Father Rocco, who was this couple's sponsor for their emigration, only a few months after their arrival. Very strange! Was it more than a coincidence?

Josie sighed, "I'm just completely shocked at this information, Mafalda. Let me help you down the stairs. I'm so tired today, I really need to take a nap. I'm sorry you came all this way for such a short visit but thank you for bringing me this news. I really appreciate it. I don't know what to do . . . I have to find Giacomo and tell him . . . Father Rocco was his employer . . . he married us . . . "

They carefully crept down the wooden stairs together, arm in arm, hugging each other at the bottom and kissing on both cheeks in the European way. As Mafalda waddled off toward the church, Josie prayed that her parents were safe. She invoked St. Michel Angelo's protection for everyone in her growing family for she felt that a storm, far in the distance right now, was heading their way.

Chapter 40   March

"Where's dinner?" Giacomo yelled as he stomped the water off his boots at the front door of the apartment. Wet coats were hanging on the few pieces of furniture they owned, as Josie had just arrived home a few minutes earlier. The smell of food traveled through the tiny room from the kitchen where she stood in her stockings stirring the pasta fagiolo warming on the ancient stove. She nodded to her husband; she was too tired to talk.

When it rained, Giacomo was always in a bad mood. He had to work in it all day, getting soaked to the skin with no chance to warm up except at lunchtime, if he could find some shelter. He was also getting ribbed by his co-workers about Josie working and he was tired of explaining to them that his young wife wanted to work to help out the family. They teased he wasn't "man enough" to support his wife since it was practically unheard of for Italian women to work outside the home, unless it was in a family business like a grocery store. Or if she was a widow. His buddies told him stories of shenanigans that women they knew had gotten into when they had gotten a job: the boss feels them up at work, they don't get paid sometimes, they have affairs with co-workers, on and on. One woman even got pregnant by her boss, his buddy swore. Giacomo turned a deaf ear to those stories but they were hard to ignore. Not much about his wife was traditional, he thought, and he did like the extra money she brought home. Anyway, this was America, and things were different in this country, right?

They sat down and ate in silence. After dinner, Josie cleaned up and sat down to rest. Giacomo had a cigarette and finished his wine.

"You hear anything more about Father Rocco? he asked.

"No, Mafalda didn't get the next newsletter for the church yet. I just sent my parents a letter a few days ago. I doubt it's even there yet. I can't believe he's dead, God rest his soul."

Giacomo was quiet. From the minute he heard the news, he knew foul play was involved. A priest as important as Father Rocco didn't just commit suicide by jumping off a wall. Never. It was a sin in the Catholic Church to take one's own life and if a person did, it meant no entry into heaven. That just wasn't the Bishop's style. His suspicions could not be proven without more information but he just couldn't shake the idea that his former employer's death was somehow connected to the man that he had killed in the cathedral. Father Rocco had never told him who that man was or why he was there. Obviously the bishop was the target, but why? Did Father Rocco have enemies from his past? Enemies that would kill to get what they wanted? It just didn't add up, but he had to be more vigilant now, especially at home.

March came to Easton like the proverbial lion, blustery, cold and rainy. Josie walked back and forth to work some days wondering if she was going to be blown away like a kite, never to be seen again. And it always seemed to wait until she was on the way home to start to pour.

Her body was changing, she was getting bigger in the belly and soon she would have to get clothes that were larger to accommodate the new girth. She asked the department boss if she could have some of the larger scrap pieces of fabric left over from some of the alteration jobs that she was cleverly able to sew together to make some presentable maternity tops. Since she didn't work on the floor, she didn't have to look like a model but she didn't want to look like a peasant in homemade clothes, either. Five skirts— that's all she had, one for each day of the week—were rotated among her loose blouses and tops that she wore under a couple of decent sweaters. And she had two dresses, frumpy affairs that were very out of date. She only had two pair of shoes, and they were getting a little tight too. She never thought you could gain weight in your feet!

"Where's dinner?" Giacomo yelled again from the front door as he stomped the water off his boots. The tiny apartment only had one closet which was already full so there were always clothes, coats and shoes thrown about.

"Just a minute more," she took his lunchbox and thermos from him and sighed. Her meals had become very basic and they were eating more leftovers since she had started her job. Some nights they didn't even have meat, just vegetables and pasta.

"What's this?" Giacomo gave her a look of distain. "Leftovers again?"

"Pllleassse! I was too tired to stop at the store and it was raining! You can pick up food anytime you're not satisfied with the service here, my darling." She threw him a tired smile, then plopped down hard into the chair.

"Ay, YOU wanted to go to work! Don't give me any backtalk! Women!" he made a swiping gesture with the back of his hand.

They ate again in silence, both too tired to fight or talk. The baby was starting to move around a lot, especially at night when Josie was in bed. At first it was just a fluttering sensation, like a little muscle spasm, then as time passed, it became stronger and

305

more frequent. There were some times where it would thump like a drum!

A few days later, Josie was surprised to find a letter addressed to her in the mailbox. So few people knew where they lived that it immediately made her wary, but when she opened it, she whooped for joy—it was from Sophia! She and Nick invited Josie and Giacomo to dinner at their home in Allentown. She wrote back to her right away so she could get the return letter in the mail when the postman came. She couldn't wait to tell Giacomo, she was so excited.

Saturday came and they boarded the bus that took them to the end of the line, where they picked up another bus that took them to Allentown, the next town west of Easton. Nick met them at the bus terminal--in a car!

They hugged and shook hands and slapped each other on the back like long-lost relatives. The women were near tears as they embraced, remembering the trip across the ocean that had brought them to this new land. Giacomo peered enviously at the car, a Ford Model T, that Nick was driving.

"Where'd you get the car, Nick?"

"You like it? It's my brother's. He let me borrow it for the night. Pretty neat, eh?"

"I'll say." Giacomo walked around the vehicle, checking it out, not feeling quite so envious now since he knew Nick hadn't bought it himself. He kicked the tires with his foot.

"What does your brother do, Nick?"

"He runs a construction company. I work for him, scheduling jobs, hiring contractors, keeping track of equipment, stuff like that. It's pretty good work."

Sophia and Josie climbed in the back seat arm in arm, giggling like two schoolgirls. As Nick started up the car, he offered Giacomo a cigar. "For when the baby comes," he winked.

They drove through the streets of Allentown as cigar smoke filled the air. The city looked just like Easton with its hills and row houses, factories and stores. A short time passed and they arrived at their house, one of the row homes tucked in among the hundreds in the town. Their home had a small front porch that overlooked the street. "Come in!" they spoke in unison.

The house was larger than Josie's apartment and was furnished with decent appointments without being ostentatious. Many things looked like hand-me-downs from relatives or friends that were in serviceable condition, yet the way Sophia put the rooms together made the overall impact very impressive. She was happy for her friend that they appeared to be doing so well.

"Do you want some wine?" Nick poured a glass for Giacomo and Sophia. They settled down at the kitchen table and Sophia brought out a small antipasto appetizer of cheese, olives, and prociutto ham. Nick wanted to know all about Giacomo's job and what was going on in the old country, while Sophia peppered Josie with questions about her pregnancy and her job.

"What's it like having to go to work every day?" she intoned as she started to boil water on the stove for the pasta. The rich smell of tomato sauce hung in the air.

"Well, it's very different from staying at home, I can tell you that! I work with nice people doing alterations in an upscale department store, but I don't wait on customers, the salesgirls give me my assignments. It's a good thing because I don't speak much English but I can understand a lot. The best part is getting to use their machines. They have everything—thread, needles, fabric—it's great! I don't have to buy anything. And my boss gives me some scraps of fabric that I can take home. She even lets me use the machines when my shift is over."

"How about the baby?"

"He's getting bigger and he moves around a lot. I say 'he' but it could be a 'she.' I walk a lot and that helps keep my strength up. He even kicks me sometimes! We're saving some of my salary to buy baby things, clothes and a crib. They said I could work at home when the baby comes but I don't know if I can manage all that and a baby . . . We'll see."

Sophia looked wisely at her friend. She had morphed from an inexperienced teenager into a full-fledged woman, about to become a mother. A far cry from that unsteady girl on the boat coming over. This girl was in control of her destiny, it appeared.

Nick and Giacomo were on their third glass of wine as dinner was served. Everyone seemed to talk at the same time as they caught up with each other's lives, hands flying in fluid gestures that punctuated the stories they were telling. Sophia's meal was a masterpiece of traditional Italian cooking: baked chicken, pasta with marinara sauce, a side dish of broccoli rabe, Italian bread—lots of bread—finished off with a green salad. Sophia even made a cake for dessert. They ate until they were so full they had to push back their chairs to make room for their stomachs. Giacomo had a couple more glasses of wine and the men went outside for a cigarette.

"So how are things at home, my darling? Are you and Giacomo getting along all right? Is he excited about the baby coming?"

"Oh, Sophia," Josie sighed. "He doesn't get too excited about much. I guess he's happy, it's so hard to tell, you know. He's not a talker. . . It was such an adjustment for him when I started the job, but now he likes the extra money so he doesn't complain so much." She looked at her friend knowingly.

"When that baby comes, you must let me come and help you. You will need some help, *cara*, and I can come and stay with you when you need me."

Josie was grateful for her friend's offer but she had no idea where Sophia would sleep or even if Giacomo would allow it. "Thanks, Sophia. Let's wait and see what happens."

"Well, you take this." She handed Josie a series of numbers written on a piece of paper. "It's my brother-in-law's phone number. You can reach me in an emergency. Can you get to a phone?"

Phones were so new to the world that they were few and far between. "I think the Church has one. I'll ask Mafalda if we can use it to call you when I give birth so you'll know."

The door opened and in walked Nick with Giacomo hanging onto his neck for support. They shuffled over to the sofa and Nick plopped him down like a sack of wheat. Giacomo's eyes were glazed and he was slurring his words. He was drunk!

Josie tried hard to hide her embarrassment and watched Nick attempt to talk Giacomo into drinking some coffee. He wanted more wine, not coffee, more wine! Giacomo wanted to celebrate although it was obvious he couldn't even stand up. "Nicky, bing me anudder glass, wouldja?" he entreated his host.

"No, paisano, no more wine. You need to have some coffee now."

Giacomo tried to stand up, lost his balance and fell back onto the sofa. "Come on!" he sputtered. No one was paying any attention to him as Josie apologized to her friends in the kitchen, out of Giacomo's earshot. A few minutes later they looked over to see him fast asleep, snoring. Josie was mortified.

An hour passed and it was time to head home. Nick woke up his drinking buddy who initially tried to swing at him with a clenched fist. He shook Giacomo and yelled at him to wake up as the man realized where he was. Giacomo pulled himself together enough to stand up and started to walk toward the car, ignoring Josie completely. Nick and Sophia exchanged worried glances as they said their goodbyes.

Sophia pulled Josie aside and whispered in her ear, "I'm worried about you. Will you be all right with him tonight?"

Josie hung her head. "Yeah, it's okay. He gets like this once in awhile."

Sophia was not convinced but there wasn't much else she could do.

"Remember what I said about when the baby comes," Sophia made Josie promise.

They dropped them off at the station as the last bus was heading out. Giacomo didn't say a word on the trip home, gazing out the window in silence. Josie, afraid of instigating a fight on the bus, kept to herself too. Inside, she teemed with resentment at her husband. He couldn't even stay sober one night when we were guests in our friends' house, she thought to herself. Where is his self-control? His maturity? What will he be like when the baby comes and cries all night?! How can she take care of a baby and deal with him? A cold reality settled over her as the bus rumbled on into Easton. Not another word was spoken that night between the husband and wife who to the unaware onlooker, appeared to be two strangers who just happened to be riding the same bus.

Chapter 41   Domestic Life

Josie would not speak to Giacomo after his drinking bout at Nick and Sophia's. She would not even look him in the eye, let alone let him touch her. He knew he had overdone it and had no defense, but really, can't a guy get drunk sometimes? he thought. I work hard all week and I deserve to let off some steam, so what's the big deal? She's just jealous because she can't drink since she's pregnant. Well, *I'm* not pregnant, so why shouldn't I drink my wine? Nick understands—he's a guy. Sophia, well, it doesn't really matter what she thinks. If that wife of mine gets on her high horse and starts giving me a hard time about this, she'll see what happens. . . he rationalized his behavior so well that he convinced himself that he did nothing wrong.

Life returned to the rhythm of daily routine for the couple. But the gulf between them was great and neither of them knew how to address it. As spring slowly but surely awakened the natural world, the lives of the Constanzas moved along in troubled silence. They only spoke to each other when necessary about mundane things such as bills and grocery shopping. When Giacomo reached for her in bed at night, she would brush him off and tell him, no, she wasn't feeling like it, she was tired. After several rejections, he just stopped asking. He couldn't tell if she was still angry or if she really didn't feel well.

The only person Josie talked about her personal life with was Mafalda. Deeply religious, Mafalda counseled her that she should turn to God for answers, and pray extra hard to Jesus to have a healthy baby and to keep Giacomo in a job. Josie knew she meant well, and she continued to pray as she usually did, but she had a nagging feeling that God wasn't getting her messages lately.

Giacomo became more and more distant and started drinking every night. He began stopping at the Italian-American Club after work for a drink before he went home for dinner. He liked going to the club; everybody knew him and there was always someone to have a drink with. Some nights he didn't get home until 10 o'clock. Josie put his plate of food covered with a towel in the ice box and he ate it when he got home. She knew that the nights that he stayed out late, he would come home drunk and he would be hungry. To avoid any interaction with him, she would go to bed and feign sleep while he crashed around the kitchen and ate in the dark, the room lit only by the streetlight that shone through the window.

Weekends were the worst. On Saturdays he would go out in the early evening and not get back to the house until after midnight. When he got home, he would wake Josie up and insist on having sex with her. He would have trouble staying erect and would get mad at himself and then her, blaming it on her not being responsive to his needs. Rather than start an argument that she knew was futile, she half-heartedly helped him along in his awkward attempts, waiting for the moment when he would either climax or fall asleep. It was exhausting for her to lay beneath him while he tried to move inside her, and fumbled with his manhood which after so much wine, just wanted to rest.

One Sunday morning, Josie got up to go to church. Giacomo still lay passed out on the bed as she got washed up from the night before and dressed for mass. She was almost out the door when he woke up.

"Where are you going?" he barked.

"To mass," she responded matter-of-factly.

"Get over here," and he patted the bed insistently.

"Giacomo, I'm going to be late for mass. Please, not now."

Giacomo shot out of bed naked and in three quick strides he was at the door. He grabbed her by the coat sleeve. "I said get over here! I'm sick and tired of you telling me no!"

Josie, having developed more of a bulge in the course of her pregnancy, was caught off balance. She grabbed for a chair back to steady herself and in that moment, Giacomo picked her up and threw her on the bed, pulling off her coat and the clothes underneath and shoving up her skirt.

She yelled, "No! Not now! Giacomo, no!" trying to push him away, but his lust made him deaf to her entreaties. He was very hard and very impatient. Josie would not stop squirming around under him. "Be still!" he demanded. She continued to resist his advances and then, without thinking, he smacked her across the face. Her head whipped around as she took the blow, then she lay dead still, humiliated to her soul as tears streamed down her cheeks. Her husband dug into her with such force she thought his penis would come out of her mouth. With five or six thrusts, he was spent and lay between her legs, heaving. She could feel the spot on her face sting where he had hit her.

He got up and cleaned himself, put on his pants, shirt and coat and went outside for a cigarette. He turned at the door to look at his wife, all tangled up in her clothes and coat, crying silently on the bed.

"Don't ever talk back to me again." The door slammed.

Josie waited a long while before she got up. The baby seemed unharmed and other than her face hurting, she was okay. If you consider being forced to have sex by your husband 'okay,' she thought. Going to mass was out of the question now. She was too unnerved by the incident to travel anywhere. She felt dirty and degraded; she couldn't face anyone. She wasn't even angry, just intensely humiliated. And sad. So very sad.

What did she do to make her husband treat her so badly? She thought about their lives together and nothing she did seemed so bad that he would hate her. I thought I was being a good wife, she mused, but I guess I'm not. What am I doing to set him off like that? I must be more attentive, more sensitive to his needs . . . but when I am, he shuts me out. When I try to talk to him, he clams up or leaves the apartment. Just how does he want me to behave? How will I know if he doesn't tell me? I know I'm not very experienced in these matters—maybe that's it. I'm so confused.

Her conversation with herself left her with more questions than answers. The reality, she was slowly beginning to realize, was that perhaps he was incapable of loving anyone. Was he too scared to open up to her? Was he too afraid of seeming weak? The only thing she was absolutely sure of was that her new husband had succeeded in one thing. He managed to make her fear him. She really just wanted to love him, and have him love her back. Right now, after what just happened to her, she was weighed down with sadness and shame.

And fear. The fear was the worst part of it. Could she learn to live with him in fear? She sank to the floor and began to cry, wailing her heart out in frustration.

Chapter 42   More News

Giacomo was holding a letter as she walked in the door. She said nothing to him as she took off her coat and sat down at the table. He turned it over and over in his hands and looked at the postage. It was from Citta St. Angelo. Josie put out her hand, signaling him to give it to her. She saw it was from her parents, quickly tore open the flimsy envelope and started reading.

"What does it say?" Giacomo demanded. She continued to read, then gasped.

"It says Father Rocco was murdered! The police finished their investigation and they determined he had been pushed over the wall and fell down the hill behind the church. They say he broke his neck in the fall but there were other bruises on his body put there before he died. Oh, my God!" she crossed herself and continued to read.

Giacomo paced across the kitchen floor with his hands in his pocket.

"They say the police found another body in the cloister garden, a man. His body was buried under one of the fruit trees. It looked like he had been there for awhile, he was so decomposed," she shot Giacomo a steely look.

"What else? Tell me!"

"They still have no leads in the case and asked everybody in town if they had seen anything suspicious in the beginning of December. Nobody seemed to know anything. My parents were interrogated by the police too but they didn't say anything. They don't really know about. . . " her voice trailed off. "What do you think this means?" she absently placed her hand over her belly.

"It means the killer is still out there free and he will do anything to get what he wants. I don't know what that is, but if he'd kill a Bishop for information, he's probably pretty desperate."

"Do you think he's looking for us? Does he know about us? Are my parents in danger? What are we going to do? Giacomo, can he find us here in America?" The idea that they may be in danger now embedded itself into the conversation, making them both uneasy. But then after a moment, they both realized that they were actually talking to each other. More was said in the last ten minutes than the sum total of their communication over the last week. Fear of a common enemy can be a convenient unifying force, a fact Giacomo knew all too well.

Josie recounted in her mind the events that led up to their emigration. She pictured the new clothes that she had made for the statue of Archangel Michael and how proud her parents had been of her work. And Father Rocco—he had been pleased too. How different her life had been then. . .

Suddenly she remembered the secret pocket that she had made in the Archangel's cape at the Bishop's request. Giacomo didn't know about the pocket, she was sure. In these past months, so much had happened that it completely slipped her mind, but now she remembered it in vivid detail. The Bishop had made her swear never to tell anyone. That level of secrecy must mean that something very important or valuable would be hidden in the pocket. But it was such a small pocket, what could he want to hide right there in the cathedral in plain sight? Something very small, like a coin? Or a piece of jewelry? Maybe . . . a necklace? Or a ring? Why didn't he hide it in his office? It was very confusing and now she would never know the answer—and she wasn't there to check the pocket to see what was in it, if anything was there. Could it be that Father Rocco never had the chance to hide anything there at all?

Should she tell Giacomo? She wrestled with the idea. A secret is a secret and she swore not to tell anyone. She couldn't break her vow to the Bishop! It would be very unlucky to do so, and she needed good luck right now. I'd better keep it to myself, she thought. But if anything ever happened to her family, or Giacomo's family, or even to Giacomo because of her secret, how could she live with herself? Does a person's death release you from your obligation of secrecy to that person? Aieee! So much confusion! How could she sort this out? Puzzlement engulfed her brain as she sat at the kitchen table and stared at the letter written on the gossamer-thin paper used for air mail communications.

Giacomo was also deeply troubled by the news. Everyone in Italy was familiar with the reach of the *Cosa Nostra*, the Sicilian Mafia brotherhood who murdered, stole, extorted and engaged in every criminal activity from prostitution to drug smuggling. Citta St. Angelo was far from Sicily and had seemingly been passed over by the *Cosa Nostra* for many years, mainly because it was a backwater place with little money and no logistical or strategic importance to them. Could the Mafia be trying to infiltrate the town? And why would they kill such a high-profile target as a Bishop? Usually they stayed away from ecclesiastical figures since when their members died, they usually wanted a Christian burial and at least a tiny chance at redemption for their violent lives. He couldn't shake the thought that the man he killed had threatened the Bishop, which meant that they knew each other in the past. But how? Giacomo was frustrated and powerless to do any investigating from his new home in America.

He had to assess the threat to his family, however. What was the chance that he could be tracked to Easton? Would the men that killed Father Rocco be able to locate him after their long journey? They weren't exactly hiding yet they were hardly prominent citizens of the town. They were keeping a low profile, as were most of the new immigrants in the great America. Right now there were too many questions and not enough answers. Giacomo decided to be extra-vigilant and to insist that Josie be the same.

Chapter 43 Mafalda

Mafalda charged down the hill like a woman possessed, her face beet-red with the exertion of walking fast and the look of a banshee as her clothing swirled around her. Her piano legs thumped on the pavement with each stride. By the time she got to the bottom of the steps of Josie's apartment, she was breathing hard and sweating with exertion.

"Let me get my hands on Giacomo, that little weasel!" she said out loud as she wrung her hands like she was kneading bread dough.

To find out whether Josie and Giacomo were home or not, she would have to climb the stairs, a feat she was unable to accomplish in her present condition. So she stood at the first step and bellowed, "Come outside, you miserable excuse for a man!" at the top of her lungs. She panted and waited. When no one appeared, she banged on the railing, yelling, "Giacomo! You piece of cow dung! Get out here!"

"What the hell do you want?" He opened the door and stood at the top of the stairs in his undershirt and pants.

"Get down here! I want to have a word with you. Right now."

Josie's head could now be seen in the doorway, curious to see what the ruckus was about. Giacomo could see Mafalda was mad. What was so unusual was that she came all the way down from the church to talk to *him*. She rarely talked to him. What was so important that she would do that? He knew she couldn't navigate the trip back up the hill without a long rest and maybe a ride, or some sort of Divine intervention.

He walked down the stairs to meet her while Josie stayed behind. In the brief time they had known the woman, they had never seen Mafalda so worked up. She looked like a bull that had just been teased mercilessly with a red cape.

"Whaddya want?" Giacomo asked matter-of-factly, leaning on the bannister.

Mafalda looked down at him and didn't say a word. She moved very close to him, put her hands on his shoulders and pushed him backwards, hard enough that he lost his balance and fell to the ground on his rear end. "Hey, what the . . . ?" he exclaimed.

"You sorry excuse for a man," Mafalda spoke, low and controlled. "You call yourself a husband? What kind of a husband hits his pregnant wife? What kind of a husband hits her so hard she has a bruise on her face for the whole world to see? You must be so proud of yourself! Get up! Get up!" She nudged him with her foot.

Giacomo looked around to see if any of the neighbors were watching. They were the only people in the alley. He had to get up for he had no chance of defending himself from the massive Mafalda if he was on the ground. She towered over him, and if she happened to fall, she would crush him with her huge body. He slowly raised himself up, saying, "That's really none of your business, Mafalda. None of this is any of your business so . . . "

"None of my business, eh?" and she pushed him down again. "How does that feel, huh? You're not such a big shot now, are you? You piece of crap."

Giacomo was trying to decide if he should stay down or defend himself against this force of nature. Was provoking her more a good idea? She was still a woman, even though she was the aggressor. Did he want to get physical with this woman? It was different when he lost his temper and hit Josie. She was his wife. She belonged to him; Mafalda was practically a stranger. He thought better of it.

"Why do you have to hit your wife?" Mafalda challenged him. "You can't deal with her any other way?"

Giacomo was silent. It was hard for him to find a rationalization for his actions.

"I'm waiting for an answer." Mafalda's hands were on her hips, making her look half again larger than her actual size, which was enormous.

"I don't know. . . I just get so mad at her sometimes. Like when she talks back to me."

"So she's not allowed to have a conversation with you without your permission, is that what you're saying?"

"Uh, no, I mean, I don't like it when she goes against me, I mean, when she says things that turn out to be right—that's not what I mean." Giacomo found himself in a verbal trap; argumentation was not his strong suit. He shifted his weight on his feet and scratched his head.

"It's hard for me to put it into words," he hung his head meekly. "I don't mean to hurt her."

Mafalda stared at him long and hard. No excuse on earth that he could give her would explain his hitting a pregnant woman, especially one who was her friend.

"Let me find out that you hit Josie one more time, now while she's pregnant or anytime, and I will wring your neck like a chicken and mash you up for dinner. Then I'll tell Father Philippi to excommunicate your sorry ass from the Church. You might've beat your peasant women over in Italy but your wife is NOT a peasant and you're NOT in Italy anymore. We

don't like women-beaters in America. You got it?"
She punctuated the last statement with her finger in his
chest.

Josie looked down upon this scene with a
mixture of gratitude and shock. She never said
anything to Mafalda, or to anyone for that matter,
about Giacomo hitting her. It was a private matter
between him and her, husband and wife. She was
thankful that Mafalda had defended her but worried
about Giacomo's reaction when she left. Would he
learn a lesson or blame her?

Giacomo looked contrite as he answered
Mafalda's threat. "Okay, okay, you're right," he
admitted. "No more hitting."

"Swear it," she breathed in his face as she
moved closer to him, flecks of sweat mixed with saliva
hitting him as she spoke. She was not going to lose the
advantage. "Swear it on your mother's grave."

"I swear. On my mother's grave." He looked
up at Josie who was wiping tears from her eyes. He
could see the bruise above her cheekbone starting to
turn yellow and a few shades of blue.

"This better be the last time I come here. Now
go get me some water," she commanded. Giacomo
marched up the steps and brushed past Josie, who
scurried down to be with Mafalda.

"You didn't have to do that, Mafalda," she said quietly.

Mafalda looked at her and said, "Your father would beat the crap out of him if he knew that he hit you, wouldn't he? Well, he's not here, but I am. You tell me the next time he lays a hand on you. You hear me? No more hitting."

Josie agreed. She heard the door slam as Giacomo brought some water down the steps to Mafalda. He left right away without saying a word. Mafalda lowered herself slowly onto the first step and chugged the water down, wiping the sweat from her face. The two women hugged each other as they sat on the step, both gathering their strength—Mafalda for the trek uphill back to the church and Josie to face Giacomo when she returned to the apartment.

Chapter 44   The Stranger

Giacomo seemed like a changed man after Mafalda's confrontation. Josie saw him trying hard to be more communicative, more attentive. She recognized that he was making an effort to patch things up as her stomach got larger and her body reminded both of them that she was soon to give birth. She entered her last trimester as the full heat of the summer descended on the mountains of eastern Pennsylvania, muggy and humid. She wondered how long this behavioral change would last or if it was permanent. Until the next glass of wine?

Josie started taking the bus to work most days, only walking in the cool of the morning if she didn't have things to carry. It was too much to pick up groceries and carry them home at the end of the day when she was tired. Giacomo didn't care as long as dinner was on the table when he got home.

She knew everyone on the bus, even nodded or said hello in Italian to the ones she knew that spoke her language. They all were coming or going to work at roughly the same hours in the day, morning and evening, and they were mostly men. A few women rode the bus while she was on it but they weren't going to a job; they were going somewhere else—shopping, visiting, taking care of children or relatives. Riding the bus created a sort of brotherhood as complete strangers united in the ritual twice a day, then parted to lead their separate lives. The brotherhood of the transportation-less.

So it was unusual to see a new man on the bus one hot late afternoon in August. Josie and the other riders casually checked him out as he asked the bus driver a few questions—in Italian. It was not Josie's dialect, but she could understand the rough words well enough. He asked if this bus went to downtown Easton and how far away it was from the train station. The driver, who was Italian, answered him in detail, even asking where he was from, but the man ignored the question and stood in the aisle as the bus was full and there were no seats. He seemed to be surveying the riders on the bus with more than passing interest.

Giacomo had talked to Josie about being careful and observant of her surroundings. He had been uneasy about her going to work but didn't want to alarm her in her condition, so he downplayed his concern about Father Rocco's murder. But he *was* concerned, more for his wife and unborn child than for himself. He knew what criminals could do—he had seen it in the slums of Rome and Naples during the war. They preyed on unsuspecting people when they

331

were at their weakest and most vulnerable. If he could have his way, he'd lock her up in the house and stand guard outside the whole day. Of course, that was not possible so all he could do was teach his wife to be alert.

She came home that night and reported the stranger on the bus to Giacomo. He grilled her for information about the man.

"How old was he?"

"About forty."

"How was he dressed?"

"Like a working man, but his clothes looked a little out of date. He had a cap on and a black mustache. He spoke Italian, but not our dialect."

"Did he have a coat or jacket on?"

"As a matter of fact, he did. I thought at the time that it was pretty hot to be wearing a jacket. Why?"

"Sometimes people hide things in jackets." Things like weapons—guns, knives. Giacomo left out that part.

"Did he have a suitcase?"

"No. Nothing. Strange, when he asked where the bus went and where the train station was. If he was traveling, you'd think he'd have at least one suitcase."

"You need to pay close attention to things now when you're on the street, eh? Would you remember this guy's face if you saw him again, Josie?"

"Yes, I'm pretty sure I would. I'll tell you if I see him again."

"Make sure you don't talk to him. *Capische*?" Josie shook her head.

"It's probably nothing, but you never know." Giacomo tried to reassure them both.

Sure enough, two days later, the same man was on the bus. He looked like he hadn't changed his clothes. He didn't talk to anyone, didn't smile, just looked around. Josie listened carefully to the few words he said to the driver and thought she could identify a Sicilian accent, but she couldn't be certain. This time the man took a seat across from her. She avoided his gaze and told Giacomo when she got home.

"Did he follow you when you got off the bus?"

"No. I checked. Nobody was following me on Northhampton Street or down the alley."

Giacomo looked thoughtful. "I'll take tomorrow off and ride the bus with you. I want to see this guy."

The game of cat and mouse began. Josie and Giacomo boarded the bus at 7:30 a.m. the next day and within two stops, the strange man was climbing up the front stairs. He walked past the couple in search of a seat and as he passed, Giacomo looked him straight in the eye. They locked eyes for a second as the bus lurched forward and the man grabbed onto the seat next to where the Constanzas were sitting. No words were spoken but Giacomo recognized a man up to no good. Was it the scar on his face, his cocky swagger, or his rough-tough attitude?

They rode on, waiting to see where the man got off. Giacomo could feel the guy's eyes on him and Josie as they chatted about their day. He knew something wasn't right when they arrived at the end-of-the-line station and they all had to get off the bus. There were only two other passengers besides Giacomo and Josie and the strange man was one of them. He leaned against the station wall and lit a cigarette, looking like he had all the time in the world.

"What should we do?" Josie whispered to her husband. "I have to get to work sometime today!"

"We'll get on the next bus downtown and see what he does. Let's grab a cup of coffee."

When they got back, the man was nowhere in sight. They boarded the return bus to Easton and took seats in the rear so Giacomo could see anybody who got on. He couldn't shake the feeling that this man was looking for *them*. Several other passengers got on but the man did not show up. The bus driver released the brakes and the bus rumbled off towards the city. Giacomo thought he might've been wrong about the man after all.

At the next stop, not more than five blocks away, the stranger was back. He climbed onto the bus, paid the fare, and started searching for a seat. As he made his way toward the back, he recognized Giacomo and Josie and couldn't miss the intense stare that Giacomo threw at him. He took a window seat next to an old woman and pretended to take a nap. Now there was no doubt in Giacomo's mind that this man was following them. He wasn't sure of his next move but he had to get Josie to work. They agreed that she would get off one stop past Fineman's and if the man got off also, Giacomo would get off with Josie. If he stayed on the bus, so would Giacomo. He did not want to lead him to Josie's workplace, or to their apartment, for that matter, so he had to be sure that they were not followed.

Josie rang the buzzer at the stop past Fineman's and she and Giacomo got ready to disembark. The man didn't move as they climbed down the rear exit, Giacomo first, helping Josie down behind him. As the bus creaked and began to pull away, Giacomo searched the windows facing their stop for the man's head. He found him staring fixedly at the couple and as their eyes met, Giacomo made a V with his index and middle fingers, touched his eyes and turned his hand toward the stranger in the window in a universal gesture that said, "I'm watching you." And now he knew that the strange man with the Sicilian accent was watching them.

This is a whole new ballgame, he mused.

Chapter 45   Working from Home

Knowing that someone was watching them with the intent of doing them harm was very disconcerting to the Constanzas. When would he strike out at them, if at all? Where? Could Giacomo outsmart or overpower him? They didn't have a gun, only kitchen knives and two-by-fours as weapons. The stranger had somewhat lost the element of surprise, but he still could hurt them, especially Josie, as she was the most vulnerable. Josie's pregnancy could not be hidden at this stage; she was very large and could not move very fast. Gangsters of the *Cosa Nostra* did not hesitate to hurt family members to get what they wanted. Everyone knew that.

But they couldn't afford to go into hiding either. Or disappear.

Giacomo didn't want Josie to go back to work. He didn't want to go to work himself, now that the stranger was lurking about. He wanted to stay at home and protect Josie and his baby. But there were two schools of thought here, Giacomo tossed over in his mind—if they changed their routine, it would be obvious that something was up, but if they continued their day-to-day routines, blending into the fabric of society in everyday Easton, acting like nothing had

337

changed, it was possible the strange man would not be able to identify them for certain and maybe he'd move on.   On the other hand, neither of them could afford to stop working now that the baby's arrival was close at hand. What to do?

In a rare but necessary act of unity, Giacomo discussed the situation with Josie. They decided that Giacomo would continue his work routine, since his income was vital, and he would tell his boss that he might have to leave work suddenly in an "emergency." His boss would think it was the baby coming. Josie was to ask her boss if she could start doing her work from home since she was in the eighth month of her pregnancy anyway. It was hot and she was fat and uncomfortable; her feet swelled and she went to the bathroom every 15 minutes, it seemed. She was ready for a break!

So it was that the next Saturday, a couple of workmen from Fineman's Department Store lugged a used sewing machine to the second floor residence of Giacomo and Josie Constanza, along with a small cabinet that held a rainbow selection of threads, needles of all types and sizes, hem tape, bias tape, assorted buttons in various sizes and shapes, coat hangers and other notions that would be needed to set up a home tailor shop. Josie was ecstatic.

Giacomo looked upon the new acquisitions with a hint of jealousy. "They must really like you at that job," he commented.

"They do. I guess they like my work," Josie responded dismissively. She knew they did, because she was very good at what she did. But she didn't want to rub Giacomo's nose in her good fortune.

"Well, now you can stay home and I won't have to worry about you so much."

Josie leaned in to give him a peck on the cheek. "You don't have to worry about me." Patting her large tummy, she said, "This is what we have to worry about."

She was right. In a month, six weeks at the most, they would have a baby. A real baby! They had no baby furniture, clothes, a stroller, diapers, nothing. It was time to get started preparing for the arrival of the little one. Josie remembered that Mafalda had told her the Church would help some, when the time came. She thought to herself, the time is coming pretty soon now, so I'd better talk to Mafalda and to the priest. Giacomo would not be involved in that conversation or any doings that included Mafalda, so she would have to make those arrangements herself. Which meant at least one trip to the Church.

With these safeguards in place, Josie felt a little more secure. However, Giacomo had driven home the idea that safety was an illusion when it came to criminals, who looked for the one instance when their victim's guard was down to pounce. He even convinced her to carry a kitchen knife in her purse. Not every having experienced any violence in her life, Josie wasn't sure if she could stab anyone with it, but she could sure try. She thought it might be like an elephant trying to stab a jaguar!

A week went by with no new "sightings" of the man. A courier from Fineman's brought Josie alterations every third day or so, then the next time he came, she returned the work she had completed and wrote up an informal bill for her supervisor. She took full advantage of the machine and sewing products to make herself several new maternity tops and to expand a skirt to wear at home. Most of the time she wore bedroom slippers—her regular shoes no longer fit. She was even able to alter a bra to give her swollen breasts more room. She managed to make a couple of tunic-style shirts for the baby but she had no idea what size the child would be. As she got closer and closer to her delivery date, she missed her mother more and more; she longed for the presence of another woman to talk to about her impending delivery. Mafalda would have to do instead--she had been through this five times. Besides a careful trip to the grocery store, walking to the Church was her only outside foray. She felt like she was in hibernation.

One humid morning in early August before it got too hot, Josie was determined to walk up to the Church to see Mafalda and ask about some baby items. She had managed to save a little bit of money to buy cloth diapers and Giacomo had pulled a rocking chair from the side of the road and had carried it home to fix for her to use when she was nursing. She also wanted to reassure Mafalda that Giacomo was behaving himself and seemed to be getting into the spirit of preparing for the child's arrival. Most of all, she wanted to talk about the delivery. She knew women did this all the time—delivering babies was accomplished at home in Citta St. Angelo, usually with the help of a midwife, and only rarely did a woman go to the hospital. She was surprised that in America women went to the hospital to have their babies as a matter of course. She was prepared to go to the hospital if necessary; she even had been to a doctor a few times. But she really would prefer to have the baby at home—if she had a woman to help her. Josie did not want Giacomo around when she delivered. This was women's work.

The sun was bright even at the early hour she left the house and laboriously trudged up the hill toward the Catholic Church. The city was already bustling with activity as cars and buses passed her on the street, honking their horns and belching smoke as their drivers downshifted to negotiate the hill. Some people who were riding bicycles had to dismount and walk up the hill because it was too steep to pedal. She looked beyond the curve of the road to see the Lehigh River tumbling toward its rendezvous with the Delaware not more than a half mile away.

"What's the hurry?!" she advised the water as if it understood the language of humans.

Josie paused for a minute to catch her breath. The baby was moving a lot today, maybe protesting the walk up the hill. In another ten minutes she drew up to the steps of the front of the Church, resting another minute before climbing them. "They didn't make this easy for pregnant women," she murmured.

She didn't go into the sanctuary but went right to the priest's quarters where she knew Mafalda would be working. As she waddled along, she passed several parishioners she had come to know who nodded to her and wished her good fortune in Italian. One old woman made the sign of the cross at her belly as she passed by! Josie thought the woman reminded her of the old nonnies always dressed in black with their hair in a bun who attended the *catedrale* every day in Citta St. Angelo. A pang of homesickness hit her as the baby kicked her in the side to remind her that things were getting crowded in her belly.

Mafalda was thrilled to see her. She made her some iced tea, a new beverage to Josie, made possible by the Church's acquisition of an ice-maker. Josie marveled at the little ice cubes that came out of the metal trays so uniform and neat. They talked about baby matters as Mafalda reassured the young woman that she would be fine during her delivery, she was young and strong and even though it would be painful during the delivery, all that would be forgotten when she held the new life she would bring into the world.

"Just think of all the women who had their babies in the fields, or in a barn or even in a cave!" Josie laughed at that, picturing herself having a baby in an Indian teepee or in a grotto in the mountains. Mafalda reminded her, "Mother Mary had baby Jesus in a stable, remember? Pray to her for strength and she will help you get through it." Josie pondered the miracle of Jesus's birth for a moment and commented, "If she could do it, so can I."

Just then Father Philippi came into the kitchen, greeting Josie warmly. She took the opportunity to ask if he had heard any news from Citta St. Angelo but he hadn't, to Josie's fairly obvious disappointment. "I'll be sure to let you know if I find out anything," he promised. As he turned to leave, Mafalda followed him into the hall while Josie drank the rest of her tea. She could hear them talking but didn't know what the conversation was about. Mafalda swept back into the kitchen with a sparkle in her eyes.

"Have I got good news for you!" she exclaimed.

"Tell me, Mafalda!"

"Father just told me that a couple in the parish who also had a baby just a few weeks ago lost their poor infant very suddenly. Father just buried the unfortunate thing and the parents are besides themselves with grief."

"How is this good news?" Josie queried, knitting her eyebrows at the thought of such a terrible experience for parents to go through.

"E vero, it is a tragedy, for certain." Mafalda crossed herself with a touch of the dramatic. Josie waited while her friend seemed to say a prayer for the soul of the little angel whose time on earth had been so short.

"Father says that the couple is so distraught that they want to get rid of all of the baby things they bought for the arrival of their little girl. They can't bear to be reminded of their loss, so they want to give the things to the Church as soon as possible. Father says that you can pick the things you need and use them for your baby. You'll be all set up. Whadd'ya think?"

Josie couldn't believe what she was hearing. What a windfall!

"Oh, my God, Mafalda, I can't believe it! Are you sure it wouldn't be bad luck for my baby?" She looked down at her large tummy so full with child.

"It's the answer to your prayers, no? How can it be bad luck? You must honor the parents' wishes and accept their gift. Someday you may be able to do the same for someone else. But for now, thank the Lord and go tell Giacomo."

"I . . . I don't know what to say. Thank you, Mafalda. You are a true friend. I'm going to stop in the sanctuary and thank God and St. Michel Angelo for such blessings." Tears hung in Josie's eyes as she pushed herself out of the chair.

She couldn't wait to get home to tell Giacomo.

Chapter 46   The Stranger Redux

By the time Josie left the church, it had warmed up considerably. She wasn't bothered by the heat at first; she took off her sweater and headed down the hill, carefully walking against the incline, balancing herself so as not to fall. She couldn't wait to see Giacomo that night to tell him of their good luck which, sadly, was at the mournful expense of another couple who would never hold their baby again. But she couldn't think of that—she had to focus on the windfall they had accidentally received and the kindness of the unknown donors. I wonder when we can pick up the baby things, she thought to herself as she swayed side to side with each step down the sidewalk.

As she stopped for a breather, Josie couldn't help but feel like someone was following her. She sat on a bench at one of the bus stops and noticed a man a half block or so behind her come to a halt and lean against the wall of a building. She thought he was looking at her. He looked just like the man she had seen on the bus but he was dressed in different clothes. It was hard to forget that bushy mustache. She got up and started to walk again and he started to walk too.

346

She doubled back to the bench at the bus stop and he stopped, pretending to pick something up on the sidewalk. They were tracking each other out of the corners of their eyes, trying hard not to make eye contact. She was sure now that he was following her. The nerve of the man to follow her in broad daylight with so many people around and cars on the road. She thought about going back to the church but that meant she would have to pass right by him and she didn't want to do that, so she kept on going.

A little further down the hill, the terrain leveled out and she was able to walk a bit faster, not exactly fast, but with a more balanced stride. At one point she would have to turn right onto Ferry Street and she would be out of his sight until he caught up with her. That would be the time for her to take evasive action, but what could she do? She was very warm from the exertion and was thirsty, but more than that, she had to go to the bathroom. How chilling to know that someone was following you and you were so vulnerable! she thought. Her hand touched the kitchen knife in her purse to reassure her, but of what she didn't want to imagine.

She was coming up to the corner and had to think of something, quick. A few storefronts from the corner was an Italian bakery that she had patronized a few times. That's it! She'd duck into the bakery and

347

ask to use their bathroom—they couldn't say no to a pregnant woman, could they? She could then see if he passed by through the window. As she rounded the corner, she took off as fast as she was able to move to the bakery door and flew inside.

"*Buon giorno, come 'sta oggi?*" said the woman behind the counter.

"*Bene, bene, e voi?*" Josie smiled her most charming smile and tried to angle her body out of sight of the front windows. "Everything looks so good today! I want to eat everything in sight! Eating for two, you know. . . " and she put both hands on her big stomach.

The woman shook her head knowingly. "I have four, I know what you mean."

Josie sneaked a look out the window and saw the man across the street. It was difficult to say whether he knew she was inside the bakery or not. He lit a smoke and walked up and down the block casually, with measured paces, but Josie knew better.

"Can I please use your bathroom? The baby makes me want to go all the time, you know? Would you mind?"

"Of course, right this way." The woman led Josie into the rear workroom where a large, sweaty man who had a light dusting of flour attached to every hair on his body was rolling out dough. He nodded to

Josie and his wife and gestured with his head to where the bathroom was located. *"Molto grazia*, signor," Josie smiled.

She actually was happy to use the bathroom as the tea she had drunk earlier was working its way through her system and she welcomed a chance to rest. The bakery was stifling hot and she started to perspire. She finished up quickly, making her way back to the sales floor where it was a little cooler, and bought a loaf of bread from the woman. After thanking her again, she slowly opened the front door, looking to the left and right and especially across the street. The man was nowhere in sight. Josie breathed a sigh of relief. She lost him! Good thing, she mused, since she was only a block and a half from home. The heat was oppressive as she marched, refreshed, down Ferry Street toward the river and turned left at the alley that led to her house. A breeze had just begun to kick up.

She passed the black woman who lived a few doors down from her, hanging her freshly-washed laundry out to dry. Generally, they didn't have much to say to each other; Italian immigrant men and the Negro men often competed with each other for jobs and they avoided interaction with each other since there was often tension between the two groups. But Josie knew the woman in passing and said hello to her as she passed by; that turned out to be auspicious a few moments later.

Josie trudged toward her building, one of a group of run-down two-and three-family wooden structures built so close to each other that you could see right into the windows of the house next door. Each one had a postage-stamp sized yard which usually was taken over by the resident on the first floor, and generally had a makeshift fence delineating its boundaries. Josie was about to open the gate to get to the stairs leading up to her flat when out of nowhere, the man who had been following her appeared from the space between two of the houses.

She fumbled with the latch on the gate but he gained on her so quickly that she let out a cry when he reached her. They were still outside the gate but Josie was so mad that he had outsmarted her and now knew where she lived that she couldn't contain her anger.

"Leave me alone!" she shrieked as he made a move to grab her. She pushed him off but he recovered instantly. "What do you want with us?" she yelled. "Go away or I'll call the cops!"

"No you won't, lady. Shut your mouth if you want that baby to be okay, hear me?" he snarled in her face and grabbed her wrist. Josie struggled to get her hand free.

A few houses down, the Negro woman was watching the encounter. She knew the man was not Josie's husband. Everyone on the block knew Josie and her husband, the May-December couple who seemed so mismatched. Giacomo had a reputation in the neighborhood and it wasn't exactly flattering. This girl—she seemed to attract some unsavory characters. But she *was* pregnant and the man was hurting her.

"Stop! Let go of me! My husband will kill you if he finds out!" Josie screamed as she wrestled with the man. Her only defense now was to make some noise and hope someone would notice. Not many people were home in the middle of the weekday. She couldn't get into her purse to get to the knife with only one hand and he was about to overpower her.

"Hey Josie, everything all right over there?" the Negress hollered at her and the man as they continued to grapple with each other. "Y'all need some help, honey? I get my husband fo' ya, here he come!"

The Sicilian hesitated for a split second when he heard the voice behind him.

"Josie, he be comin' right now! Walter, git outchere right quick!" she bellowed as her voice filled the alley.

The man let go of Josie's wrist and pushed her into the gate. Josie was wailing by now. She took the blow to her back but managed to stay on her feet.

"This ain't over, you bitch." He pushed her again for emphasis. He turned around just in time to see a huge black man carrying a baseball bat coming fast toward him, followed by the woman who had yelled for him, still screeching, "Hang on Josie, we's comin'!".

"Tell your husband I want my ring," he sneered at Josie and he took off running down the alley and disappeared.

Chapter 47   Rain

"Ring? What ring?" Giacomo was beside himself with fury. Josie was shaken to her core as she recounted her run-in with the man with the mustache who seemed to now know all about their family. Giacomo, always quick to suspect a conspiracy, believed Josie wasn't telling him everything.

"What did you tell him?! You led him right here! What were you thinking!"

Josie sat wide-eyed and stupefied that her husband would be so callous as to blame her, the victim. He wouldn't let her explain that she had tried to evade him by ducking into the bakery. The baby was moving around considerably in response to the stress and she had a bad case of heartburn. All she wanted to do was lay down and rest.

"Giacomo, I did everything you told me to. He was not following me home, he was here when I got here. What can I tell you? He outsmarted me! If it wasn't for Walter, he would've attacked me—he tried! I did the best I could . . . "

"Aaaaahhh, crap!" followed by a string of expletives was all Giacomo could say. He beat the table top with his closed fist. He looked at Josie, whose head was now resting on her arm on the table.

Giacomo studied his options while his wife drifted off to sleep. The only thing that made any sense to him was that this man and his ring was somehow related to the man Giacomo had killed in Citta Saint Angelo while defending the Bishop. What kind of a ring was it? A wedding ring? A bishop's ring? He suspected that Father Rocco's death was tied up in this scenario but he had no idea why. It mystified him that all of this bloodshed could be because of a ring. He had no ring, Josie had no ring, she said she didn't know of any ring, so what did a ring have to do with anything? Until he could figure out that part, it would be hard to defend his family or figure out the stranger's next move.

Giacomo gently shook Josie to wake her, then helped her to the bed where she promptly fell back to sleep. He patted her hair and then went out on the porch to smoke a cigarette and think. The wind had picked up, he noticed, and it wasn't so hot; he had trouble lighting his cigarette.

Pacing back and forth, he surveyed the alley and the neighborhood from his vantage point. Having the high ground was always an advantage. He thought about the two entrances to his apartment, one in the front of the house which was always locked and rarely used by either the upstairs or downstairs tenant, and the back entrance, accessed by the stairs. The apartment consisted of one large room that he suspected used to be two rooms, a small kitchen and a separate bathroom with a toilet and a lion-claw tub. If the man was alone, Giacomo had the advantage if he tried to come up the back stairs, unless the man had a gun, which was very likely. All bets were off if he had a gun. If he got into the apartment, there were only a few places he could hide without being seen. But he knew that he couldn't be there all the time, so what about Josie's safety if he wasn't there? Now he was sure the man knew where they lived and would be staking out the place; it wouldn't take long for him to figure out their schedules. What could he do? He bristled in frustration as he recognized how tenuous his position there was.

The only thing that made sense to him was to take Josie to Nick and Sophia's until this was resolved. With Josie so close to delivery, she had to be in a safe place, and he was sure Nick would not object to taking care of Josie temporarily. He would stay in the apartment and try to flush the stranger out, forcing a confrontation and a resolution. Maybe it was all a mistake and the man would move on once he found out they knew nothing about a ring. Maybe not . . .

Giacomo looked up at the sky and noticed that heavy, black clouds were moving into the Delaware

Valley. It looks like rain, he thought to himself. Maybe some rain would cool things down.

It was not long afterwards that it did begin to rain, a slow, steady downpour, not rain that comes and goes with a thunderstorm, but the kind that sticks around. It rained the whole rest of the day as gusts of wind blew the drops around in all directions. When Josie awoke, Giacomo was there warming up some food for dinner.

"You're going to Nick and Sophia's until this is over."

She nodded in compliance, offering no resistance. "Here's his brother's telephone number. I'll start packing some things." She ate the food as Giacomo left to find a phone.

Giacomo walked in the rain up a slight hill heading toward the center of town and the Italian-American Club where he knew there was a phone. He hadn't been going there as much lately since his encounter with Mafalda; he was trying to turn over a new leaf and behave more like a husband about to have a child. He did like the atmosphere there, though, the camaraderie, the Italians who gathered there to drink to the Old Country and reminisce in his language and with his customs—truth be told, there was nothing he *didn't* like about being there, other than the fact that he spent too much of his hard-earned money and usually got drunk. The Italians all looked out for each other; everybody knew each other's families and relatives, their triumphs and failures, their day-to-day efforts and setbacks. Except no one there knew of Giacomo's "issue" but he thought that it might be time to change that.

He asked the bartender if he could use the phone and gave him a quarter as an incentive. "I won't be long," he assured him. Still not used to the newfangled device he now held in his hand, it took him a second or two to get the hang of it. He slowly dialed the number Josie had given him and got Nick's brother, as he expected. In Italian, he told Sal that he needed to get a message to Nick about Josie coming to stay with them for a week or so. Sal knew about Josie and Giacomo so the call came as no surprise to him. He would give Nick the message.

"Eh, Sal, one more thing. Can Nick borrow your car to come pick up my wife? She's not in good shape to take the bus and I can't take off work right now, *capische*?"

"Sure, sure," Sal agreed. "I'll go right over dere and tell him. I guess he'll come tonight when the rain lets up." Giacomo heard the click on the other end, wondering if anyone else was listening on the party line.

The downpour didn't seem to affect attendance at the club one bit. There was a pretty good crowd there for a late Saturday afternoon. Families were there having a drink before dinner and there were a number of children of all ages running around the dining room. Italians took their kids with them everywhere when they went out as a family. Giacomo ordered a beer at the bar and after a few sips, he was feeling more relaxed. He wasn't quite ready to go back out in the rain so he sat at the bar and pondered his next move. What was this ring business, he kept asking himself? Is it possible that Josie knows something about it she's not telling him? Or is this guy just fishing around, looking for the joker that *really* has his ring? It must be some important ring, he reminded himself, or the guy was just a wacko out for revenge. Hmmm, that's an angle, he thought. What if this is all about revenge and not really about the ring? But revenge against who? He never saw this man before and he was pretty sure Josie didn't know him, either. He didn't look at all like the man he fought off the Bishop back in Citta St. Angelo. The Sicilian man whose body the police exhumed from his fruit-tree grave, he recalled, was shorter and more muscular than this guy. Could this all somehow be related to the Bishop? It was more than coincidence that two men, the Sicilian and the Bishop, were killed right before and right after he and Josie left for America. Nobody could remember the last time there was a murder in the town, let alone two. Too coincidental.

And of all places, this new stranger followed the couple to Easton, Pennsylvania. Of the millions of immigrants that came through Ellis Island, this guy finds *us*. The only people who really know what went on in that church last December when the Bishop was assaulted. In one city of a hundred thousand in this huge country, he tracks us here. Yeah, he thought, it has to be connected, it all seems to fit, the timing, the locations, the people involved. The only thing missing was the motive.

A man bumped into him walking by the bar and jostled Giacomo out of his reverie. *"Scusi, scusi, senor*, my apologies," he mumbled contritely. Giacomo let it go; he didn't want a bar fight to bring attention to himself, not today. Knowing Giacomo had a short fuse and could jump into a fight at the smallest provocation, the bartender came up to him to refresh his beer, asking him, "Hey, did you hear about the flood warnings?"

"What flood warnings?" The two men on either side of him turned to hear the news too.

"This rain, it's part of a nor'easter. That's the northern version of a hurricane, like they get in Florida. It's going to be around for awhile, a couple of days at least. With the wind and the rain, there's a flood warning for the whole Delaware Valley, especially here in Easton. The announcement was on the radio to watch out for low-lying areas that could flood. You guys be careful!"

Crap, thought Giacomo. I wonder if Nick will be able to get here to pick up Josie.
He looked out the window to see sheets of rain drenching the streets and the grey, low-hanging clouds appeared to be fixed in place. Rain was coming down harder now and it looked like it would never stop. Garbage cans and plants that were outside were strewn around like trash. A few dead tree branches were in the road. Giacomo thought to himself, maybe the weather would keep the stranger away.

Then he saw him, standing under an overhang of a building across the street. The same man that had been following him and Josie. He was sure playing the cat and mouse game well.
Giacomo gestured to the barkeep for another beer. When he brought it to him, he asked, "Is there a back entrance I can use?"

"Yeah, you got it. Through the kitchen. Just don't make a habit of it, okay?"

Giacomo grunted his assent, took his beer and slowly made his way to the kitchen. He opened the door, tightened his cap on his head and his jacket around him, and began sprinting through the rain toward home and Josie.

Chapter 48   More Rain

Josie woke up to the sound of rain blowing against the windows of their apartment. Where was Giacomo? she wondered. What was taking him so long? If she sent him out to get baby food and he didn't come back for three hours, was she going to have to deal with a screaming baby while he was out having a few drinks? She was not in a mood to be patient now that she was big as a house, her breasts were tender and her back hurt. So where *was* he?

Then it occurred to her that he might have encountered the man who was tailing them. For a brief moment, the idea of losing Giacomo flashed through her mind and she cringed. As much as the two of them disagreed and fought with each other, they were a team and Josie wouldn't know what to do without him. Oh my God, she thought. What if this man kills him?! How would she survive with a newborn in this new country that she was just beginning to know? The idea paralyzed her with fear and she quickly pushed it out of her head. It's not possible, it can't be. All the man wants is his ring. We'll figure something out. We'll be okay. She said this over and over to herself until she convinced herself that there was no danger, that it was a case of mistaken identity. The alternative was too much to comprehend right now.

She turned off the light, quietly went to the back door, opened it a crack and looked out, hoping to see her husband bounding up the steps. All she saw was buckets of rain dashing against the wood of the porch and rivulets of water running down the dark alley. So much rain, she thought; so much water can't be good. The street looked like it was beginning to flood—it was no wonder with the amount of rain that had fallen, with no letting up in sight. It had even cooled down considerably. She was glad she wasn't out in it. The wind would blow her away like a sailboat! Please hurry, Giacomo. Please come home.

She busied herself cleaning up the kitchen and starting to prepare the night's meal, all the while keeping one ear on the sounds of the rain, the push of the wind on the panes. She listened hard for the creaking of the back porch steps that would herald Giacomo's return. Or *someone*'s arrival, she reminded herself. The baby was active today, moving around and pushing against his mama's womb as if to say, "I'm ready to come out! Let me out!" Soon, my darling, soon, but not too soon, Josie crooned to her belly. She and Giacomo had to get this threat resolved before any birth could happen. You must stay in there until it's safe, *caro*. Soon, I promise, soon. She looked out the window at the dark descending early on the town because the clouds were so heavy with rain. The rain that was falling with a vengeance now and the wind was blowing steadily. What a storm!

The next thing she knew, the electricity in the apartment fluttered and then went out. Josie looked out the window again and saw that none of the houses around her had power, either. She searched in the twilight for a candle to keep on hand. Great, she thought, no lights. That would make it even easier for the man to break in. Losing power also reminded her of how much they'd come to rely on the new supply of electricity. In America, only the poorest people did not have power and in the cities, it was reliable and steady so much that folks often took it for granted and didn't really think about until it went down. In Citta St. Angelo, when they finally got an electric hookup, she was just a little girl and there were always outages— they became a part of life over there. Not here in big, rich America!

Josie lit the candle and started to pray. She invoked every diety she knew, especially her patron saint, Michel Angelo, who had helped her so often in the past year. God, Jesus, the Holy Spirit and the host of angels were all earnestly petitioned, but she saved her most fervent prayer for the Holy Mother, the Virgin Mary. Lately she had developed a comfortable kinship with her as she prepared herself to enter the ranks of motherhood. She wanted to be as pure of heart and as worthy as she could when the time came to bring new life into this world. Ave Maria, ave Maria, Bless me, Mother . . .

Her contemplation was sharply interrupted by a tremendous sound that reverberated throughout the neighborhood, followed by a high-pitched, piercing noise like metal being torn apart. The ear-splitting noise went on for a few minutes, scraping sounds that combined with what seemed like a locomotive hooking up with a series of boxcars, boom, scraaaaaaaaaaape, another boom, then the sound of water being pushed around. What could it be? The immense sound lasted longer than an explosion. Fear mixed with curiosity got the better of Josie as she rushed out to the porch. She saw other neighbors out in the rain—they heard it too. It had stopped but then it happened again: BOOM BOOM, scraaaaaaaaaaape. The sound filled the air, overriding the noise of the rain falling on flat surfaces, roofs and window panes. Were they being attacked in the middle of a storm? Were planes dropping bombs on them?

"What IS that?" Josie yelled to some people standing under umbrellas in the alley near her house. "What is this big noise?"

Nobody seemed to know.

Within a few minutes they heard sirens blaring. Something big must've happened, but what? No one wanted to venture out into the wind and the now-flooded streets to find out. Josie went back into the house to wait for news. She wondered if Giacomo had been able to call Nick and Sophie and if they were coming to pick her up. And when would her husband come home? Will he come home at all? And—God forbid—what if he doesn't?

Josie sat down in the most comfortable chair they owned and waited. And worried.

Chapter 49   The Bridge

No one could've foreseen the wrath and chaos that Mother Nature brought upon the Delaware Valley with the arrival of the Northeaster. Over a foot and a half of rain fell on the Pocono Mountains north and west of Easton in a 24-hour period. Every creek, stream and gully filled with water that went rushing into the Lehigh and Delaware Rivers in its urgency to get to the ocean. Trees, vehicles, livestock, structures—anything in its path—was swept into the flow. The Delaware Valley soon became a raging, uncontrollable highway of water and debris, thundering down its channel toward Easton, where it met its sister river, the Lehigh, which was equally full of debris and just as angry. The mass of water converged in Easton, just a block south of the iron bridge that spanned the Delaware and connected the towns of Easton in Pennsylvania and Phillipsburg in New Jersey. And a short block away from the residence of Josie and Giacomo Constanza.

Where Easton's side of the river was built on higher ground, Phillipsburg's downtown area was lower. The bridge's roadway fed directly into its main street. The shops and buildings on the New Jersey side were literally built up against a large rock cliff that was

300 feet high behind them.   When the rivers flooded, so did Phillipsburg's downtown. Everyone there had to evacuate but before they did, they moved their valuables to the second floor of their buildings, then they fled to higher ground. This was not the first time Phillipsburg's downtown flooded.

The bridge's connection to the Easton side was different. To access the bridge, the road sloped downward for half a block to account for the raised level of the terrain. Horses and carriages and later, automobiles, had to brake along the descent before they reached the level surface of the two-lane bridge. Like so many other bridges of that era, the Delaware Bridge was constructed of iron with a superstructure of iron latticework that made it look a bit like the Eiffel Tower. Built as a suspension bridge, two support columns which rested on two enormous cement pylons carried the weight of the bridge on iron cables. The bridge had been in use since the late 1880s and was the only crossing available for 20 miles in either direction.

"Josie! Josie! Come down!" Walter yelled from the bottom of the steps of her house. The wind and rain had subsided briefly. His wife, Alicea, and the other neighbors were gathering in the alley to find out what the explosive noises had been and they were walking down to the river in a group.

"Josie, come with us!"

Josie was tired of waiting in the house for Giacomo so she put on her coat and made her way carefully down the wet steps, clinging to the railing, carefully placing one foot in front of the next. Her coat was really too warm for the temperature but it was her only rainproof outer garment. Only the top buttons could be closed. Her expanded belly made it impossible to fasten the lower ones. She didn't intend to be gone long in case Giacomo showed up for he would probably be mad that she had left the house. At least she was with a group of people. She *had* to know what the noise was!

The crowd made its way to the waterfront and a collective murmur passed through the group. Even from a half-block away, they could see that the level of the normally-placid Delaware was unnaturally high as debris and objects bounced up and down on top of the water racing by. As they got closer and rounded the corner, they saw the source of the loud noise.

The Delaware Bridge had been ripped apart by the water and the middle of the bridge was gone! The girders that held up the roadway had been hit by the debris-laden water, repeatedly assaulted by the backup of a huge pile of rocks, wood and metal and with the force of the river behind it, the bridge could not fight back. It collapsed and the water tore through the hole, pushing the girders and suspension cables, roadway cement and latticework through into the channel on the other side. A huge, jagged brown hole right in the middle of the bridge where the road used to be greeted the onlookers. Some of the construction material made its way to the bottom of the river right away, but as the debris mass moved downstream, not a half mile away, it merged with an ally. The Lehigh, slightly smaller but just as full, brought its entire load of runoff to deposit into the Delaware in a chaotic, smashing collision of flooded giants. Debris clashed and collided as the waters merged, creating a massive whirlpool where the furious rivers intersected.

The neighbors at first could not comprehend the magnitude of what they saw. It was incomprehensible that Nature could cause such damage. The magnitude of water, its speed and volume, its force and deadly power was awe-inspiring, to say the least. People in the crowd started to gasp and cry as they watched whole trees, cars, parts of houses, dead animals and innumerable pieces of unidentified objects whip and swirl by them. Their initial shock was turning into reality just as the wind began to pick up again and a few drops of rain started to fall.

"Look over there!" Someone pointed downstream. They started to move toward the park at the promontory a short distance away overlooking the exact point at which the two rivers met. In normal times, they would be 80 feet above the water level but now they were only about eight feet up. Some people held back; it was frightening to get too close to the fast-moving water. The men moved closer to get a better look while the women held back, hanging onto each other.

A massive pileup of debris, probably from the bridge, had collected against one of the cement support columns that held up the railroad trestle a half mile downstream. The trestle itself, a much newer structure than the bridge, was built so high above the water that it wasn't threatened by the flood. Yet the debris pile created a logjam which collected more and more flotsam as the water pounded it from both sides. The pile got higher and higher with each deposit from the river.

"Listen to the noise when debris hits the pile! It's so loud!" It was true. As debris caught on the pile, a smashing sound could be heard above the cacophony of rushing water. Like little car accidents, the sound of crushing metal and tortured wood breaking up could be heard across the watery divide in the town itself. No wonder the bridge breaking up sounded like bombs were dropping on their city! They all stood immobilized by the power of the flood, eye witnesses to the intense force of nature unfolding in front of them.

A police car appeared in the wet street. The officers told the crowd they had to go back home since it wasn't safe at the waterfront. The rivers were still rising, they said as they herded the crowd back up the street. Josie waddled up to one of the policemen.

"My husband he is no home. You see Italian man here, only one maybe two?" she asked in her limited English, gesturing a wide circle indicating her neighborhood.

"Go home, ma'am. We'll send him home if he's on the streets. Best place for you is at home." He waved dismissively at her, shooing her away like a fly. Josie was getting used to such treatment since many people in America felt threatened by the steady stream of European immigrants with strange customs and languages arriving at their country's doors, taking American jobs.

The rain was starting again and the wind picked up. They had no choice but to go back to their homes and wait it out. Walter and his wife walked by Josie to help her.

"How is you doin' Josie? Dat baby wantin' tuh come out yet?" she inquired.

Josie had a hard time understanding her accent, but she did comprehend her meaning. "Baby is good, thank you. Me good too. Want to find Giacomo. You see?" They shook their heads no.

"But we'll keep lookin' fo' him and ifn' we finds him, we sends him home."

These were the first and only black people Josie had ever met. She thought they were pretty decent people, in spite of what some white people said about them.

"Molto grazie, my friends." It was raining harder and she was soaked. A dull pain was settling in her lower back. I need to get home soon, she told herself.

Out of the corner of her eye, she barely noticed some movement at the edge of the park they had just left. The park bordered on some old buildings on the riverside, long abandoned, that had been factories at one time, using the flow of the Lehigh to power their machines. A dark, wet mass of something that looked like clothes was moving on the ground. There it was again! Through the rain she was sure she saw something move. She felt impelled to find out what it was when she told Walter she would see them back at the apartments.

"Yo' bedder not dilly dally in dis weather, Miss Josie," he chided.

"I come back in one minute," she promised. "I be quick!"

Chapter 50 The River

Giacomo ran right into the man he was trying hard to avoid. Running through the water, rain pelting his face, he didn't see him as he rounded the corner to the alley until it was too late. Bam! The two men collided and fell into the flooded street. Neither realized who each other was until they got up, soaked and staggering to maintain their footing.

Giacomo recovered first and landed a right jab on the man's jaw. He reeled but kept his balance, trying to recover as they were both buffeted by the wind.

"Who are you?!" Giacomo demanded, full of fury. "Why are you following me? I don't have any ring!" he yelled in Italian. He sized up the man who was taller than him but thinner. The man didn't respond but took out a pair of brass knuckles and slipped his hand into them.

Giacomo dodged the next blow, wheeled around and started to run away from the house, hoping to lead him away from Josie. The water was up to his calves, making running nearly impossible; the man chased him several arms' lengths behind as they both high-stepped through the torrent in the street. The Sicilian had longer legs but Giacomo was quicker on his feet, making them about evenly matched. He rounded the corner of the long, brick factory building that an industrialist had built in the last century between the street and the river, and he stopped and listened for a split second. He could hear his pursuer splashing right behind him.

Without hesitation, Giacomo kicked the guy in the shins as he charged around the corner.
He went down right in front of Giacomo, face first in the water. Giacomo had to scramble over him to get away, but while he was straddling his legs, the man flipped himself over and grabbed Giacomo's pants and yanked him down on top of him. Rolling and flailing in the water, the Sicilian wrestled with his prey, landing a couple of blows on Giacomo's wet head.

The two men managed to break free of each other long enough to get out of the street and find the grass of the park next to the factory where the footing was better. They stood facing each other, crouched in defensive postures, looking to see who would make the next move, when Giacomo heard someone calling his name across the street. "Giacomo!!!"

It was Josie. Oh no, he thought. Not now!

He turned his head a fraction and yelled, "Go home! NOW!"

The Sicilian heard the voice and took advantage of the interruption in Giacomo's focus. He clobbered Giacomo in the face with the brass knuckles, landing three blows in sequence to his forehead and cheek. Blood gushed from one of the hits and the pain seared his brain, but he had to get rid of Josie or they would both surely be hurt.

"GO HOME JOSIE!"

However, Josie had other ideas. She had found a thick tree branch in the street and now approached the Sicilian from behind, plowing through the water with one purpose in mind—to help Giacomo. No matter that she was eight and a half months pregnant and her lower back hurt, she was undeterred. Apparently the stranger had not heard or seen her while he was beating on Giacomo's face, but she couldn't hide her presence for long. The sound of the rain helped mute her sloshing as she came closer and closer to the two men.

As he paused from the thrashing he was giving Giacomo, he heard a swishing sound directly behind him and the next thing he knew, a heavy blow to the back of his head sent him stumbling off his victim. Not knowing where it came from, the Sicilian retreated further into the park. There are two of them now, he thought. Time to retreat. In his confusion, he didn't realize his second assailant was a pregnant woman or that he was moving closer and closer to the river's edge.

Giacomo recovered hastily from the onslaught and he saw his opening. He followed the Sicilian, wiping the blood from his eyes and the water from his face so he could see better. The man seemed disoriented as he staggered toward the iron fence that enclosed the park's edge and kept visitors away from the drop down to the channel of the river. Except today the drop to the river was about four feet below the fence, not the usual eighty, as the channel continued to fill with the rising floodwaters. His adrenaline was sky high as he closed in on the man, forcing the final confrontation that would end this threat. He had Josie's tree branch in his hands.

"Stay back, Josie!" he ordered.

The Sicilian was holding the back of his head with his hand as Giacomo charged him. The tree branch landed on his forearm like a bat hitting a home run, and Giacomo heard the satisfying crunch of a bone shattering. The man screamed in pain as he leaned against the fence. He was cornered and he knew it. Again Giacomo hit him with the branch on the shoulder of the arm he had just broken, pushing the man further into the fence in retreat.

"Who are you?! Who are you?!" Giacomo yelled at the top of his lungs, coming at him again with the branch.

"You have my mother's ring! I want it back! Luigi Longo wants his ring!"

Josie heard all of this as she hovered, drenched, in the background. The violence she was watching overwhelmed her yet she realized now that this man meant to kill Giacomo and it was a struggle to the death. Thank God she found the tree branch since that enabled him to go on the offensive, in spite of his serious wounds.

The two men continued to scuffle in the rain and the wind, pushing and shoving each other against the fence but it was clear that Giacomo now had the upper hand. Suddenly from her vantage point, Josie saw the fence bow outwards toward the riverbank as sections of the ground beneath it gave way. The fence began to unravel as it separated from its supports.

"Giacomo! The fence! Look out! Noooooo!"

The weight of the two men's bodies against the fence snapped the rods holding it together and for a moment, they teetered on the edge of the channel. Giacomo wanted to push Longo into the water but if he did, he would lose his balance and go in right after him. The next thing he knew, Josie was standing there, speechless. He stretched the tree branch out to her and told her to hold on to it. Josie slid down to the ground and held onto the branch for dear life as the rain and wind pounded them all.

No more than a few seconds passed as Josie prayed to God, Jesus, Mary and St. Michael Angelo to spare their lives.

As if he had been miraculously revived, Luigi Longo started the struggle anew, grabbed Giacomo and in a last-ditch effort, tried to pull himself onto solid ground. They wrestled for a moment, slipping in the mud, Longo with a broken arm and shoulder and Giacomo maintaining a delicate balance holding the tree limb as a lifeline to his wife.

"Let go of the branch, Josie!" he commanded. "Let go!"

Josie froze at that moment and couldn't bring herself to let go of the one thing keeping the two of them together. She just couldn't do it. She braced herself against the pain in her back that had been building throughout the fight and was determined to hold on.

But Giacomo saw things from a different perspective. Longo was dragging him down with him and Josie would surely follow them into the water if she didn't let go.

"LET GO NOW! JOSIE, LET GO!" he screamed decisively.

She released her hold on the branch and she watched, horrified, as both men slipped between the broken fence into the raging waters of the Delaware River.

Chapter 51   Labor

The rain was pounding her, the wind whipped around her, and all Josie was conscious of was scanning the raging floodwaters for any sign of Giacomo. The two men had fallen in together down the four-foot drop, made a splash that she could hear, then disappeared in the brown, turbid flow and quickly passed out of sight. "NOOOO!" she wailed.

"Giacomo! Giacomo!" Josie screamed at the top of her lungs. "Giacomooooooooo!"
But there was no response. The sound of the wind and rain took care of that. She got up and walked along the fence line to try and see him to no avail. She got to the farthest point of the promontory where the fence was still intact and couldn't go any further. She burst into bitter tears as sobs coursed through her.

She was slowly becoming aware of her body. The dull ache in her back had become much stronger and in spite of being completely drenched by rainwater, she noticed a different wetness between her legs. Her legs were weakening and a profound heaviness settled around her lower torso, as if the baby was being pulled toward earth by gravity. THE BABY! Was it time to have the baby? Shaken to her core about the loss of Giacomo, Josie had to now come to terms with delivering her baby—by herself? Oh God, no! This is too much to ask of me, she prayed. I have to get home, call the police, get help for Giacomo. I can't have a baby right now!

Summoning every bit of strength and fortitude in her being, Josie headed toward home in the torrent, head down, sobbing with grief. There wasn't a soul on the flooded street—she was completely alone. She stumbled in pain and had to stop as her lower back was wracked by such an intense pain that it took her breath away. There was no doubt now; her water had broken and she was in labor. "I have to get home," she whispered to herself. The baby was coming.

She looked up ahead of herself to gauge how far she had to go to the alley. Up ahead she could just make out the shape of the black man, Walter, who called out to her. "Josie! I's comin' fer 'ya. Stay there!" Gladly, she thought. Gladly.

Walter's long stride brought him to her in no time. He saw she was in distress, so he swooped her up in his arms and carried her through the downpour to her apartment. She kept saying, "Giacomo's gone, the baby coming" over and over. He couldn't understand what she meant by Giacomo being gone but he certainly understood the part about the baby. As he hauled her up the wet steps, her body seemed to go limp like she fell asleep, so he entered the dark apartment and laid her on the bed, wet clothing and all. He had to go get Alicea, his wife. She would know what to do. She was a midwife.

Soon Alicea had taken over the apartment. She stripped off Josie's wet coat and clothes and found a dry nightshirt. She told Walter to boil some water on the stove and to find as many towels as possible. She looked around the apartment and didn't see any baby items at all, so she assumed they had not expected the baby this early. Alicea had noticed that the baby seemed to have dropped when she saw Josie earlier. She also noticed that her water had broken and the child's descent down the birth canal was obvious. Josie was in full labor; it was just a matter of time until the baby made its appearance. The exhausted girl was sleeping now but she'd be awake soon enough. All they could do was wait.

Alicea didn't have to wait long. Josie's next contraction came about ten minutes later.

"Josie, you is in labor, honey, an' I's gonna hep you get yo' baby borned. I's a midwife and I birthed lots of babies, so don' you worry none, we's gonna do dis together. Okay, honey?"

Josie nodded as if she was in a trance. A contraction wracked her body and she shuddered with the pain. She kept repeating, "Giacomo, Giacomo?"

"He ain't here now, Josie, so you needs to listen to me, hear? Now I wants ya to breathe real deep and let it out slow-like in puffs, all right? Show me how you can do dat, okay?"

Josie took a breath and did as the woman said. She was scared of the pain that came more and more frequently now as the baby made its way further and further out of her uterus. Her thoughts kept going back to the scene with Giacomo and Luigi Longo when she let go of the branch and fell down into the river. It turned over and over in her mind, shocking her each time, and preventing her from focusing on the childbirth. She felt almost detached from what was going on in her own body, although the pain served to remind her every time a contraction began, burning through her torso like fire. Then it would stop and she'd rest, coached by Alicea, and the images would come back: the look on Giacomo's face as he plunged down into the abyss, Longo's curse words as he was swept to an inevitable death. She couldn't get the horror of that scene out of her head.

Alicea was getting concerned at the girl's inability to concentrate on the task at hand. Of course she had a lot to worry about. Where was Josie's husband? Alicea couldn't understand why he wasn't here by Josie's side to help with the birth of his child.

Suddenly Josie sat bolt upright and started to get out of the bed. "I have to call the police," she mumbled, like a possessed woman. "They have to save Giacomo. They have to get him out of the water."

"Out de water? What you mean, Josie? Who in de water? Ain't no police out dere now, girl. Dey's a storm goin' on. Come on back here and lie in de bed. Let's get this chile borned."
She led the girl back to the bed, amazed that she could even move when the baby was crowning.

"Where Giacomo at, Josie? Does you know where he at?"

Josie nodded, crying. "He's in the water. He fell in the river." She couldn't say anymore until the next contraction passed. They were coming repeatedly now.

"How you know dat? How you know he be in de water? Did you see him fall in?"

"Si. He was in a fight with another man. The fence broke and they both fell in and disappeared. I was right there. I saw it happen. Can you call the police?" Josie begged.

Walter and Alicea were stunned by this news. They had left Josie for a few short minutes on their way back from the bridge. How did they miss all of this?!

"Right now you is goin' to have yo' baby. Dat baby wants to come out so bad, you gots to hep it get out, y'hear? Now when I say push, I wants ya to push real hard and hep dat baby come outs, ready now, deep breath and PUSH!"

Josie strained against her body, pushing as hard as she could. At that point, all thoughts of Giacomo disappeared in the incredible pain she experienced as the baby's head worked its way out of her vagina.

"Again, Josie—PUSH! Push hard, girl!"

It wasn't long before Alicea could grab hold of the child's head and with a few more pushes, it plopped out of Josie straight into the midwife's practiced hands. Walter was there with towels and water as Alicea held the baby upside down and gave it a smack to get it to take its first breath.

"Josie, it's a girl. You have a baby girl!" Josie heard the wail of the shocked child who had just entered the unforgiving environment of the outside world. Alicea clipped the cord, cleaned up the baby and laid her on Josie's chest and directed her to let her suckle at her breast. She waited for the afterbirth that followed a few minutes later and was glad to see that it was intact. The midwife noticed that Josie gave the child an indifferent glance, then seemed to drift off to sleep with the baby on her chest.

Alicea and Walter looked at each other in silence. "Lord, she gots her troubles, for sure," Alicea commented. She sent Walter to their house to bring them something to eat.

While he was gone, there was a sharp knock at the door. Alicea wasn't sure if she should answer it but the pounding continued while voices cried out, "Josie! Giacomo! Are you there?" She was afraid they would wake up Josie and the baby so she peeked out of the window and saw a man and a woman standing on the porch in wet clothes and shoes, holding a bag.

"Come on in," Alicea whispered with her finger against her lips. Nick and Sophia entered the tiny apartment, saw Josie and the baby sleeping in the bed and figured out what they had just missed. "Who are you?" they asked in unison.

"I's the midwife, Alicea, Josie's neighbor," she smiled warmly. Walter came in a few minutes later and introductions were made as they explained the whole story.

"We've been driving for hours," Nick explained. "The roads are flooded everywhere! We've never been to Easton before and we couldn't find the house . . . I wish I'd been here to fight off that mobster with Giacomo. And to help Josie--damn!"

Sophia sat next to her friend on the bed, stroking her forehead. Josie looked like she was beyond exhaustion. Sophia took the sleeping infant in her arms and admired her, all pink skin with a shock of black hair, wrapped in a towel. The baby squirmed, opened her eyes and smiled at Sophia. "Oh you sweet thing!" she cooed with delight. Nick looked on at the scene bathed in candlelight and thought, this looks like a fairytale instead of the nightmare it really is. Oh, God help us.

Chapter 52   Vendetta

Giacomo was not the hero type. He was thrust into this situation in Citta St. Angelo with little choice. He had to defend his employer and protect the girl, Josie, but he never expected to get caught up in any mob-related vendetta between the leader of the *Cosa Nostra* and the Bishop or the Church. He wasn't even sure what was going on there . . . Nonetheless, here he was, fighting with a mobster who had traveled to America to settle a score that had something to do with a ring. He thought to himself, my whole life has been upended because of this guy and his claim to a ring that I had nothing to do with. And now I'm about to lose my wife, my child, maybe even my life for a stupid ring! I can't believe this idiot is about to drag me into a flooding river and he just won't die!

As the two men felt the fence breaking under their weight and they both dropped into the Delaware's raging water, Giacomo was able to kick Longo in the ribs as he pushed him away a second before they hit the water. He didn't want to be wrapped around Longo for they would both certainly be dragged underwater. He wasn't sure Longo could even swim-- even more reason to be free of him. Giacomo was a good swimmer under the best of circumstances, but he had just been beat up in a fight and was now in a fast-moving current full of all sorts of debris in the driving rain. Whatever small chance of survival he had depended on him staying focused and not panicking. That was going to be *very* difficult, he knew. Especially after leaving his pregnant wife on the river bank. It was with great satisfaction that he saw Longo's thrashing body pass him as he yelled "Help me! Help me! I'm drowning!" Good bye and good riddance, Giacomo mused.

Survival was the only thing on his mind. He kicked off his shoes and wriggled out of his jacket. Struggling to tread water, he looked around at the debris racing by him, hoping to grab onto something that could help him stay afloat. All manner of objects passed by him—metal pieces of bridge girders, whole trees, lumber, parts of buildings, pieces of cars, it was like a floating junkyard. He saw a beam from what must've been a house moving fast towards him and he lunged at it, grabbed it and held on for dear life. He wrapped both arms and a leg around it and continued to float down the channel, bobbing up and down and gasping for air.

The sky was a twilight grey and it was still raining. He could see a little way in front of him as he moved downstream. What struck him as unusual were the sounds of the debris crashing against other debris and the sheer volume of so much water moving so fast. It was so loud! A few seconds later, he heard a tremendous roar close at hand becoming louder and louder like a freight train rushing by. He was coming up fast on the Lehigh River's confluence where it met the Delaware, forcing its water to merge with the larger river in a massive clash like a liquid bomb. In a flash, he and his floating beam were engulfed in a fast-moving maelstrom, spinning around on his piece of wood in a counter-clockwise motion, now being pushed back upstream towards the park where he fell in, then being sucked south again by the whirlpool. He was swallowing a lot of water, finding it hard to catch a breath, as the water washed over him again and again. The beam bobbed up and down in the current and he went underwater every time it was submerged. Giacomo was not a religious man, but he prayed for his deliverance to get back to his wife and family.

By a miracle, his floating raft seemed to clear the massive whirlpool only to be met with another obstacle. Giacomo heard more crashing ahead of him, but this noise was the sound of debris hitting debris that was stopped, solid matter collecting in a sort of logjam. It was different from the sound of water crashing on water. He could still only see a few feet ahead of him, but he knew that the railroad trestle crossed the Delaware just a half-mile or so south of where the Lehigh met the larger river's channel. He knew the trestle was too high for the floodwaters to threaten it, but what about the supports? He couldn't remember how many there were but he knew such a high structure that carried freight trains and locomotives had to be supported by a number of sturdy bases. Many times from his house he had heard the whistles of the trains crossing the trestle in the night when it was quiet. How close was he to the supports? Was he doomed to crash against a cement pylon and be crushed by the debris behind him? His adrenaline gushed at the prospect.

He was tiring and he knew it. Not many men would've been able to withstand the punishment he had just gone through and stay afloat in the dangerous flood he was fighting. If he didn't get help or a break soon, he knew he would perish. Realistically, he was amazed that he had survived this long under the circumstances, yet it had only been about ten or fifteen minutes since he had fallen in! It was only because he was young and in such good physical shape, and he had such a burning determination to see his unborn child, that he was able to find the strength to continue.

"God above and all that is holy, help me survive!" he yelled to the sky.

No sooner had the words left his mouth than his beam slammed into a pile of debris. For a few seconds it stopped, giving him a chance to see where he was. My God, he thought, I'm stuck on a trestle support! The water split into two paths and poured on either side around a large pile of debris that had built up over the last few hours, stuck on one of the trestle's cement pylons. The pile shifted and groaned as the water brushed past it, sometimes collecting a new trophy piece of flotsam. Giacomo thought it seemed fairly sturdy. Or, he surmised, as sturdy as anything could be in that situation. As it turned out, the cement base he and his beam were stuck on was near the Pennsylvania bank of the river, out of the most intense flow of the water and in a sort of reverse eddy formed by the whirlpool of the two colliding rivers further upstream. He finally had a chance to catch his breath and assess his position.

The cement part of the pylon was about ten feet tall. Above that were steel girders and bars that were constructed to support the trestle in a pattern that became increasingly wider as it got higher. By the time the support column reached the track, the trestle's walls were substantial, although huge spaces among the beams were designed to let air through. Giacomo thought that if he could climb high enough, he might be able to ride out the flood until somebody saw him and could come and rescue him. Could he manage to climb high enough? He had to try. Or go back to floating down the channel in the water.

With great care, he crawled up onto the debris pile, trying not to shift it with his weight. It seemed to hold his weight. He wondered how much debris was actually below the level he was on; it must be enough to resist the force of the water plummeting downstream. That was encouraging. Moving from piece to piece, he clawed his way a foot up, then another foot, testing each movement against the stability of the pile. It held. So far so good.

He looked up. The cement still towered about six feet over his head. He could see the ledge where the girders were bolted to the base. So close, he thought. I can do it, I can get there.

Then something slammed into the debris pile and the entire mass shifted. It's moving! Giacomo slipped and fell almost into the water again, catching himself at the last second before he would've been swept away.   Hang on, hang on, he told himself. The physical exertion was taking its toll on him but the mental stress was worse. He began to doubt that he could make it, that he would survive, he was so tired, his arms hurt from holding on, the muscles in his legs were starting to cramp up . . . then the pile stopped moving. Oh my God, it stopped, he thought. But for how long?

Gathering his wits about him, he forced himself to focus. Take a breath, man, breathe!

He grabbed the first thing he could find in the pile of broken flood trash and hauled himself up. Again, he found footing that was stable enough to hold his weight. Looking to the left, he saw the familiar shape of his wooden beam, the friend that had gotten him this far. He reached for it, knowing it would be heavier than it was in the water, and he was right. But in this instance heavy was what he needed, and because the wood had been roughed up in the water, there were indentations that Giacomo could use as footholds. His hands caught splinters as he worked the beam to a vertical position and braced it in the middle of the debris pile, resting it against the pylon at a 45 degree angle. He talked to the wood: "You only have to stay there for thirty seconds, just a half a minute while I climb up. Can you do that for me, my friend? Just thirty seconds." It seemed like a reasonable request in the middle of a life-threatening place.

Was his mind playing tricks on him? He thought he heard a voice over the cacophony of the floodwater. There it was again. A woman's voice was crying, "Giacomo! Come home!"

It was faint but he knew he heard it. There it was again. "Giacomo . . . "

With every ounce of strength he had left in his battered body, he scrambled up the beam like a spider, three-quarters of the way to its top, grabbing for any handhold he could find for balance on the cement. At first there was nothing to hold but then he found the end of a girder. Just as he kicked off his foot to bring his leg up onto the ledge, his wooden beam collapsed back into the debris pile. He heaved his drenched body onto the ledge, hanging on as every muscle in his hands and arms screamed in protest, but he made it. Wet, beat up, beyond exhaustion, his body ready to disown him, he still made it. He secured his seat among the holes in the girder design, weaving his arms and legs into the holes so he wouldn't fall if he fell asleep and he let the rain pelt against him. He was safe—for now. He would survive.

Thank you, God. Thank you, beam from someone's house. He glanced down at the debris pile below him and saw it move ever so slightly, then more and more, and within a few minutes it had broken up completely and was floating piece by piece down the Delaware.

Josie, I'm coming home. Wait for me, I'll be there. Exhaustion took over and he fell into a deep sleep, wrapped around the girder bars of the trestle like a snake.

Chapter 53   Rescue

"Josie, you have to eat something. Come on, just a little taste." Sophia nudged and cajoled her friend, just like she did on the ship when they crossed the Atlantic.

"I'm not hungry. I don't want any." She could hear the baby wimpering in the background. "Just let me sleep."

"Josie, you have to eat. You have to be able to nurse your baby. She's hungry! Come on, have some broth." Josie just turned away from her friend.

Nick and Sophia had taken over caring for Josie and the baby to let Walter and Alicea go home. Alicea told them what to do to get the baby to nurse and although Josie was cooperative, she had no strength and little enthusiasm for the child she had just borne. Nick was restless and spent a lot of time on the porch watching the weather and thinking about Giacomo, wondering if he was dead or alive. He didn't hold out much hope for anyone who fell into a flooded river, but Giacomo was strong if he wasn't drunk, and if anyone could survive, he could. He was a scrappy son-of-a-bitch! He thought about leaving Sophia with Josie and going out to look for him, but although the wind had died down, it was still raining and no one was in the streets. They had brought some food with them, enough for a few meals that would last a day or so.

It was anyone's guess what would happen after the storm broke.

Sophia tried again and again to get Josie to eat. She held the baby, comforting her and encouraging her to nurse. She got Josie up once or twice to go to the bathroom and she almost fainted. That convinced Sophia to renew her efforts to get some food into her.

They spent the night sleeping on the floor.

The morning dawned clear and bright as if nothing had ever happened to the Delaware Valley. After two days of a fierce hurricane, the townspeople crawled out of their homes like moles to observe the damage the storm had left behind. There was plenty to see. Sirens were heard in the distance. More and more vehicles could be seen on the roadways, which were still flooded in many places. People wearing high boots were canvassing the neighborhoods to assess the damage. Nick saw Walter from the porch and waved.

"Need some help?"

"Sure do, you gots some gloves?" Nick nodded in assent.

The two men roamed down the alley, picking up trash they could move to the side of the street to clear the roadway. They worked their way down toward the waterfront, sloshing through huge puddles of water that came almost to their knees in places. There was mud everywhere. Bits of garbage were strewn all over the place like confetti. Most homes were intact but porches, window sashes, awnings, garbage cans, anything that was loose had blown away. The men saw broken windows on storefronts on the main street where debris had been blown into the panels of glass, smashing them and letting the rainwater in.

They made their way to the bridge crossing. Nick couldn't believe what he saw—the central section of the bridge was gone as if a giant had sawed right through it. The floodwaters, brown, ugly and full of the objects of an upstream world, still rushed through the gaping hole in the bridge. They could see some people on the New Jersey side in Phillipsburg looking at the inundated business district of their town. What a mess! The men realized that they were cut off from the western portion of New Jersey until repairs to the bridge could be made.

"Le's take a look ovah chere," Walter indicated downstream and they walked to the promontory overlooking the two rivers. Slogging through the flooded street, they got to the park and were astounded to see that both rivers were so high. They noted the broken fence and a large chunk of earth that had been swallowed up by the Delaware. The cannon was still in place.

"Don' git too close," Walter warned. "De earth ain't too sturdy ovah dere."

"Look at that railroad trestle, Walter. It's still standing! Look at the junk piled up on the bases. Amazing!"

"Hey, whazzat? Yo' see dat white thaing on de bottom of dat base on de right dere?"

Nick tried to discern what Walter was talking about. Squinting his eyes, he scanned the bases of the trestle's supports but didn't see anything.

"Dere it go agin, I seen it. Somethin' white shakin' back an' forth. See it? What'chew think dat is?"

It was difficult to see anything a half-mile away but Nick was fairly sure he saw the same white fluttering object Walter was pointing out to him. "Is that a bird?"

"Don' know. It stops den it starts agin. Don't think it ain't no bird. It jus' be in de same place the whole time."

"It's like somebody's waving a flag. Do you think that could be a person stuck up there? Come on, Walter, let's go find out!" They were both up for an adventure.

They hurried back to the alley and got Nick's brother's car. Walter guided them uptown a few blocks where there was little flooding on the streets and they crossed over the Lehigh on the Third Street bridge, fortunately undamaged by the water. Floodwater still crashed beneath them but the bridge was higher than the Delaware bridge, and traffic had started to cross back and forth already.

"Walter, get the binoculars under the back seat of my car, would you?"

They traveled over the railroad tracks to the train station, desolate now of passengers because of the storm. They parked the car and started to walk the tracks until they reached the Delaware where they looked down at the floodwaters below them.

"I'll be damned!" Nick exclaimed. "There's a man down there! Let me have those binoculars!"

Walter got as close to the track's edge as he could and yelled at the top of his lungs.

"Hey you! You okay? We gonna get hep fo' ya! Hang in dere!"

The man waved what they now understood to be an undershirt back at them to signal he had heard them. As Nick focused the lenses on the man wrapped around the trestle, Walter kept yelling, reassuring him.

"Mother of God, it's Giacomo Constanza!"

The two men jumped up and down with joy, slapping themselves on the back. They now yelled Giacomo's name and promised to go get a rescue party to free him.

"Hang on, Giacomo! We're coming for you, buddy! Don't move! We'll be right back!"

Nick was crazy with excitement and a huge smile lit up Walter's face. They hiked back to the station, jumped in the car and drove like fiends to the Easton Police Station, where they begged the already overworked cops to mount a rescue mission. Amid the chaos of one of the greatest disasters to ever hit the region, some men were found who could negotiate a rescue.

Four hours later, a tired, bloodied and bruised man collapsed into the arms of his friend and neighbor, Nick and Walter. A crowd had gathered as word had gotten out that someone had survived the flood by hanging onto the train trestle. Everyone watched in silence as the firemen walked the half mile to the trestle, carrying very thick ropes. One rappelled down the outside of the steel girders and reached where Giacomo was hanging on. The ropes were lowered and tied off. The fireman secured the half-dead man in a harness and prepared to hoist him up to the tracks on the outside of the structure as he climbed alongside him up the girders, stabilizing him. The burly firemen above made slow but steady progress, and with great effort they were able to haul Giacomo up to the level of the tracks. As they pulled the man by his belt onto the train tracks, heaving him over the precarious edge high above the turbulent floodwaters below, all Giacomo could do was sob the words "Grazie" as a huge cheer went up from the crowd. They could tell by looking at him that he had been to hell and back but he had survived! Like the biblical Noah, he had survived the great flood--it was a miracle!

The firemen supported him as they carried him to the car where Nick and Walter were waiting to drive him home to Josie and Sophia. The crowd exploded in cheers for the firemen and the rescued man and waved them on, chanting "Hero! Hero! Hero!" They followed the car all the way across the bridge and down Ferry Street to the alley where Giacomo lived, cheering the whole way.

Chapter 54   Home

Sophia heard a commotion in the street below and stepped out onto the porch to see what the noise was all about. She could hear yelling and car horns blaring in the distance like someone had just won an election. What could it be? she wondered. Were people so happy that the storm was over that they were celebrating in the streets?

She was worried about Nick. He had been gone quite awhile with the black man, Walter. Where did they go? She had finally gotten Josie to eat a small amount of bread and drink some tea but the baby was fussy and she wasn't sure her friend's milk had come in completely. Josie was like a zombie, detached and emotionally drained as she tried to come to grips with the idea that Giacomo was gone. How long would it take to find his body? What if they never found it? How would Josie have closure if there was no trace of him? What was to become of her and the child? Sophia shuddered at the prospects her friend was facing.

Sophia knew that despite the rough times these two people had gone through, they loved one another, each in their own way, and that they would have made good parents. She knew from her own marriage that it wasn't all peaches and cream, that there were tough times, disagreements and challenges, but a people stuck them out, worked through them, and came out stronger for it. Now Josie wouldn't have that chance. It was such a shame! She felt terrible for her friend.

What is that commotion? It's getting louder. She could hear a crowd of people yelling something in a staccato rhythm. She wanted to leave Josie to go find out but she didn't think that was a good idea. Maybe Nick would know when he got back.

"Sophie! Can you take the baby for me?" Josie called to her friend.

Sophie took the little being in her arms. "Josie, do you have a name picked out for her yet?"

"A name?" Josie looked puzzled. The baby wasn't due for another three weeks. She wasn't ready for the child. She wasn't ready for any of this. "A name? I . . . I don't know, I thought it was going to be a boy. I don't have a name for her."

"Well, let's think of a name. What's your favorite name, Josie?"

She responded with a blank stare. I don't want to deal with this now, she thought.

"Well, what's your grandmother's name?" Sophia was insistent. She didn't know that Josie had been adopted. The child needed a name and Josie needed to get her mind off her grief. If the baby had a name, she reasoned, she would become more of a person to Josie. This child would have a name soon if she had to name her herself. "How about Maria? Or Antoinette? Or Gladys?"

Josie put her head in her hands and started to cry. "I can't, Sophia. I can't name her without Giacomo. A name is something that both parents decide together. I can't do it without him. . . " She sobbed again and again.

Sophia put the sleeping baby in the dresser drawer that they had lined with towels as a makeshift cradle. She held Josie close to her to try to take away some of her pain. She needed to grieve, her friend who had lost her husband and had borne a child in the same day. They held each other while Josie cried, letting the pain out of her heart, giving at least a small portion of it to her great friend. Slowly her sobs subsided and she wiped her face on her nightshirt.

"What is that noise outside, Sophie?"

"I heard it before. Some people are making a commotion, I don't know why. Nick will be back soon—I'll ask him then. I know what we should name your baby!"

"What?" Josie asked with a glimmer of interest.

Sophia thought of the Italian word for 'pain.' *Dolore.*

"Josie, how about Dolores? She was born at a painful time but you won't feel this pain forever. Her name will remind you of this sad time but as she grows, you will learn how to forget your pain and enjoy your daughter. It's a beautiful name, and she's a beautiful girl. What do you think?" Sophia thought she had finally reached Josie.

"I-I think you're right. It's a good name." Josie tossed the name around in her head as some of her mental fog lifted. "I like it. I think Giacomo would approve too." She started to tear up but caught herself. She went to the quiet baby with the shock of black hair resting peacefully in the dresser drawer and picked her up.

"What do *you* think about that, eh? Would you like to be called Dolores? Can that be your very own name? Maybe . . . Dolores Angelina since you look like an angel."

The baby looked straight at Josie and gurgled. She crinkled her nose and moved her lips in a tiny smile. "All right, Dolores, it's just you and me now, and Aunt Sophia and Uncle Nick."

They heard a car pull up in the alley bearing down on its horn—BEEEEEEP, BEEEEEEP, BEEP BEEP, followed by loud voices making a commotion. They both went to the window overlooking the porch and saw Nick's brother's car. "They're back!" Sophia exclaimed excitedly. Josie put the baby down and sat dejectedly on the bed, resigned and ready for more bad news. But Sophia insisted that Josie come with her so the two women stepped out on the porch to greet Nick and Walter together. They saw the crowd that had gathered around the car, neighbors and strangers Josie had never seen, still clapping and whooping and cheering.

"What are they yelling about, Sophie?" Josie asked on the verge of tears again.

Nick and Walter walked to the far side of the car and opened the door. They half-carried a dirty, beat up, shirtless man around the car and into the tiny yard.

"GIACOMO!" Josie screeched. She tore down the steps, almost falling on her nightgown. "Oh my God, GIACOMO!" she sloshed through the mud in her bare feet.

The two embraced long and hard. Giacomo could barely stand up but Nick and Walter stood by to catch him if he fell. Both were overcome with emotion, crying in each other's arms and kissing each other, Josie repeating over and over, "You're alive! You're alive, I can't believe you're alive!" Giacomo couldn't even find words to speak.

Nick had to break them up as he reminded Josie that her husband needed to eat and then rest. He thanked the crowd for their goodwill and support as they dispersed now that they had witnessed the reunion. He and Walter helped Giacomo up the stairs into the apartment where Sophia had been making some food. They helped him into the bed but before he could fall asleep, there was one important introduction that had to be made.

Josie brought their new daughter to her husband with tears in her eyes and announced, "This is Dolores. Say hi to your daddy, little girl."

Giacomo had just enough strength to touch the baby's face as she squalled in protest. "Good lungs," he quipped. He fell asleep before he could eat anything.

Nick recounted how Walter had seen Giacomo perched on the railroad trestle and described the rescue to an overwrought Josie. They would have to wait for him to wake up and gain some strength to hear the rest of the story. "All in good time," Sophia said. "At least he's home in one piece. Thank God."

Josie looked at her sleeping husband and her heart filled with pride that he had survived such a horrific experience. She could only imagine what it had been like in the water after being beaten by Luigi Longo. She didn't dare think of what had happened to *him*. Suddenly she was overcome with waves of other emotions as she thought about what the future held in store for the new family. She had honestly been overjoyed that he had returned home alive, and she thought she felt a spark of his love for her in his sincere embrace. Did he finally find the emotional source that he had been denying himself these past months? He had saved her from the mobster and had nearly sacrificed himself in the process. She knew that it was hard for him to show emotion; it was not in his nature. He was a pragmatic realist who tended to see the world as a dangerous place, full of mistrust. For that very reason, Giacomo was her hero, her protector and for that she respected him and found renewed love for him. Would that be enough in the years to come?

Giacomo stirred as he interrupted her musings. He pushed up from the bed with a start and Nick caught him, holding his shoulders, saying, "Slow down there, you're all right now, Giacomo." His words relaxed him and he fell back against the pillow.

"What's this?" Josie pointed to a spot of blood on the bedsheets near his right elbow. She moved the sheet to see a nasty, deep cut about three inches long on his bicep that had reopened in the rescue. The cut was deep, through the muscle and almost down to the bone.

"You have to get that stitched up, Giacomo! Nick, can you take us to the hospital?"

"No hospitals!" Giacomo grunted.

"Come on, now, who knows what got into that cut? You could get a big infection from the floodwaters, and what if it doesn't stop bleeding?" Nick protested.

"No hospitals!" Giacomo reiterated with force.

The three friends looked at each other, wondering how they could argue with a man who fought like a soldier to survive, only to lose his arm from stubbornness?

"I have an idea," Josie said. She went to the icebox and got what was left of the red wine. "Giacomo, you must drink all of this wine, just leave a little for me. *I* am going to stitch up your wound."

He willingly obliged and was half-drunk by the time Josie had gathered some hot water, clean towels and her strongest needle and thread. With Nick holding his arm still and Sophia as her assistant, Josie first washed the cut, spreading it open to get out any embedded debris, then poured the remaining wine into the wound to disinfect it. Giacomo protested a little but didn't have the strength to fight them. When the needle was threaded with a strong, heavy black thread, Josie carefully began puncturing the edges of the cut, pulling the thread taut with each pass through the skin. She thought that his skin wasn't much tougher than the heavy damask fabric on Saint Michael's cape. She sewed with a singular focus—to save her husband's arm—four, five, then six stitches, neat and orderly, and tied off the thread at the end, trimming it with her scissors. She finished the job spreading a few more drops of wine over the incision.

"Nicely done, Josie!" Sophia was impressed. Giacomo moved stiffly to look at his arm, emitted a grunt, and fell back to sleep. Josie stood up and exhaled a mighty sigh.

Her mind raced back and forth as she thought of the events of the last few days and the letter she would send to her parents. A very long letter. Her mother's words rang in her ears, "Italian girls do not get divorced." She was in this marriage for life, now even more committed than ever with the birth of her child. Even if things got bad, she somehow knew that she could survive almost anything after this experience. Josie said a silent prayer to Saint Michael to guard their family and help them recover and prosper.

Josie moved to Nick and Sophia and gave them a grateful hug. "You are the best friends anyone could ever have," she cried. "I don't know how to thank you."

"Let's just be friends forever, Josie. That's thanks enough," Sophia smiled as Nick shook his head in agreement.

Josie looked at the people spread throughout her apartment and felt a great resolution, a sense of peace and blessing descend upon her. Like a blessing a priest gives his congregation during mass. She thought of the Bishop whose benediction she imagined had just been given to her family and friends. She thought for a minute of the clothes on the statue of Saint Michel Angelo. How were they holding up? she wondered. For some reason, she picked up her coat, the beautiful hand-made wool coat that she had made in Italy with such skill, the coat that represented her past and her roots. It was muddy and still wet in spots and was missing a button or two. Sophia watched her smooth the coat out on the kitchen table to see if it needed repair.

"Oh, Sophie, look, the lining is ripped."
Sophia and Nick came to the table to see the damage.

She carefully worked her hand from the bottom of the coat underneath the lining up to one of the arm holes. There were several seams that met in that spot so the fabric was two layers thick, not including the lining. Was it wet there too? Was it ripped? Josie felt something unusual as her fingers examined the seam.

"That's funny. There's something hard inside the seam."

She took a seam ripper and gently expanded the lining rip to expose the seam to the light.

413

There, sewn into the seam of the fabric by a hand that did not belong to the coat's maker, was a flawless, three-carat diamond wedding ring.

###

ACKNOWLEDGEMENTS

I would like to thank the following people who have helped me in my journey to get this book into print. First, my son Karl, who finally got his degree in Digital Media in his forties and put it to work creating the cover of this book. I also want to acknowledge my artist husband, Robert Mier, who painted the cover art and put up with my frequent directions to fulfill my vision. A great debt of gratitude goes out to author Marcia Meara, whose books were an inspiration and who helped guide me through the forest of self-publication. Other kudos go to my macro-editor, Valerie Russell, my colleague at Seminole State College, and Andrea Lee, my micro-editor.

My greatest thanks go to my mother, Linda Shawde, who agreed to record an oral history of her early life to preserve the stories of her parents, and to my grandmother, Lena Mazzochetti, who recognized that I was her only grandchild interested in the Old Country. May they both rest in peace.

The second installment of the Abruzzo Annals will likely be published in 2017.

39609030R00232

Made in the USA
Middletown, DE
20 January 2017